RISE OF THE
GRAY NINJA

SPI

© 2020 SPI Publishing

Printed in the United States of America

www.grayninjabooks.com

Unless otherwise indicated, all Scripture quotations are from The ESV Bible® and New International Version® ...and ultimately from God

Scripture quotations [on pages 180, 237, 173, and 256] are from The ESV® Bible (The Holy Bible, English Standard Version®), copyright © 2011 by Crossway, a publishing ministry of Good News Publishers. Used by permission. All rights reserved... again.

Scripture quotations [on pages 116, 117, and 256] are taken from The Holy Bible, New International Version® NIV®

Copyright © 1973 1978 1984 2011 by Biblica, Inc. TM

Used by permission. All rights reserved worldwide. And universal if aliens actually exist.

Paperback ISBN: 978-1-64786-450-7

Library of Congress Control Number: 2020902765

Cover Design and Author Photo By: SPI Studios

TABLE OF CONTENTS

PROLOGUE

A beautiful pink and orange sunset covers Old York, a town located in the middle of the state of New York. The downtown area appears peaceful as shopkeepers close their stores and head home for the night.

Once the sun goes down, a silver car emerges into downtown Old York. The car stops in an empty parking lot next to a florist shop, where a colorful assortment of flowers is still visible through the shop's main window. The glare of a lone streetlight shines through the window, illuminating the flowers.

All of a sudden, a small, silver star-like projectile is hurled at the streetlight. The light vanishes, and the flowers seem to fade into the darkness. A man quickly exits the car and moves behind the building, advancing into the shadows behind it. The unseen figure is an older man with gray hair and a wrinkled face.

However, when the figure steps out to the other side, his appearance has changed. He is now wearing a gray and dark blue ninja-like suit with silver armor pieces, including a silver helmet that resembles a ninja hood. Strapped to his back are two ninja swords and a staff, among other weapons that are attached to the front of the outfit. The figure proceeds through the streets of the downtown area, moving stealthily in the darkness. Car and street lights do not expose the ninja, as he takes advantage of every bit of cover in his path.

The ninja stops at an alley and quietly moves into it. With stealth, he gets behind a dumpster, and peers out from his hiding place.

He is not alone. Five other figures, dressed in black, are already in the alley. The ninja in gray comes out from his hiding place and advances carefully towards them. He reaches for his staff, grips it, and lunges at his opponents. The elderly ninja swiftly knocks down two of the figures and then disappears back into the darkness. The remaining three turn in alarm and look down at their fallen companions. As they reach for their weapons, the ninja re-emerges out of the shadows, twirling two silver fork-like weapons called sais.

One of the three figures raises a knife but does not attack quickly enough. The ninja spins around, and a mighty kick sends the man with the knife flying against a trash can. Another figure whips out a gun and fires it at the elderly ninja.

The bullet ricochets off the ninja's shoulder armor, and the stealthy fighter rotates to escape the gunman's line of sight. When the gunman also shifts to face him, the ninja punches him down with the hilt of a sai.

The last of the dark figures aims his gun at the ninja but fires too late. The stealthy warrior has already returned to his cover behind the dumpster. The ninja's remaining adversary breathes heavily as he slowly advances towards the ninja's hiding place with his gun still raised. The faint glare of a streetlamp shines faintly on this part of the alley, and the man unknowingly walks into this light.

The ninja gets a better look at his opponent's getup, which he finds all too familiar. Designed with dark colors and the emblem of a scorpion, the ninja recognizes it as the attire of the Scorpions, the most dominant gang in the town of Old York.

"Put your weapon away!" the ninja demands, watching his adversary's hands shake.

"NO!" the gang member shouts, with fear in his tone.

"I don't have to hurt you," the elderly ninja adds from behind the dumpster. "There is a way out of this! What Scorpio offers won't help you!"

"He's already helped me! He's given me a purpose, shown me a better path!"

The ninja's opponent points at his fellow gangsters, who are still on the ground, defeated.

"Master Scorpio gave them a purpose, too!" the gangster adds. "AND YOU JUST HURT THEM!"

The ninja stands up.

"I do not seek to harm this town," he replies. "BUT TO DEFEND IT!"

Suddenly, multiple ninja throwing stars— called shurikens— fly towards the gang member. Instead of having sharp tips, these are non-lethal. Nevertheless, they bring the ninja's opponent to the ground, and the gun slides out of the gangster's hands. The ninja in gray stands over his opponent, as the gangster weakly raises his head.

"Remember," the ninja says to him. "No matter what you do or where you are… you can still change. The way out is available. For *you*… and for *anyone*."

The elderly warrior picks up his weapons and starts to leave. The gangster reaches for his gun, grabs it, and gets to his feet. He aims the firearm at where the ninja just was, but there is only darkness in front of him.

CHAPTER 1: "FIRST DAY"

Zach Rylar rushes out of his house, with his school clothes and backpack on. A yellow school bus approaches from down the street.

The scruffy-haired high schooler races down his empty driveway, watching as it flies past his front yard and becomes tinier in the distance.

Zach lowers his head and sighs.

"If only I were faster," he says to himself.

"So... you seek to become faster," Zach hears from behind him.

Zach Rylar does a 180° and faces an elderly gray-haired Japanese man, who is wearing a light blue jacket.

Zach recognizes him almost instantly.

"Grandpa!" Zach exclaims. "What are you doing here?"

"Just doing my regular jog."

"I didn't know you go jogging," Zach states, with some disbelief in his mind.

His grandfather chuckles.

"Even old men like me need their exercise, Zach," he replies.

"Yeah, but jogging? Aren't you like... eighty?"

"Let's just say... I've made physical activity a big priority throughout my life, and I've been trying to get back into it a lot lately," Zach's grandfather explains. "On my run today, I noticed your neighbor at the bus stop, but... I didn't see you."

"Yeah," Zach says, lowering his head again. "I missed it."

His grandfather turns to the empty driveway and then turns back to Zach.

"Does your... mother have the same job?"

Zach nods.

"Yep... the same one where she leaves before I wake up and gets home late at night," Zach responds with another sigh. "I just wish my dad was still around."

As Zach's grandfather looks at him sympathetically, an idea comes to Zach's mind.

"Wait... Grandpa, is your car nearby?" Zach asks. "Could you drive me to school?"

His grandfather chuckles again.

"Why would you use a car when you already have a good means of transportation?"

"What? My scooter?"

"No," the elderly man says with a smile. "Your legs!"

Zach throws up his arms.

"So what, we're just going to run all the way to Lennwood High?! School starts at 8:30, and it's like five miles away!" Zach protests.

Zach's grandfather pulls out a small, black, rectangular object with rounded edges. Zach watches as his grandfather looks down and presses on it with his fingers.

"Actually, it's 3.1 miles away," Zach's grandfather informs him, showing Zach a map on the phone.

"I'm not really in shape, Grandpa," Zach admits and looks down at his body.

"How can you get there?"

"Get where?"

"How can you reach a goal?" Zach's grandfather asks rhetorically. "You desire to be faster, and the path to getting there– and to school on time– is available. You just have to be willing to walk on it."

"Fine," Zach gives in, tightening up his backpack. "But how will we get there on time?"

He takes his phone out of his pocket and checks the time.

"It's 7:55," Zach adds. "Which means we have thirty-five minutes."

"To reach our goal, we must persevere. Work hard, Zach, and through your endurance, you can achieve great speed."

Zach takes a deep breath and stares down the sidewalk. *Okay,* he thinks. *This will all be over soon.*

His grandfather starts to jog down the sidewalk, and Zach follows closely behind him.

"School is this way, right, Zach?"

"No."

"Oh."

They stop, and Zach's grandfather examines the map on his phone. Zach dashes over to his grandfather and helps him to start a route to Zach's school, Lennwood High.

The older man thanks him and proceeds to play upbeat, contemporary music through the phone's speakers.

Rhythm and melody fill the air as Zach and his grandfather run down sidewalks, cross streets, and pass a countless number of houses. At times, Zach catches his grandfather's gaze shifting into the neighborhoods as if he sees something Zach doesn't. All Zach sees are houses, trees, people, and cars.

A mile into the run, Zach stops to catch his breath.

"Zach, please continue!" his grandfather commands.

"*Please*! I'm exhausted and drowning in sweat!"

"Zach… we are one-third of the way there. Do you think you have the strength to finish this?"

While drenched in sweat on the hot August morning, Zach Rylar contemplates his situation and realizes that he has a few options. He could quit now, turn back home, and feel better. Or he could keep going, with a chance of making it to his first class on time, yet feel so drained during the school day.

I could call in sick, Zach thinks, but another thought comes to his mind. *But if I push through this, I might actually make it there on time.*

"Okay," he finally says. "Let's keep going."

Zach's grandfather smiles. He and Zach run alongside each other on the sidewalk, with the music still playing. Occasionally, Zach stops to walk, which his grandfather briefly allows. Nevertheless, Zach's grandfather encourages his grandson to finish strong.

After about thirty minutes in total of movement and music, the duo reaches the parking lot of the school. Beyond the parking lot, stands a connected set of big, brown brick buildings that form Old York's Lennwood High School.

Zach and his grandfather run around the overcrowded school parking lot to avoid all of the vehicles and pedestrians. Zach's calves seem like anvils as he forces his legs to keep moving. While still in motion, Zach pulls his phone out of his pocket and rechecks the time.

"8:26," it reads.

With every step beside the parking lot, Zach feels as though another force is weighing him down, but he keeps going. His eyes look beyond the parking lot. They lock onto the steps that lead to the front doors of the school, as determination fills him. As Zach and his grandfather move closer and closer towards it, passing by students, Zach maintains his pace.

All of a sudden, he trips on a rock and falls to the ground. Pain shoots into Zach's left arm. Zach rubs dirt off of it, and his grandfather helps him get to his feet.

"Press on, Zach! We're almost there!" Zach's grandfather encourages him.

Zach examines his arm and realizes that it is just a minor scrape. He continues to run, with his grandfather beside him.

Finally, the duo reaches the steps and stop to catch their breath.

"Well..." Zach states, panting. "We're here. I guess I'll see you later, Grandpa."

Zach turns to face the school.

"Wait."

Zach turns back to face his grandfather, detecting pride on the older man's beaming face.

"I see... so much potential in you, Zach," he says. "So much. How you fought today tells me that you are very special. If you aren't busy, let me drive you to my place after school. I have something to show you."

"I don't have any plans," Zach replies with a shrug. "I guess I can make it."

"Excellent!" Zach's grandfather exclaims, still smiling. "Now go... and FAST! I don't want you to be late."

****

Zach Rylar races up a flight of stairs in Lennwood's Science building and frantically searches through his backpack. He whips out his schedule and glances at it.

"Room 202... Room 2... 0... found it!" Zach says to himself.

He looks at the time on his phone again and realizes that he is a few minutes late. Zach peers into the room, noticing his teacher writing on a whiteboard with his back to the class. The classroom contains six rows of desks, with five of them in each row. Zach sees a Mexican boy that he recognizes to be his neighbor, Ryan Hampkins, on the other end of the classroom. I might be able to get over there without being seen, Zach thinks.

"And so that is why it is important to follow the rules," Zach hears the science teacher say, as he is still writing on the whiteboard with a dry erase marker. "Without rules to follow, what basis would we have for justice?"

The teacher does a 180° to face the class. Zach waits for the teacher's eyes to return to the whiteboard again before making his move. As Zach waits, he notices that his chemistry teacher has a ginger beard and hair, and is wearing a sand-blue suit. Just as Zach predicts, the bearded teacher rotates back to face the whiteboard and continues to write.

Now's my chance!

Zach rushes quietly into the room, heading towards the back of the class. He walks around all of the desks and approaches the corner of the classroom where his friend is.

Before Zach makes it to the other side of the classroom, he hears a firm voice from the front of the room.

"HEY, YOU!" the voice booms. "STOP RIGHT THERE!"

Zach rotates 90° to face the teacher's hawk-like stare. All of the students in the class also stare at Zach, as nerves build up inside him.

"What's your name?" the bearded teacher asks.

"Uh... Zach Rylar," Zach replies nervously.

"Heh, you almost got marked absent," the teacher states with a snicker and erases something on a piece of paper nearby him.

Zach turns his gaze over to Ryan, who is looking up at him. Ryan points to an empty seat to the left of him, and Zach steps towards it.

"HOLD ON!" Zach's chemistry teacher stops him.

Zach freezes and turns his eyes back to the teacher.

"Tell me a little bit about yourself, Mr. Rylar."

Zach's hands begin to shake as more sweat drips down his forehead. His face is already red from the run, but it gets even redder.

"I'm uh... sixteen. A Junior here at Lennwood," he says. "I um..."

Zach frantically tries to think of words to say in his mind as so many eyes are staring at him.

"You have any hopes? Dreams? Aspirations?"

"I... hope this class will be easy," Zach responds, and some of the students in the class snicker.

The chemistry teacher sighs and waves his hand.

"Alright, sit down," he instructs, and Zach sits in the seat next to Ryan.

Ryan Hampkins has been Zach's next-door neighbor since they were toddlers. The teen has black, wavy hair moved to one side and is wearing a camouflage shirt.

"Why are you so sweaty?" Ryan whispers to him.

Zach chuckles nervously.

"I kind of had to... run here," he replies awkwardly.

"Nice, dude!" Ryan congratulates him in a whisper.

"OKAY!" their chemistry teacher exclaims loudly from the front of the room. "Now that I have gone over why rules are important, it is time to get into the rules themselves."

He turns around and writes on the whiteboard some more.

"Rule number one…" he declares as he writes. "My name is Mr. Earnheart."

"That's not a rule," someone blurts out a few desks to the left of Zach.

"I'M GETTING TO THE RULE!" Mr. Earnheart shouts back. "My name... is pronounced URN-HEART... NOT ARN-HEART! Rule number one is DON'T PRONOUNCE MY NAME WRONG!!!"

"This class sounds like fun," Ryan whispers sarcastically to Zach.

"Rule number two!" Mr. Earnheart continues. "Do not bring lizards into this classroom! This is a Chemistry class, not Biology…"

When the class is over, Zach and Ryan exit the classroom and walk through a sea of people to get to their lockers. Lennwood High's setup consists of three-story buildings, all standing in a square-like formation, with different subjects in each building. The buildings have hallways in between that connect the buildings and contain the students' lockers. Ryan and Zach have Chemistry on the second floor of the science building, so they walk down a flight of stairs to head to their lockers on the ground floor below.

The two friends spent a lot of time together over the entire summer, so they don't need much time to catch up.

"Rule number 53!" Ryan imitates Mr. Earnheart as they are approaching their lockers. "No ostriches in the classroom!"

"Rule number 54," Zach adds with a smile. "No dancing on the desks!"

Ryan and Zach laugh as they reach Zach's locker.

"Well… I'm gonna switch out my books," Zach tells his friend, starting to turn the combination on his locker. "What class do you have next?"

"Gym," Ryan replies. "How about you?"

"Math."

"I'm sorry to hear that," Ryan sympathizes, while Zach unzips his backpack and exchanges his chemistry textbook for his math textbook.

Zach's neighbor seems to be thinking of something, Zach realizes, as Zach notices a smile forming on Ryan's face.

Ryan snickers.

"What?" Zach questions him.

"Remember our freshman year? When we had Algebra with Mr. N?"

"Ohhh yeah!" Zach exclaims. "I miss those math games."

"WHAT'S UUUPPP!!!"

All of a sudden, Zach does a 180° and stands face-to-face with an old friend. He recognizes the face of Mike Alford, who is a tall, African-American guy with a shaved head.

"Mike!" Zach responds, giving him a high five. "It's been so long!"

"Yeah, it's been what… three years since I moved?" Mike questions himself. "But now, I'm back!"

"Awesome!" Zach exclaims happily. "How have you been?"

"Pretty good, pretty good," Zach's friend from middle school replies. "I've done a lot of custom model building since then. Mostly RC stuff."

"Nice!"

"What have you been up to, dude?"

"Not too much," Zach admits.

"Just hanging out with me a lot of the time," says a voice from beside Zach.

Zach turns and recalls that Ryan is standing beside him.

"Oh yeah. Mike, do you remember Ryan?" Zach asks.

"You guys are neighbors, right?" Mike questions Zach.

"Yeah," Ryan answers the question. "We've been friends for like, all of our lives."

"Wow," Mike comments, impressed. "Well... I hope I can also get to know you better, Ryan."

Mike readjusts his grip on his backpack and starts to walk past them.

"Gotta go to my robotics class," he tells them. "I'll see you guys at lunch?"

Zach and Ryan look at each other, and then turn back to him, nodding.

"Yeah, that sounds good," Ryan replies.

Two class periods later, the three friends sit at a lunch table in the school cafeteria. Zach and Mike spend some time catching up, as Ryan devours the school pizza.

"Dang, dude! You're destroying that!" Mike comments.

Ryan looks up at him and smiles.

"The pizza isn't half bad here," Ryan tells him.

Mike takes a bite of his pizza.

"Mmm!!! Okay, this is way better than the food at my old school!"

"So why did you leave your old school?" Zach asks him. "It wasn't the food, was it?"

The pizza Mike is eating slips out of his hand as his eyes fixate off into the distance. Zach is puzzled by the silence of his energetic old friend. To Zach, Mike has always been a super talkative and outgoing guy. However, right now, he seems reluctant to say any words at all.

"I lost…" Mike starts to say.

He suddenly lowers his head and puts it in his hands. Zach's heart beats faster, and his nerves seem to kick in as he hears his friend sniff. Mike then takes his head out of his hands and wipes away tears.

"I lost my bro," he continues, trying to keep his voice steady. "He just got involved in the wrong crowd and…"

As Zach watches his friend put his head back into his hands, he can't help but feel uncomfortable. He wants to sympathize with his longtime friend, but anxiety has overtaken the dark brown-haired high schooler. *What if I say the wrong things? What if I make things worse?*

Zach thinks back to when his father died, and wonders if talking about his own experience might help the situation. Zach knows deep down that he doesn't feel comfortable with getting too personal, so he tries to justify an excuse in his mind.

That happened seven years ago, he thinks. *When I was nine. I've moved on since then.*

"That sounds really hard," Zach hears Ryan tells Mike. "I'm sorry it happened."

Mike sniffs.

"Thanks, Ryan," Mike replies, grateful.

He lets out a chuckle.

"I think I already like you."

Laughter soon fills Zach's ears, as Ryan and Mike start to get acquainted. Zach pretends to laugh along with his friends, but on the inside, all he feels is insecurity.

****

After saying goodbye to his friends, Zach Rylar walks out of the lunchroom alone. Instead of walking with them through the hallways of the school, he decides to take a shortcut.

While multiple, connected buildings make up Lennwood High, there is also a large, open area in the middle of the high school. Zach cuts through this courtyard to get to the gymnasium for his fifth-period gym class.

Lennwood's gymnasium is at the back of the school. There are side doors in it that connect to the hallways of other buildings, but its main doors lead out to the courtyard. As Zach is on his way there, he notices something in the middle of the open area, standing beneath the flagpole.

Huh. This thing wasn't here last year, Zach thinks.

It is a statue of a knight, who seems to be boldly raising his sword in one hand. In his other hand, he is holding a red jewel. There is a plaque in front of the statue, which Zach bends down to read.

Its inscription describes that the knight, which is Lennwood High's mascot, is holding a fake replica of an object called The Knight's Jewel. The jewel will be on a trophy that will be given to a sports team every year.

Zach stares up at the statue and admires how confident the knight appears to be. He breathes a sigh, envying the knight's confidence.

Yet as Zach looks down on himself, the conversation that he had with his grandfather after the run comes to his mind.

"I see so much potential in you, Zach," Zach remembers his grandfather saying. "So much. How you fought today tells me that you are very special. If you aren't busy, let me drive you to my place after school. I have something to show you."

When Zach's school day ends, he remembers the conversation again. After the final school bell rings, students burst out of the buildings and rush towards the parking lot. Zach Rylar is among them, but instead of heading toward the buses as he used to do, he looks around for his grandfather's car.

What does Grandpa's car look like again? Zach asks himself, realizing that he does not know the answer.

Fortunately, Zach spots his grandfather beside his car, which turns out to be a silver model. The two relatives greet each other, and Zach sits in the passenger seat of the vehicle.

"So... what exactly am I going to be doing at your house?" Zach asks his grandfather as the car exits the parking lot and gets on the road.

"You'll see," Zach's grandfather simply responds.

The rest of the car ride is mostly in silence, aside from a few general conversation questions and answers. Zach stares out the window, viewing the uncountable number of trees they pass by.

Eventually, Zach and his grandfather reach the outskirts of Old York, where there are barely any houses, and fields, hills, meadows, and trees permeate most of the land. Zach's grandfather pulls the silver car over to the side of the road, as a tall, round structure on top of a small hill comes into view.

The car doors open and close as Zach and his grandfather step out and proceed to walk up the hill. A small path made of stones leads up to the structure, and Zach follows his grandfather up the pathway. Once they make it to the top, they come to two tall wooden gates. A wood fence of the same height stands on either side of the gates, connected to them.

Zach's grandfather starts to unlock the fence doors.

"Why did you want me to come here, anyway?" Zach asks again.

"I will explain," his grandfather replies while turning the key in the lock.

He puts his keys away, and with both hands, opens the large, wooden fence doors. As Zach follows him inside, the teenager's eyes move around the structure. His grandfather's ordinary white one-story house is on the opposite side of the property, while the tall wooden fence surrounds the property. The ground on the inside of this wall is flat, with no visible blade of grass anywhere on it.

"When I first came to Old York..." Zach's grandfather starts to explain, and Zach turns to look at him. "...I found peace in this town. But as time passed, the crime increased."

"Wait," Zach interrupts. "What does this have to do with me? I thought I was going to help you with some yard work or something. Do you need me to help you plant grass?"

"Let me continue," his grandfather tells him. "From the outside, Old York seems like a peaceful and normal town. Yet in the shadows, some threats have not gone away. Instead, they are growing in strength and numbers."

He turns to Zach and seems to look straight into his grandson's eyes with seriousness.

"One gang stands above the rest, Zach... the Scorpions. This gang has avoided the police and is rising in power. I could not just let this happen, so I..."

Zach's grandfather pauses.

"You what?"

"I decided to stand up to the Scorpions myself," he finishes. "Zach... I, Kenshin Haruta, am a ninja."

Chapter 2: "The Decision"

Zach bursts out laughing.

"HA HA HA HAAA!!! Very funny, Grandpa!" Zach exclaims. "For real, though, why did you want me to come here?"

"I am serious, Zach. I gave up the life I knew and returned to the training of my past to become a ninja again. And I brought you here with the hope that you will join me."

"Join you? What do you mean?"

Kenshin Haruta's serious expression becomes even more serious.

"Zach... I want to share what I have learned. Recently I have been seeking to find a student to help me fight for Old York."

"And you think I could be this student?" Zach asks in disbelief.

His grandfather nods.

"Hold on... so what you're telling me is that you're a ninja... and you want to train me to become a ninja to help you fight... a gang?!"

"I know it's hard to believe, Zach, but what I am saying is true."

Zach still doesn't believe him but considers the possibility. I mean, he's pretty fit for his age, Zach thinks. What if Grandpa really is a ninja?

"So… you fight?" Zach questions. "You're an eighty-year-old, and you fight gangsters that have guns?!"

"Yes, yes, and yes," Haruta responds. "It may seem impossible that I have survived, but I have learned over the years to master the six core elements of ninjutsu, which have helped me greatly in battle."

"The six… what?"

Kenshin Haruta chuckles.

"I will explain later," he states and starts to walk into his house. "For now, let me show you some other things that can help you."

Zach Rylar follows his grandfather into the house, which is a simple, one-story home, painted white. Beyond the front door is a small living room and a kitchen behind the living room. On both sides of the kitchen are hallways. The left one leads to other rooms, while the right hall leads only to a closet and something on the floor in front of the closet. Zach watches as his grandfather sets one knee on the wooden floor and reaches for this metal-like object. The object is large and rectangular, with a handle and keyhole on top of it.

Kenshin Haruta grabs onto the handle, and the hatch opens, revealing a set of stairs that lead below. Zach follows his grandfather down the stairs as his eyes curiously move around the basement-like room.

Kenshin pulls onto a small string on the ceiling, and a dim light illuminates the room. Two pillars hold up the roof in the middle of the room. Next to these supports is what appears to Zach to be a small pool of crystal-like, sparkling water.

20

As he and his grandfather step off of the stairs, Zach turns his head leftward to see an assortment of handheld weapons on the wall.

But something else catches Zach's attention. His eyes focus on the back wall. Against the wall is a closet, and to the left of that closet is something that surprises the teenager. He has never seen anything like it before.

Zach Rylar walks over to it, with his gaze fixed upon it.

"This… is the Gray Ninja Suit," Zach's grandfather declares.

The ninja suit is held up profoundly on the wall, composed of gray, dark blue, and distorted silver colors. It contains protective armor pieces on the shoulders, knees, elbows, wrists, and chest. A silver circular helmet, in the shape and design of a typical ninja hood, rests on top of the suit.

"The 'Gray Ninja'?"

"Exactly, Zach," Kenshin Haruta replies. "It is who I am, and whom I hope you will also be someday."

"How well does this hold up against bullets?" Zach questions, examining the armor.

"The armor was forged from a metal called invinsium. Ever heard of it?"

Zach shakes his head.

"Good. You shouldn't have. It is extremely rare, and I know of no one else who has it," the ninja master says. "How I acquired the metal is a story for another time. However, the armor is strong enough to repel bullets."

"But it's not made completely out of armor," Zach points out.

"No," Kenshin Haruta responds. "That would make it too heavy. This is a suit for a ninja, not a samurai. However… the fabric is strong. It cannot stop a bullet, but may keep you from being cut by knives and other weapons."

"May?"

"Any amount of protection you have, Zach, will be for nothing if you aren't skilled with the six core elements. Even if you do master the elements, you can still get hurt."

"What are these elements you keep talking about?" Zach questions him.

"The six core elements of ninjutsu..." the ninja master states. "...are Strength, Speed, Stealth, Endurance, Balance, and..."

Zach waits for his grandfather to finish.

"And... what?"

Kenshin Haruta smiles mischievously.

"Patience, Zach."

"Are you going to tell me the last one or not?"

"No, Zach. That is it. Patience is the last one," Zach's grandfather tells him with a smile.

Zach sighs.

"If you let me train you, I will teach you how to master each one of these elements," Kenshin Haruta continues. "It will be tough... but will improve you physically and mentally."

Zach's eyes turn to the weapons on the wall. He sees a staff, swords, nunchucks, and other ninja-like weapons that he does not recognize.

"I don't know, Grandpa," he admits, feeling a bit uneasy. "What if I get hurt? What if these gangsters you're talking about... kill me?"

"Fear is holding you back, Zach," his grandfather states. "You are afraid of what could happen and whom you may encounter."

"Well yeah, there are some scary people out there."

"As a ninja, you will learn to conquer fear. For fear has a lesser effect on those who strive to overcome it."

"I guess you're right… but I'm not sure about this."

Kenshin Haruta motions for Zach to follow him again and leads his grandson to the pool of water. As Zach looks into the water, it seems to sparkle.

"A long time ago, I fought to protect this water," Zach's grandfather tells him.

Several empty cylindrical canisters are on a stand nearby, and the ninja master grabs one of them.

"It may seem like normal water at first…" he continues and scoops some into the canister. "But this is no ordinary water. I call this… 'Water of Purification.'"

Kenshin Haruta gently grabs Zach's left arm and then pours the canister of water onto it. During the run, when Zach fell, a nasty scrape opened on it. But now, as a soothing feeling rushes over the wound, the scape seems to close.

"It's… it's healing water!" Zach exclaims and looks up at his grandfather in shock.

"Yes… unfortunately, its amount is limited, and if known to others, would be too highly coveted. So I insist on only using it for emergencies. Besides… the water does not work if a person is past the point of recovery."

Even though Zach just witnessed his wound heal, fear still grips him.

"Grandpa… I still don't know about this," Zach confesses nervously. "I mean, going against a gang? That has a bunch of guns?! It's… it's insane that you've survived for this long, but me? I could die! I mean, I'm only sixteen!"

Zach's grandfather looks into Zach's eyes with a serious look on his face.

"Zach… I would not ask you this if I didn't care about you, and I, believe me, Zach... do care about you. I know we haven't been that close, but I still want what is best for you. This is your decision to make, and I will give you time to think about it. I'll take you home, and will pick you up again tomorrow after school if you're okay with it. If you will reach your decision by then and decide to try this out, we can do so. Do you agree?"

Zach nods slowly.

****

"Mom! I'm home!" Zach announces as he opens the front door of his house and enters his living room.

All Zach's ears can pick up is the faint ticking of the kitchen clock.

"And... she's not here," Zach says aloud, sighing. "As usual."

The teenager takes off his backpack and tosses it aside. He plops down on his living room's couch, kicks off his shoes, and peels off his socks. He grabs a remote on the coffee table in front of him and aims it at the living room TV.

I guess I'll watch some YouTube, he thinks.

He turns on a rerun of one of his favorite shows. The show is a comedy about a hacker and robot that are on the run from a secret agent.

At one point, Zach's phone vibrates in his pocket. He raises it and views the message on the screen. It is a text from Ryan Hampkins, his next-door neighbor.

"Hey. Wanna hang out outside today?" the text message reads.

Zach pauses his show and considers his friend's question. He stares at the message and then looks up at the TV. His eyes move back to the text, as laziness overtakes him.

"Not tonight, sorry," Zach replies.

He turns off the phone, sets it on the coffee table, and resumes the show.

An hour passes, and Zach's stomach growls. He pauses the show again, grabs a huge bag of chips from the pantry in his kitchen, and heats a hot pocket in the microwave. Returning to his spot on the couch, Zach Rylar shoves chips in his mouth. He hits the play button on the remote again and continues to watch the show for another minute.

BEEP!

Zach pauses the show a third time and walks back into his kitchen to grab the hot pocket.

While he is in the kitchen, he faintly hears a car door slam from outside. Zach peers around the kitchen wall and gazes at the living room window to see a figure in a hood approaching his front door.

Suddenly, the doorknob to Zach's front door starts to jiggle. Zach gets behind the kitchen wall, his heart racing.

What do I do?! What do I do?! Zach thinks frantically.

BANG! BANG! BANG!

Someone is pounding on his front door.

Zach reaches in his pocket for his phone, but his stomach sinks as he realizes that he left it on the coffee table. He peers around the corner, and his eyes meet up with the phone.

Okay. I have to be quick, Zach tells himself in his mind.

He charges towards the coffee table and snatches the phone. All of a sudden, he hears a tapping sound on the living room window.

Zach freezes.

He looks up to see the guy in the hood peering through the window and instantly recognizes the face of his next-door neighbor.

With a sigh, Zach lets him in.

"So you are home!" Ryan exclaims mischievously, facing Zach in the doorway.

Ryan is wearing a camouflage sweatshirt with a hood that he lowered after Zach opened the door.

"Was that necessary?!" Zach questions, with anger in his tone.

"What? Did that scare you?" Ryan teases.

"No!" Zach defensively responds, his face red. "You just shouldn't do that to people!"

"I wouldn't do that to just anyone, lol," Ryan responds.

"Yeah, well, I told you that I wasn't able to hang out outside today."

"I was just knocking to ask if you wanted to hang out inside instead."

Zach facepalms, but lets his neighbor inside anyway.

The two friends spend a few hours together, playing video games and eating junk food. Zach eventually sends Ryan home and then starts to get ready for bed.

The next day, Zach awakes to the sound of his alarm clock. He jumps out of bed and smiles at the time on the clock.

Doesn't look like I'll be late for school this time, he thinks.

"Hey, man!" Ryan greets Zach when Zach makes it to the bus stop.

"Sup, Ryan?" Zach greets back.

"I'm good-" Ryan starts to reply, but corrects himself. "I mean- not much!"

"Heh, I make that mistake all the time," Zach admits.

The school bus pulls up to their bus stop, and the two high schoolers get in it. Zach walks through the aisle of the bus, scanning for an open seat. Ryan sits down on one with only one person already on it and motions for Zach to sit across the aisle from him.

Zach does this, but accidentally bumps into the person already sitting there.

This guy, who is wearing a hooded sweatshirt, whips around and gives Zach a look of resentment.

"Sit somewhere else!" the guy in the hoodie orders.

Zach stands back up.

"Sorry, I just want to sit next to my frien-"

"YOU CANNOT SIT HERE!"

"HEY, SWEATSHIRT! LET HIM SIT THERE SO WE CAN GET A MOVE ON!" Zach hears the bus driver yell.

Sweatshirt Guy glares at Zach and clenches a fist.

"This is my seat! You sit here, and I'll break your nose!" he threatens in a hostile whisper. "Whatcha gonna do about it, huh?! Whatcha gonna do about it?!"

Timidity overwhelms Zach as he compares the guy's strong-looking physical appearance to his own.

Zach steps back from Sweatshirt Guy slowly and turns to a girl in the seat behind him.

"Can I sit here?" Zach asks her.

The girl takes off her headphones.

"HUH?" she asks loudly.

Zach repeats his question, and she nods. The girl puts her headphones back in and stares through the window as Zach sits down next to her. The bus drives away from the stop, heading to Lennwood High.

Zach's phone vibrates in his pocket. He lifts it up and reads a text message on his lock screen. It is from his grandfather.

"Don't forget. You have a decision to make," it reads.

****

Zach and Ryan enter their first-period Chemistry class on time. He is following Ryan Hampkins over to their desks when-

Suddenly, Zach trips over a student's backpack and struggles to maintain his balance. His body lunges towards Ryan, who is starting to unload his backpack. Zach crashes into Ryan, who is holding an unzipped pencil case in his hand. The pencil case flies out of Ryan's hands, causing an assortment of pencils, pens, erasers, and highlighters to explode out of it.

The materials shoot towards the front of the room, where all the class can see.

Mr. Earnheart looks up from behind his desk.

"Alright! Who threw the pencils?!" Zach's chemistry teacher demands.

Zach's face turns red as his eyes lock with his teachers'.

"Ah, yes, Mr.... Rylar."

"I'm sorry! I tripped and accidentally knocked over Ryan's stuff!" Zach blurts out quickly.

Several students in the class snicker, as Mr. Earnheart shakes his head in disappointment. Zach and a couple of neighboring students help Ryan to pick up the materials.

****

Zach's foot taps anxiously as the second hand of the clock seems to move in slow motion. His fingers start to drum, and his eyes slide back and forth from his US

History teacher to the clock. To the clock, then to his teacher. Her mouth seems to be moving unusually slow this morning, even slower than the pace of the second hand. *Seven minutes till lunch,* Zach thinks.

Zach Rylar has never been a very patient person and has always been this impatient as a student. On top of that, Zach still feels awkward about what happened at the beginning of Chemistry with Mr. Earnheart. He is also frustrated with himself with how he backed down from facing the 'Sweatshirt Guy' on the bus.

"RING!" the school bell finally shouts.

Zach shoves his textbook and pencil into his backpack and speedwalks out the classroom door. He maneuvers through the hallway traffic and heads to the lunchroom.

Zach speedwalks there as fast as he can, so he can get to the front of the lunch line without having to wait to eat.

He makes it to the cafeteria quickly and somewhat close to the front of the lunch line. As Zach approaches his grub, he spots Mike and Ryan walking into the cafeteria and approaching the back of the line.

They're not that far behind me, Zach thinks. I could wait a bit to eat and talk to them.

But Zach also realizes that he is getting closer and closer to the food, and his stomach is growling. Zach forces the thought out of his mind, focusing on the food in front of him.

Zach Rylar sits at the lunch table that he, Mike, and Ryan sat at the day before. He starts to eat his lasagna before staring off into space.

Considering his grandfather's offer, Zach imagines what it would be like to be a ninja.

If I were a ninja, this day would've gone a whole lot better, he thinks. *And If I were a ninja... people wouldn't look down on me.*

"Look at this food, dude," Zach hears above him and looks up to see Mike looking down on him.

Mike sets his tray down on the other side of the table and sits across from Zach. Ryan walks over to Zach's side of the table and sits beside his neighbor. A third guy that Zach doesn't recognize takes a seat next to Mike on the opposite side of Ryan.

"Yeah, I know. It tastes like plastic," Zach remarks.

"Whatchu mean?" Mike questions in disagreement and taking a bite of his lasagna. "Nah, this is delicious."

The unfamiliar Caucasian teen with spiky brown hair looks at Zach.

"Hi, 'Person I Don't Know.' What's your name?"

"I'm Zach, Zach Rylar."

"Please to meet you, 'Zach, Zach Rylar,'" the brown-haired teen replies. "My name's Seth, Seth Davis."

"Nice to meet you," Zach responds respectfully.

"Seth's one of my new neighbors since I moved back here," Mike explains to Zach. "He lives a couple of houses down from my new place."

"Yep," Seth says. "I also moved here last summer. I mean, I was kinda forced to, anyway."

"Why were you forced to move?" Ryan asks him, and Zach realizes that they have already gotten acquainted.

"My dad may or may not have won the lottery, and like everybody in our town wanted money from us," Seth states with a cheerfulness about him. "So, we had to change our names and move far away."

"Wow," Zach comments.

"Don't believe him!" Mike tells Zach with a laugh. "This dude says some of the silliest stuff."

My grandfather is a ninja, Zach wants to say, but keeps it to himself.

Zach and Seth meet up again later that day, as they realize that they are in the same physical education class. The whole class changes into their uniforms in the locker room and then meets the class's teacher in the gymnasium. Two volleyball nets stand in the middle of the basketball court.

"OKAY, CLASS!" the gym teacher yells to the students. "TODAY WE WILL BE STARTING A UNIT IN VOLLEYBALL. I WILL EXPLAIN THE BASIC RULES, AND THEN WE WILL DIVIDE UP INTO FOUR GROUPS."

After he finishes explaining the rules, Zach and Seth join the same group and move over to their side of the first net.

"You ready to win?!" Seth questions Zach enthusiastically.

"It's our first day of this... it's probably only practice," Zach replies.

"THIS MAY BE OUR FIRST DAY OF THIS, BUT THIS WILL BE A COMPETITION!" their gym teacher shouts. "FIRST TEAM TO TWENTY-FIVE POINTS WINS. IF YOUR TEAM WINS, YOU FACE THE OTHER WINNER. THE TEAM THAT WINS OVERALL WILL EARN BONUS POINTS FOR THE CLASS!"

Zach's teammates get into different positions. Zach stands in the middle and pretends to look ready.

The coach tosses the ball to someone on the opposing team. The teenager with the ball walks to the back of his side of the court.

"You heard the coach! First team to twenty-five wins!" he declares and then serves the ball.

The ball heads straight for Zach, and he attempts to hit it, but only deals a mighty blow to the air left of it. The ball bounces on the floor.

"Come on, dude!" someone behind Zach says.

"I– uh– wasn't ready!" Zach defends.

"Hey, that's okay!" Seth encourages him with pride. "They're not going to beat us!"

The volleyball goes back and forth over the net, and each time the ball hits the floor, a team earns a point. The score seems relatively close, and before Zach realizes it, it is his turn to serve.

Zach's heart pounds as he throws the ball into the air. He tries to hit it, but it jams against his pinkie finger.

"Ow!" Zach cries out as the ball goes out of bounds.

His team just looks at him with disappointment as Zach quickly moves back to his position.

The rest of Zach's serves are about the same, and the game eventually becomes 24 to 23, with Zach's team behind. The opposing team serves the ball, and just like at the beginning of the game, the ball heads straight to Zach.

Zach's right-hand moves towards the incoming ball. WHAM!

The ball goes flying.

However, instead of going over the net, the ball heads east and slams into Seth. Seth hits the ground.

The opposing team laughs and cheers.

"That's game!" one of them taunts. "We won!"

Zach's teammates glare at him. Zach walks over to Seth and reaches out to help him up.

"I'm sorry, dude," Zach apologizes nervously. "Are you okay?"

"Yeah, yeah… I'm fine," Seth responds, getting on his feet. "Did we win?"

Zach gulps, shaking his head with shame.

As everyone else in Zach's class goes to the locker rooms, Zach walks into the bathroom.

He slams the stall to a bathroom behind him, as anger builds up inside of him.

What is wrong with me?!?! Zach fiercely thinks to himself. *Why does this always happen?! First, I'm too slow and can't even make it on my bus on my first day! Then, I couldn't sneak into class without being seen, and today... how was I so clumsy today?! I can't even help my team in a stupid game of volleyball!*

He thinks back to last night and how he mistook Ryan for an intruder. *What if it was an intruder? What would I be able to do about it?! And what would I be able to do if that dumb guy on the bus fought me? Why can't I do anything right?*

Zach's thoughts translate to action as he pounds on the wall of the bathroom stall. In realization of his outburst, he frantically listens for eavesdroppers. Relieved to hear no one, Zach continues his thought.

"What can I do?" Zach whispers to himself, as a lump forms in his throat. "I'm no good to anyone like this…"

****

When the school day is over, Zach races down the steps in front of the parking lot. Zach's grandfather is standing in front of his silver car in the parking lot, wearing a light blue jacket and holding onto a walking stick. Zach speedwalks over to him.

"So," the ninja master says to Zach as they open the doors to the car. "Have you reached your decision?"

"I have," Zach responds, and sits in the passenger seat.

Kenshin Haruta sits in the driver's seat, and the two of them close the doors to the car.

"I want you to train me. I want you to train me to become a ninja."

Chapter 3: "The Six Core Elements - Part 1"

"Every day... I just feel... inferior," Zach tells his grandfather during the drive to the elderly man's home. "Other people always seem to be on top of things, while I'm just... late... or... behind. I'm slow and clumsy and-"

"Have a lot of potential," Zach's grandfather finishes for him. "Zach... you're not a failure."

"I guess not but-"

"But the fact that you were willing to tell me these things, and that you'll let me help you tells me a lot. It tells me that you aren't someone who gives up easily. Your desire for success is very strong, Zach. However... as a ninja, you will learn that success may not be what you think it is."

Kenshin Haruta's silver car pulls up in front of his house's tall, wall-like fence. He and Zach get out of the vehicle, walk up to the doors, and Zach's grandfather proceeds to unlock them.

To Zach's surprise, his grandfather's place has been transformed. Instead of just dirt, a training course has been set up on the compound. Zach spots a pull-up bar, target dummies, a balance beam, and other equipment on the ground in front of the house.

"I figured it was about time I remodeled the place," Kenshin Haruta states with a chuckle.

"All of this stuff... you... you knew I would say yes."

"I didn't know for sure, but I had faith," his grandfather replies.

"Faith?"

"Yes. Faith is the assurance of things hoped for, the conviction of things not seen."

"You hoped that I would say yes, so you set all of this up with that expectation?" Zach questions.

"You're on to something, Zach. Faith often requires action for it to be real, for it to stay alive. As a ninja, you will have to discern the right time to take action."

Zach listens intently to his grandfather's words.

"I have faith that Old York will one day no longer be under the reign of the Scorpions," Kenshin Haruta continues. "So almost every night, I take action and seek to slow down their progress."

"Tell me more about these... Scorpions," Zach tells his grandfather. "They're not actual scorpions, are they?"

"No, but they take on the title of the dreaded creature because of their leader, Scorpio," Zach's grandfather explains. "Scorpio and I were once allies in a gang war. He was a vigilante, like me, who despised gang violence. But he was corrupted by the very thing he hated and formed his own gang, the Scorpions. With his new followers, Scorpio was able to conquer the other gangs and make the Scorpions reign supreme."

Kenshin Haruta's calm and joyful mood has turned into a more serious one.

"They act like scorpions. They inflict pain upon others, especially those weaker than them. That is something I do not tolerate."

He motions for Zach to follow, and after Zach does, they reach the pull-up bar, which is held up in the air by two poles in the ground.

"As I mentioned before... there are six core elements of ninjutsu," the ninja master teaches Zach. "The first of these is Strength. Contrary to popular belief, Strength is not simply the ability to lift weights and get bigger muscles. Strength is the improvement that gets you there. Strength is having the courage to try a hard task even if you feel too weak to accomplish it, and then becoming better because of that experience."

"So what you're saying is...?"

Sensei Haruta's expression transforms into a lively, mischievous one.

"Try ten pull-ups," he commands with a grin.

"Um... okay," Zach simply responds.

Zach jumps and grabs the bar with both of his hands. Zach's puny arms raise his body, and his chin moves above the bar. Then, he lets his body go without losing grip of the bar.

"One," he spits out and attempts to lift his body up again.

"Come on, Zach, I know you can do it!" his grandfather encourages him. "Don't think about the ten... just this one now!"

"Two," Zach says weakly as his chin is raised above the bar a second time.

"Yes! Now focus Zach! Focus on doing one more!"

Zach loses his grip and falls to the ground. His grandfather helps him up.

"I'm sorry, Grandpa. I can't-"

"That's 'Sensei,' my student," Sensei Haruta interrupts him. "And yes... yes, you can."

All of a sudden, Kenshin Haruta moves closer to the bar and grasps onto it. Zach watches in amazement as his eighty-year-old grandfather knocks out ten pull-ups as if they're nothing.

"Wha... but... what?! How?!" Zach stammers.

"If I can do that, surely a somewhat healthy fifteen-year-old like yourself can," Sensei Haruta jokes.

"Sixteen."

"My apologies. But you understand my point, don't you?"

"Okay, I'll do it. I just need some time to rest first."

"I will let you have some, but not yet. Proceed!"

Zach obeys, taking his sensei's place on the bar. The ninja-in-training fights through the pain and lifts himself up.

"One!" Sensei Haruta counts.

Zach lifts his body up again, but his arms start to shake.

"Believe you can do it, Zach. And then... do it!" his sensei tells him.

Zach's chin makes it above the bar.

"Two!"

Zach lets his arms go, and tries to raise himself up again, but considers his arms to be too weak to continue.

"Focus, Zach!" his sensei guides him. "Focus... and press on."

Zach's chin barely makes it above the bar.

"Three! Now forget the ten, just two more, and you're done. Just two more!"

Zach's chin hits the bar, yet he still moves his chin above the bar, fighting the pain.

"That's four! Press on, Zach!"

Zach's arms feel as though they are going to explode. He raises his entire body up once more. His chin is only an inch from the bar when his arms give way.

Zach's feet hit the ground.

"Very good," Sensei Haruta says.

"I didn't make it..." Zach sighs, lowering his head.

"You may have not, but you did improve. And that... is Strength."

Zach's eyes wander to the training course.

"Is that what's next?" he asks, pointing at it.

"For tomorrow. We are finished with training for today."

"Wait seriously? That's it?"

"For today," Sensei Haruta repeats. "The sessions will be longer as we go on, but for now, we are simply going over the basics."

"So when am I going to get my own ninja suit? And what about my own weapon?"

"Don't worry, we will get to combat training soon," Sensei Haruta assures his student.

"You didn't answer my questions."

His sensei chuckles.

"Don't get too ahead of yourself, Zach. Have patience... that time will arrive quicker that you may think."

****

The next day is a Friday, but Sensei Haruta still picks Zach up from school for training. The two of them go to the ninja master's place, which Sensei Haruta tells Zach is a "dojo."

Zach tries to follow his grandfather into his house, but the older man stops Zach.

"Wait here, Zach," Sensei Haruta commands. "I will be right back."

Zach takes this moment to examine the training equipment. It is set up in a line, creating what appears to be an obstacle course.

Less than a minute later, Sensei Haruta steps out of his house, completely transformed. Instead of wearing his light blue jacket and lime green shirt, he is wearing black robes with symbols on them.

"How'd you change so fast?!" Zach questions in awe. "And what is that?"

"This is my teaching kimono," Sensei Haruta explains. "A traditional outfit for senseis like myself."

"That's cool," Zach comments.

Zach notices that his sensei is no longer carrying his walking stick, but is holding onto a different wooden object.

"What's that in your hand?" Zach adds.

"It is called a bo staff," Sensei Haruta replies. "A staff is a valuable instrument for a ninja, especially when practicing the element of speed, which will be what today's lesson will be about."

"Ninja staffs?"

Sensei Haruta facepalms.

"No, Zach. Speed. The second core element of ninjutsu."

"Is that what this obstacle course is for?"

"Yes," Zach's sensei responds, taking out his phone.

Zach stares down at the electronic.

"Let me guess," he blurts out. "You're going to time me each time I do the course, and after I'm done, tell me what my best time was, followed by some inspirational saying."

"Excellent theory, Zach!" Sensei Haruta jokes. "Now... this is the course."

40

He sets his staff on the ground in front of his grandson.

"You will begin behind my staff. Then, you will run to the three recycling bins, jump over both of them, run up the stairs, run to the side of the house, go over the railing, knock down the trash bins, run over to the pull-up bar, swing right around the bar and head to the wall beside it, climb up the wall, jump over to the other side, land by the doors outside of the dojo, run through the courtyard, and run over my staff to finish."

"Uhhh... could you repeat that, like, five more times?"

Five repeats later, Zach Rylar stands behind Sensei Haruta's staff and gets in a running position.

"3... 2... 1, GO!" Sensei Haruta shouts.

Zach dashes towards the green recycling bins and jumps over each of them. Next, he sprints up the steps, making it onto Sensei Haruta's porch. Zach turns left and heads towards a railing. He stops at the railing and carefully lifts his body over it. After his feet hit the dirt, Zach races toward four tall and sizable black trash cans. Zach punches the first trash can, but it only barely budges.

He then kicks the bin with so much force that it slams onto the ground. He pushes the second one towards the third with a powerful blow, which knocks them both over. Zach kicks down the last one and runs over to the pull-up bar. He uses one of the bar's supports to swing towards the wall and leaps in front of it.

Sensei Haruta put supports on the tall wall-like fence beforehand, giving it a resemblance to a small rock-climbing wall. Zach attempts to climb the wall, but his right-hand slips on one of the supports. He falls to the ground below, landing on his back.

"Press on!" Sensei Haruta tells him.

Zach gets back on his feet and attempts to trek up the wall a second time. His left-hand grabs onto a support, and then his right-hand reaches a higher one. Zach raises himself up, repeating this process until he makes it to the top.

As his eyes move down to the ground below, fear engulfs Zach. He fights through the feeling and jumps off the tall fence to roll on the surface below. Zach dashes towards the dojo doors, pushes his way through them, and finally sprints through the courtyard to his sensei.

Sensei Haruta just looks at him. Heart pounding, Zach stares back at him.

"Grandpa... I mean- Sensei?"

Sensei Haruta nods at his staff and nudges it with his foot.

Zach steps over the staff.

"EXCELLENT JOB, ZACH!" Kenshin exclaims, with a hint of sarcasm in his tone.

"What was my time?" Zach asks and eats a massive breath of air.

"I may tell you that at the end," his grandfather replies with a smile. "Now, get ready for lap two."

Zach nods and once again gets into a running position. After Sensei Haruta resets up the trash bins, he gives a countdown, and Zach takes off.

Zach does the course faster this time because he is more familiar with it. With great determination, Zach struggles to climb the railing but still overcomes it. He jumps to the ground and lunges at the trash bins.

A powerful punch knocks one over, as Zach's right foot brings down a second trash bin. Zach kicks a third down and proceeds to run towards the pull-up bar. One trash bin remains, blocking his path. With one massive shove, the final trash bin falls over, and Zach charges towards one of the poles holding up the pull-up bar. This pole is grasped by Zach's hand, and Zach flings himself at the climbing wall. Step by step, grip by grip, Zach advances up the wall. When one of his hands starts to slip again, he quickly grabs onto a different support with the slipping hand. He heaves himself to the top and dives onto the ground below. With one confident sprint, Zach returns to his sensei's staff.

Zach continues this process several more times until Sensei Haruta lets him know that he can stop.

"What... *gasp* was... time?" Zach asks after his fifth lap, out of breath.

Sensei Haruta picks up his staff and then shows him the blank stopwatch.

"You didn't even turn it on!"

"Exactly, Zach, You don't need time to tell you whether or not you did well. Your body can do that. Search deep within yourself and realize not only how fast you really are... but how fast you can be," Sensei Haruta tells him, and then walks to the gate with his staff. "That is all for this week. I will see you on Monday."

****

"Well, I'm glad this day is finally over," Zach says to his grandfather as the duo heads to the dojo after school on Monday.

"I take it you didn't get much out of school today," his grandfather remarks.

"No! It was literally just teachers rambling on about useless information!" Zach exclaims.

"Well, Zach-" Sensei Haruta starts to say.

"What are you going to say... that I should try to take advantage of this 'learning experience'?"

"I guess that is true, but I was going to say that your circumstance is actually really relevant to today's lesson," Sensei Haruta joyfully replies.

"Which is what, exactly?"

"Patience."

"Oh no."

When the duo enters the dojo, Sensei Haruta leads Zach into his house's hallway. He instructs Zach to use the bathroom before the lesson begins since he will be busy for a long time.

"What did you mean by 'a long time'?" Zach asks his sensei after using the bathroom. "And I thought you said the third element was stealth."

"I... am doing them a bit out of order," Sensei Haruta admits. "But that is intentional. And what I meant by a long time is... well, you'll see. Now give me your phone."

"What? Why?"

"Because how can you master the element of patience if you are distracted by a hypnotizing object of instant gratification? Sometimes you just have to set it aside to maintain concentration."

Zach reluctantly hands his phone over to his grandfather.

"Thank you."

Sensei Haruta moves over to a wooden door on the left side of the hallway. He jiggles a doorknob and opens the door.

"Wait, what?" Zach questions as he looks inside. "Is this literally just an empty room?"

The room they are facing has beige colored walls and tan carpet. Except for a plain metal chair, the room is entirely empty.

"This is your next challenge," Sensei Haruta tells Zach. "To master the element of patience."

"Okay, what?"

"Sit in the chair, Zach."

"Huh?!"

Sensei Haruta motions toward the chair. Zach makes his way over to it.

"So… what am I supposed to do?"

"Master patience," Sensei Haruta says while he shuts the door.

Zach throws up his hands.

"Yeah, you said that! What do you mean?!"

There is no response from the outside.

"When will it be over?" Zach calls.

Once again, Zach's grandfather is unresponsive.

"Sensei, I can't stay here forever! I have an essay to write for one of my classes!"

Silence.

Let's see… how can I do this? Zach thinks to himself. *I guess I just have to wait until Grandpa says the time is up. He surely won't make me wait too long.*

Zach stares off into space, trying to think of things to do to pass the time.

"Alright, hands," Zach whispers to his hands. "Get ready for a classic game of Rock, Paper, Scissors!"

Zach shakes both of his hands, and his left one 'becomes a rock,' while his right 'becomes paper.' He repeats this game several times, yet for some reason, the right hand is dominating.

"1, 2, 3, 4, 5, 6, 7…" Zach begins to count a few minutes later until he makes it to one hundred.

Zach gazes up at the ceiling in boredom and breathes a long sigh.

Suddenly, a thought comes to Zach's mind.

What if Grandpa isn't out there anymore?

The ninja-in-training stealthily tip-toes over to the door and moves his hand slowly up to the doorknob. He touches it, and at an even slower pace, turns the knob.

"Crrrrreeeeeeeak!" it screeches, and Zach peers outside.

He realizes that Sensei Haruta brought a couch into the hallway and is sitting on it, reading a book.

The elderly man looks up from his book.

"To many, patience is the hardest of the six elements to master. Do not be one of those 'many.' Focus, Zach, and press on!" Sensei Haruta tells him, and Zach closes the door.

Zach goes back to the chair but sits in it for so long that he feels like standing. I feel like standing, he thinks. *No, I feel like running!*

A burst of energy activates inside Zach. He runs around the room at least fourteen times and even attempts to run down one of its walls. His feet barely stay off the floor for less than four seconds. Still, Zach continues to try this over and over again until faceplanting on the hard floor. Struggling to get up, Zach moves his body onto the chair. It is at this moment that he contemplates the meaning of life.

"What is the meaning of life?" he randomly asks aloud to himself.

Zach Rylar spends a good five minutes, pondering the question.

Does God exist? he wonders.

Zach's mother took him to church when he was really young, and Zach remembers hearing about the deity as a child. *How is it even possible that God has always existed?* Zach asks himself in his thoughts. *I mean, I guess it makes some sense that there's a creator out there... I don't think this world or even my thoughts would able to function if everything just started randomly and from nothing.*

Zach's thoughts shift to wondering why his mother stopped taking Zach to church. *She said it was because of her new job; however, it happened right after Zach's father died. Zach also recognizes that he and his mother first started attending the church when his father was diagnosed, which was nearly two years before he died.*

Dad's funeral was at the same church, Zach realizes. *And Grandpa went there...*

Zach remembers bits and pieces of a conversation his mother and grandfather had shortly after the funeral. He recalls Kenshin Haruta's sympathetic and caring attitude and how his mother was very defensive. Zach's mother rejected her father-in-law's advice and the teachings of the church. Young Zach felt trapped by all of this. He listened to his mother, and for many years had not seen his grandfather, except during family gatherings. However, over the past few years, Zach's mother and grandfather reconnected, and have seemingly repaired things between them. Because of this, Zach's mother has been okay with Zach going to his grandfather's house after school. She believes that Zach is helping his grandfather with some work around the house and is spending some quality time getting to know his grandfather. It never comes to her mind that Zach is actually trying to master patience in an empty room.

Zach's foot taps on the floor. It picks up speed. It taps faster. His entire leg begins to shake, as his fingers drum on the chair.

Zach Rylar propels himself out of the chair. He creeps over to the door once again and sticks his ear to it. He expects to pick up the sound of turning pages, yet only detects the sound of a buzzing fly.

He begins to turn the knob, opening the door even slower than before. Zach's eyes make out the couch and his grandfather's book, which is lying closed on a couch cushion, with a bookmark sticking out of it. Zach opens the door even further and starts to take his first step onto the fluffy hallway carpet. He begins to make his way through the hallway while carefully scanning the area around him. However, once he reaches the couch, he second-guesses himself.

Why am I even trying? I should be done with this by now anyway! Why would Grandpa make me do something like this?

Zach gives up on being stealthy.

"Sensei?!" he calls for his grandfather loudly. "Where'd you go?!"

Suddenly, a blur slams into Zach and knocks him over. Zach doesn't even get a chance to see where it came from. The figure zooms past him and heads into the empty room. Zach pulls himself up to see that his attacker is wearing a black ninja outfit with a hood. The person moves over to the chair, lifts up the chair, and rips a red flag off from underneath it.

"I won!" Sensei Haruta proclaims as he lowers his ninja hood. "I captured the flag!"

Zach facepalms.

"Sensei… you should have just told me that this was a capture-the-flag based game…" Zach protests.

"A ninja…" Sensei Haruta replies. "…should be ready for anything. And patience plays an important role in this awareness."

"What does that even mean?"

"It means… to create a strong sense of your surroundings, you need to wait to really listen."

"Huh," Zach simply responds. "But didn't we just do speed before this? Won't they clash?"

THE SIX CORE ELEMENTS - PART 1

"There are times to be quick... and times to wait. Speed is also an essential element, and if used correctly, it can be mastered well alongside patience."

"Okay, now I'm even more confused."

Sensei Haruta chuckles.

"In time, you will understand, Zach," the ninja master tells his student. "In time... you will understand."

CHAPTER 4: "THE SIX CORE ELEMENTS - PART 2"

"Run around the entire dojo," Sensei Haruta commands Zach.

A day has passed. Zach and grandfather are standing outside of the dojo after school.

Zach takes off his backpack, while Sensei Haruta extends a hand. Zach passes the backpack to his sensei, who sets it beside the tall, wooden fence.

"Just around the entire fence?" Zach inquires.

"Exactly, Zach."

"How many times? Just once?"

Sensei Haruta chuckles, as Zach stares at him, confused.

"Are you ready?" the ninja master questions Zach.

"Yeah, but-"

"Then, if you want to be a ninja... GO!"

Zach is still staring at his grandfather after he says this. Sensei Haruta points his walking stick forward.

The soles of Zach's tennis shoes kick dirt back as the ninja-in-training takes off. Zach's arms cut through the wind, thrusting himself forward.

"Don't forget to pace yourself!" Kenshin calls from behind Zach.

Zach Rylar reduces speed yet continues to run along the east side of the fence. To Zach's right is a small road, the only one that leads to Sensei Haruta's place. The property itself is secluded by woods.

Zach makes it to the end of the side yard fence and turns left to cut into the open yard behind the house. Kenshin Haruta's backyard contains a storage shed, a porch with lawn chairs, a grill, and even a bird feeder. Two trees stand close to the house, while others surround the back portion of the property from several yards away.

Zach's feet stomp through the grass as he makes it to the other side. He turns left again. With the dojo now to the left of him, the ninja-in-training races back to the front. Zach's heart pounds faster, and his breathing escalates as he comes closer to another corner. His body moves left again as he advances into the front yard. Zach's eyes pick up the blue of Kenshin Haruta's light blue jacket. The older man is still standing beside the dojo doors, with his hands resting on the top of his walking stick.

"Do it again!" Sensei Haruta commands as Zach approaches.

Zach flies past his sensei and starts another lap.

When Zach reaches the front a second time, Sensei Haruta is walking towards the dojo doors.

"Again!" the ninja master instructs, without even looking behind him.

However, when Zach finishes his third lap, he doesn't see his sensei.

Zach stops for a second to catch his breath.

"Don't stop until your sensei says so!" he hears from somewhere.

Zach continues to run, going around the dojo again and again and again and again and again and again and again.

Zach has stopped counting. When he makes it to the front again, he slows down.

"Maintain the same pace!" a voice orders.

Zach looks around for his sensei but does not see him. He runs to the side yard and looks backward.

Sensei won't know, Zach thinks to himself as he stops for a breather.

Suddenly, the sound of racing footsteps fills Zach's ears. He looks backward again and to see Sensei Haruta jogging up to him.

"I just need a-!"

"A break?" Sensei Haruta questions. "Oftentimes, there are no breaks during moments of endurance. Oftentimes, breaks can lead to giving up!"

The older man waves his hand at Zach, motioning for him to follow.

"Let's try this a different way!" Zach's grandfather declares. "Run with me, Zach!"

Zach obeys and starts to run beside his grandfather.

"Match my pace," Sensei Haruta instructs. "Keep your knees high, fingers together, and eyes forward."

"But what if... *pants* we get attacked by a crazy squirrel or something?" Zach jokes.

"I'll make sure that doesn't happen," Zach's grandfather assures him. "Just focus... and press on. Be ready for anything, but make endurance your priority today."

"You could... really be a salesman, you know that?"

Zach's grandfather turns to him with a smile. The two relatives run around the dojo several more times until

Sensei Haruta finally stops in front of the dojo. Zach then stops instantly, gasping for air.

"How old are you again?" Zach asks his grandfather, still short of breath.

"I'll be eighty-one in December."

"Okay… *gasps for air* what's your secret?"

"A lifetime of self-discipline, meditation, and exercise. Training my body, mind, and spirit," Sensei Haruta replies. "Oh, and a little Water of Purification here and there."

"Can I have… *wheezes* some of that water?" Zach nearly falls over.

"I feel like I'm dying right now," the ninja-in-training adds.

Sensei Haruta chuckles.

"Trust me, Zach. You're not dying," he says with a smile.

"You know from experience, don't you?"

His sensei nods.

"I can't name off every time I've faced death, but even if I told you about the times I do remember, we would be here past midnight."

There is a brief pause, with only the sound of heavy breathing.

"I have to be honest, Grandpa," Zach opens up. "This 'ninja' thing seemed like a cool idea from the start... but it's been really tough!"

"I'll be honest too, Zach. It's gonna get tougher. A lot tougher. If you wish to continue, you will come to realize that you can apply these teachings to your life. The core elements aren't only useful for a ninja, but for anyone. If you master Strength, you will be better equipped to face the toughness of life. Mastering Speed enables you to work quickly, while the element of Patience can keep you calm through it all. Endurance is essential for pressing on, while Balance is essential to maintain focus and figure out what to prioritize in life. And Stealth... Stealth can be used to humbly pursue success."

"So... balance and stealth are next?"

"Yes, and then I will teach you how to fight," Sensei Haruta tells him. "That is... if you'd like to keep going. It's up to you."

Zach pauses for a moment, contemplating his options.

"You're not going to hold it against me if I say no?" he finally asks.

"Of course not, Zach... in fact, I have been very grateful for the time you've given me to teach you," Sensei Haruta assures him. "However, becoming a ninja requires a great deal of commitment. Is this something you feel like you should commit to?"

If I want to be better, this is what I need to do, Zach tells himself. *I'm so weak... being a ninja could really help me.*

But what if I can't do it? another voice questions in his mind. *What if I don't have what it takes to be a ninja?*

"I... I want to," Zach finally proclaims. "I'm just... not sure..."

Zach's grandfather moves closer to his grandson and pats Zach on the back.

"I know it's a lot to think about," Sensei Haruta sympathizes with his grandson. "It could be your destiny, Zach... your destiny to become the Gray Ninja and to help me defeat the Scorpions. Or it may not be... only God truly knows it all."

Zach's grandfather looks into his grandson's eyes.

"I've prayed about it, Zach... and I have felt as though you're the one I should train. I could be wrong, yet I still would like for you to meditate on it... and ask God about it. When you've determined the path you should take, let me know."

Zach awkwardly lets out a forced chuckle.

"Yeah… God… prayer… good stuff… yeah, I'll do that. That helps, right?"

Zach's grandfather smiles at him again.

"I'll drive you back to your house," he tells Zach. "Call me when you feel like you know what to do," his grandfather instructs. "It can be tomorrow, next week… whenever you're ready."

"Okay," Zach replies. "I'll do that."

****

That night, Zach sits on his bed, deep in thought.

"Could this really be what I'm meant to do?" Zach asks himself aloud. "But what if I'm not good enough? What if I get killed out there… what if people find out that I'm a ninja? Or what if-"

Zach's stomach sinks, and he forces out the words.

"What if I get someone else killed… like Grandpa… or Ryan… or Mom! What if the bad guys find out about them… then they would be in danger too!" he whispers.

I'm only sixteen, Zach adds to the debate in his mind. *How can I fight gangsters that have so many weapons and are skilled in combat?*

Suddenly, Zach remembers what Sensei Haruta had taught him about his allies in battle. About the invinsium-plated Gray Ninja Suit, the Water of Purification, and mastering the six core elements.

"I might be able to survive. And I might be able to take down some bad guys," Zach reasons with himself. "But what if I'm not good enough?"

This is a question that Zach can't seem to find the answer to. Nevertheless, the teenager realizes that he will be better off training with Sensei Haruta than going on with his life as usual.

Throughout his life, Zach has felt an emptiness, a void in his life that has never been filled. Although, at this moment, Zach convinces himself that this ninja training is what his heart has been searching for. With this thought in the back of his mind, he reaches for his phone.

"Hello," Zach greets after calling his grandfather.

"Hello, Zach!" Sensei Haruta answers. "So… have you prayed about it?"

"Yeah," Zach lies. "And I've given it some thought, and…"

Zach hesitates.

"Yes, Zach?"

"Are you free tomorrow to continue?"

****

"Stand on your tippy-toes, Zach."

"Wait… WHAT?!"

Sensei Haruta repeats his command, so Zach obeys.

"Hold that position. I will sit over here," Sensei Haruta tells him, and proceeds to sit on the steps leading up to his house.

It is the next day of Zach's training, a Wednesday. After a long day of school, Sensei Haruta drove Zach here and announced that he would be learning about balance.

"Balance, Zach, balance!"

"This… kinda… hurts!" Zach exclaims, straining to stay on his toes. "Wouldn't this technically be a part of endurance training?"

"Endurance plays a part in the element of balance, just as speed will in stealth," Sensei Haruta explains.

Zach lets go.

"Very good, Zach!"

"Is that sarcasm?"

"No, I actually didn't expect you to go for that long," Sensei Haruta remarks mischievously.

"Uh... thanks?"

Zach's grandfather stands up and tosses aside his staff. He then walks over a cylinder-like support stand in the training course and jumps on it. Then, he raises his left leg and stands on his right toes.

"Practice with me, Zach," he invites, motioning for Zach to come.

Zach jumps onto an identical support beside his grandfather. Zach tries to raise his right leg, but his whole body begins to wobble.

"Zach... focus... FOCUS!" Sensei Haruta coaches.

"I am focusing!" Zach shoots back.

"Okay, what are you focusing on?" his sensei questions.

"Focusing on balance!"

"Yes, but to do that, you must be at peace," Sensei Haruta advises Zach, taking a deep breath. "Breathe with me. Inhale... exhale. Inhale through your nose and exhale out your mouth."

The sensei and student do this together.

"Very good, Zach," Sensei Haruta compliments. "Now, keep going."

Zach continues the exercise for another minute but loses his balance again.

Zach sighs, disappointed.

"That's okay," his grandfather tells him. "We're only going through the basics."

Zach and his sensei repeat the exercise a few more times, and then Kenshin Haruta leads Zach to the wall-like fence.

"Follow my lead," he states and then climbs up the fence.

"Uh, Grandpa! I don't think that's a-!"

Zach's grandfather is now standing on the top of the fence.

"... good idea," Zach finishes.

Sensei Haruta stares patiently at him. After a moment of silence, Zach begins to climb. His experience with doing this on the Speed Training day helps him to make it to the top.

"What now?"

Sensei Haruta starts to walk along the fence, away from Zach.

"OH NO... I am not doing that!" Zach protests.

"What's holding you back, Zach? Fear?" his sensei questions. "*Abandon* fear. Leave it behind. *Focus* on *balance*."

"Okay, okay," Zach says to himself and takes a step. "Focus on balance... focus on balance."

He slowly follows Sensei Haruta, step by step.

"Good, Zach... good," Kenshin Haruta compliments as they walk down the fence. At this point, Kenshin is walking backward.

Zach's arms spin around, and he struggles to keep his feet steady.

"Focus, Zach! Quiet your mind and focus!"

Zach tries to concentrate on keeping his feet balanced, but he wobbles even more. He starts to fall, but Sensei Haruta grabs his arm.

"Try it again!"

It takes Zach a few more tries before he maintains his balance. Eventually, the duo climbs down the fence, and Zach turns to his sensei.

"I'm not good enough, am I?" Zach asks him.

Sensei Haruta turns around quickly.

"No, you are not!" he strictly tells Zach. "But that is the purpose of this training. If you were good enough to be a ninja master, we would not need to train."

He sighs.

"I'm sorry, Zach, but that is the reality. Instead of asking yourself whether or not you are good enough, ask yourself how much you can grow. How much you can *improve* and *mature* through all of this."

Zach nods his head.

"Let's take a short break... and then move on to Stealth training today," Sensei Haruta declares. "You are starting to improve, Zach, but you still have much more to learn."

****

"Ninja are masters of the art of stealth," Sensei Haruta describes to Zach after their break. "It has been said that stealth is one of a ninja's greatest weapons. It can be used to easily take down weaker opponents. We will go through phases to learn this special ability."

Sensei Haruta has led Zach through his backyard and into the forest behind it.

"Phase One: Being able to move without making a sound," the ninja master proclaims. "Allow me to demonstrate."

He steps forward and then looks up at Zach.

"Did you hear that?" he asks.

"I didn't actually," Zach responds.

Zach's sensei takes another step.

"How about that?"

"Okay, what?" Zach questions in amazement. "I was really trying to listen that time, and I couldn't hear anything! Am I losing my hearing or something?!"

"Zach… how loud do you play music in your headphones?"

Zach looks at him with concern.

"Your face, ha ha ha!" Sensei Haruta exclaims with a chuckle. "No, Zach. This is natural. And I can teach you how to master this art."

"Okay," Zach simply replies.

Sensei Haruta lowers his right foot, and with the speed of a turtle, sets his toes down first. When his toes touch the grass, the grass bends down. Then, the heel of his foot lightly touches the ground.

"Now, you try it."

Zach copies his sensei but does not hear the grass.

"Excellent, Zach," Sensei Haruta compliments, and then does the same with his left foot, yet placing it in front of his right.

Zach follows along with him. Sensei Haruta and Zach continue this exercise by placing one foot in front of the other, in a walking motion. Sensei Haruta then shows Zach that if he tiptoes quickly, he can become nearly inaudible.

"Now run like this," Zach's sensei instructs, as he demonstrates his teaching to Zach.

Zach tries it successfully.

"Okay, let's say I'm an old blind guy," Sensei Haruta pretends. "Try to sneak up on me."

He motions for Zach to start at his house's back wall. Then, Kenshin Haruta moves into the woods and stands still with his eyes closed.

Zach walks up to the wall.

"Ready, Zach?"

"Ready!"

"Proceed!"

Zach steps slowly and hears the faint sound of grass being crushed. He raises his opposite leg, and this

60

time, he sets his foot down as his sensei demonstrated. Zach repeats this, shifting his legs back and forth to advance. He then begins to make longer strides, yet still following the method he had been taught.

Sensei Haruta is still yards away, so Zach decides to try to tiptoe-run up to him. After his first steps, he is called out.

"I can hear you!" Sensei Haruta exclaims and opens his eyes.

"Dang… I messed up the run," Zach states.

"You may have, but you did really well with the stealth walk."

Zach's grandfather smiles.

"Come on, Zach. Let's practice the stealth run some more. But remember, don't doubt yourself. Stay confident… as I said before, you have so much potential. And tomorrow, we will begin a very crucial aspect of your training."

"What?"

"Combat."

CHAPTER 5: "COMBAT"

"Have you ever been in a fight before, Zach?" Sensei Haruta asks Zach at training the next day.

"Apparently, in preschool, I pushed some other kid down a flight of stairs."

His grandfather's eyebrows raise in surprise.

"I don't actually remember doing this… my mom said I did, though," Zach clarifies.

"As I mentioned before," Sensei Haruta continues. "Today will be the first day of your combat training. I will first teach you basic fighting skills, and then we will move into martial arts."

"Cool!"

"But first… I have something for you."

A confused look appears on Zach's face as his sensei motions for him to follow. Zach follows Sensei Haruta into the house and instantly notices something different about the older man's living room. Lying elegantly on the couch is something that makes Zach's jaw drop.

"Whoa…" Zach marvels, turning to his grandfather. "Is that… is that-?"

"Yes, Zach. And it is yours," Sensei Haruta replies proudly. "Since you have decided to go through with your training and have learned the six core elements... you are ready for your training gi."

Zach examines his new outfit with amazement. It is a gray and dark blue kimono with a ninja hood.

"Besides... it is better to train wearing this than a T-shirt and gym shorts," Zach's grandfather adds with a smile.

Zach nods in agreement, now holding his new gi. His eyes are glued to it.

Sensei Haruta chuckles.

"I remember when I was given my first kimono," he reminisces. "I'll teach you how to put it on... and then... we will fight."

****

On the opposite side of Old York, a police car maneuvers through traffic. A middle-aged man with a blond flattop is behind the wheel.

"Lieutenant Kowalski, come in," a voice commands over the police radio.

"10-8, Major."

"What's your progress, Lieutenant?"

"I have identified the suspects' vehicle, and I am in pursuit."

"Roger, this is Lawson," another officer says over the radio.

"10-4, Johnny."

"Richie and I are on the other side of the highway. Keep him going this way!" the other police officer instructs.

"So... I'm luring him into a trap! Good work, boys!" Roger tells them.

Roger Kowalski is on a police mission with his fellow officers and friends, John Lawson and Richard Thompson. John and Richard are slightly younger than Roger. John Lawson has brown hair and a brown mustache, while Richard has a black hair combed to the side.

Their mission is to stop two suspects who raided a weapons store and stole a truck.

Roger Kowalski pursues a red truck that is speeding through the highway traffic. His squad car follows closely behind the vehicle, as the policeman's siren causes other vehicles to move out of the way. The truck advances onto an exit ramp, heading into downtown Old York.

"Is this the right truck... red and scratched on the back of it?" Richard Thompson asks.

"Yeah, that's the right truck," Roger responds.

"These guys don't stand a chance..." John proclaims. "...against Johnny Law!"

"I still don't get why I didn't get a cool nickname like you guys," Roger jokes with a chuckle. "I mean, come on... y'all are 'Johnny Law' and 'Rifle Richie,' while I'm just 'Rodge'!"

"Hey, what else am I supposed to call you? Besides, I like 'Rodge.' It suits you," Johnny defends.

"Fine," Roger gives in.

Suddenly, he realizes that the truck is entering downtown Old York. "Okay, boys, you're up!"

"10-4, Rodge!" John Lawson replies enthusiastically.

Roger watches Johnny's police cruiser drive out of an alley and move towards the truck. The truck swerves out of the way but gets stuck in between large trucks and a bus. Two figures, dressed in black, rush out of their vehicle. They maneuver in between cars and dash down the sidewalk.

"They're heading for the neighborhood!" Richie points out.

"Looks like we're on foot," Roger declares. "Let's go!"

John and Richard jump out of their police car and run after the two figures. Roger quickly parks his squad car by the side of the road and joins the chase.

The three police officers chase the suspects down the sidewalk. The suspects reach a fence and jump over it, but Johnny and Richie do the same. However, when Roger reaches it, he stops and continues his chase alongside it.

"Ugh… I wish I was ten years younger," Roger mutters to himself.

The suspects, with Roger's associates after them, jump over the next fence and sprint into a forest. Roger, who is not far behind them, suddenly realizes that he is familiar with this part of the town. He takes a detour into the front yard of the property and charges down the sidewalk. Roger Kowalski activates his walkie-talkie and asks Johnny where the suspects went.

"We're chasing them into a cornfield… Richie, do you see them?" Johnny says over the frequency.

Roger Kowalski hears a faint, "Negative" from Rifle Richie. Roger infers that the cornfield they are referring to is the one he remembers. He makes a left turn and stops at a large field of grass. The cornfield is at the end of the field.

Out of instinct, Roger starts to run again. As he moves through it, he realizes how much harder this is than the last time he was here, which was several years ago. All of his muscles and joints seem to ache, as his heart beats faster, and his breathing accelerates. Roger tells himself to keep going, but when his knees begin to hurt, he feels like he can't help but stop for a moment.

He stops to catch his breath, putting his hands against his knees. When he looks up again, the end of the field feels way further than before.

"Johnny?! Richie?!" Roger questions over his walkie-talkie. "Are they still in the cornfield?!"

"Affirmative!" Richie replies. "I see them!"

Roger continues to run but gets even more fatigued. He pauses another time yet forces his body to push through the pain. Finally, he makes it to the cornfield.

Roger Kowalski slowly makes his way through the tall corn, with his gun raised. Suddenly, he hears the sound of corn being stepped on. He advances into an open patch and points his weapon in the direction of the noise. Two silhouettes approach through the corn.

"Freeze!" the police officer orders.

The two figures step out, and Roger realizes that it is Johnny and Richie.

Roger tries to apologize but is interrupted by Lawson.

"What took you so long?"

"I took a shortcut. Well... almost a shortcut," Roger corrects himself.

"You got tired again, didn't you?" Richie asks.

"Let's talk about this later," Roger tells them. "Where did you last see the suspects go?"

"I think they slipped by you, Rodge," Johnny replies. "Are you sure you didn't see them?"

Roger Kowalski turns around and rushes back the way he came. Pushing back ears of corn, the police officer scans the entire field, noticing woods to the right of the cornfield.

"They're in the woods," Roger declares over his walkie-talkie.

"We're right behind you," John Lawson expresses aloud.

Roger does a 180°, to see him and Rifle Richie.

"Did you see them, or are you just guessing?" Johnny questions.

"If I were trying to escape from us, that's where I would go," Roger tells Johnny. "That's where we should go, come on!"

He motions for John and Richard to follow him and starts to run towards the trees. Johnny and Richie run behind him… no- alongside him… wait, now they're in front of him…

The three police officers raise their firearms as they enter the woods.

"They're in here somewhere," Roger whispers. "Spread out!"

****

"Fighting for a ninja is different from other forms of combat," Sensei Haruta explains to Zach that day.

Zach's sensei had just gone through the basics of fighting with him.

"Ninja are masters of the six core elements. And when it comes to combat, stealth is the most important of the elements for a ninja."

"What about strength and speed?" Zach suggests. "Why aren't they more important?"

"By using stealth, ninja can confuse their opponents. Their opponents are less likely to see them, making them more vulnerable to attacks. Ninja can make their opponents less likely to see them coming. And then, ninja can use the element of speed for rushing up to them and taking them out quickly. If they try to fight the ninja, that is when endurance and strength come in. Ninja endure through attacks, and then ninja use their own strength and skill to counter their opponents' moves."

"When do patience and balance come in?" Zach inquires.

"A ninja must be patient when stealthily waiting to engage his or her opponent, so the attack can be made at the right time," Sensei Haruta replies. "The element of balance is used throughout the entire process. During hiding, a ninja must balance in any position, whether comfortable or uncomfortable. Also, during the fight-"

Zach yawns.

His grandfather looks at him sternly.

"Are you paying attention?" Zach's sensei questions him.

"Sorry, I'm just tired," Zach lies.

"Do we have to do the patience training lesson again?"

"Please, no," Zach replies.

"You'll stay focused?"

Zach nods.

"Yeah, and press on... like you say."

Sensei Haruta chuckles.

"You make it sound like my teaching is some harsh challenge for you to endure."

"Oh no, it's way worse," Zach comments sarcastically.

The ninja master grins, but then shakes his head and continues his lesson.

"Earlier today... we went through the basics of punching, kicking, blocking, and dodging."

Yeah, that took a while, Zach thinks but keeps to himself.

"And now that I have explained why stealth is so crucial, we will combine the two concepts," Sensei Haruta goes on to say.

"Is that why we're in your backyard again?" Zach asks.

"Remember your stealth training in the woods back here?"

Zach nods.

"Now, we will be combining that exercise with what I have taught you today."

Zach notices that in between the trees, there is a random trash can standing in a clearing. He points at it.

"Cool, but why is that there?"

"That… is a Scorpion."

"Are you calling the Scorpions trash?"

"That was not my intention, but that is funny," he comments with a chuckle. "Yet, Zach, the Scorpions are a dangerous threat. These training dummies are not accurate representatives of them, even though this exercise will be quite beneficial for you."

Zach's sensei raises his staff, using it to point at some trees that are several yards from the trash can.

"You will start behind those trees," he instructs. "And remember… use the core elements as you fight."

Zach nods again and gets behind the trees.

"Alright," Sensei Haruta proclaims. "BEGIN!"

****

"Are you *sure* they retreated into these woods?" Richie asks Roger over his walkie talkie.

Half an hour has passed, and Roger Kowalski, John Lawson, and Richard Thompson have all searched the small forest next to the cornfield. Unlike the forest behind Sensei Haruta's house, these woods do not go very far and are cut off by a nearby neighborhood.

"They must've escaped into the neighborhood," Johnny concludes, as they all meet up. "It's a good thing we called backup to get that truck, though. It would have caused a traffic jam."

"Yeah," Roger agrees. "I guess we can search the neighborhood next."

"Forget it," Lawson disagrees. "They're long gone by now. We'll call it in and get backup to do a search."

"It is our duty!" Roger counters. "There are two car thieves on the loose, and-!"

"And what?" Johnny Law questions. "You think they're Scorpions, don't you?"

"They could be," Roger replies. "The weapons store they robbed is in an area that we know the Scorpions have been in before! Then, they stole a truck, making sure their getaway vehicle was expendable."

"Those have been Scorpion tactics," Richie points out. "At least from a few cases."

"If this really was our lead on the Scorpions, Roger, we blew it," Johnny Law complains.

"I... apologize that I didn't get here sooner," Roger says to them.

"Rodge... I'm sorry, buddy, but you may not be cut out for this anymore," Lawson tells him.

Roger stares at him.

"That's not how I meant it," his mustached co-worker clarifies. "I just meant that you've spent a long time in the field... and maybe it's time you considered, I don't know..."

"I get your point," Roger responds. "It did take me a long time to get through that field, after all."

He fakes a laugh.

"I'm sure Chief Mulberry would give you a good job at the department if you asked him for one," Richie suggests to Roger.

"Yeah, you've done so much for Old York in the past, but maybe-" Johnny starts to say.

"What?!" Roger Kowalski questions sternly. "Maybe it's time I fought crime behind a desk?!"

"Not all heroes fight out here with guns and tasers, Rodge," Johnny Law responds. "Some do it in other ways."

"Like with a paper and pen?" Roger states.

"Probably, yeah."

Roger looks down, deep in thought.

What if I did switch to a desk job? he thinks. *I wouldn't get to be out here... I wouldn't get to take down the Scorpions with these guys.*

Roger recognizes that he is getting older, and considers all of the times he has slowed down and

"Thanks for the advice, guys," he tells his friends. "I'll keep it in mind. In the meantime, though, we should focus on the Scorpions. Taking them down should be a higher priority."

****

Zach rushes towards the empty trash can, ready to knock it over.

Suddenly, a blur comes out of nowhere and knocks Zach off of his feet. Zach looks up to see his sensei standing over him.

"What was that for?!"

"Ninja also strive to be ready for anything," Sensei Haruta teaches him.

"Yeah, well... that kind of hurt," Zach complains. "I landed on a gumball!"

"It wouldn't have... if you were ready," his sensei says, and walks over to the trash can. "Remember what I have taught you. Be stealthy when you come up to the trash can this time."

"I was, though!"

"No, you went like this!" Sensei Haruta responds, stomping on the leaves beneath his feet.

CRUNCH! CRUNCH! CRUNCH!

Zach sighs.

"Okay, fine. I'll try again," he gives in and walks back to the starting point.

With a staff in hand, Sensei Haruta remains next to the trash can, like he is guarding it. Zach crouches behind the trees again. He peers out from beneath the tree, but his sensei's gaze catches up to him. Zach quickly moves his head behind the tree, turning to the other side. He recognizes that there are more trees on the other side of this one, and he could be able to sneak over to them without being noticed. He steps forward, accidentally breaks a stick in the process.

CRACK!

"Whoops," Zach whispers to himself and proceeds to take another step.

This time, he repeats what Sensei Haruta had taught him in the previous lesson. Zach tip-toes through the grass, setting his toes down first, then his heel. He also tries to avoid leaves and sticks the best he can, and makes it to the other trees. These trees are closer to the trash can but aren't the nearest ones. Zach makes his way to the first one, tip-toe running this time, because of the more significant gap in between the trees.

Sensei Haruta is still in the middle of the clearing, guarding the trash can. He is scanning the area around him. Once he turns his back to Zach, Zach realizes that this is his chance.

Just like with Mr. Earnheart, Zach recounts.

The ninja-in-training sprints up to the trash can and pushes it over. Sensei Haruta does a 180° and aims his staff at Zach's throat.

"Now what do you do?" he questions his student.

"I'm not going to fight you, Grandpa!"

"Pretend I am not your grandpa or your sensei. I am a Scorpion, and I have my gun aimed at you. What do you do?"

Zach tries to pull the staff out of his sensei hands, but Kenshin's grip is too strong. The ninja master tosses Zach to the ground.

"Grandpa!"

"I am your sensei, Zach! Do not let our relationship as family members get in the way of your training!" the ninja master firmly tells him.

"Sorry," Zach apologizes.

Sensei Haruta extends his arm and helps Zach up.

"Now... we will try that again," Zach's sensei declares. "Except this time, when you grab the staff, get a good grip and twist, don't just pull. And do it quickly. Let speed be your ally."

Zach takes a deep breath, and then with great speed, grips the staff. He twists the weapon, freeing it from his grandfather's grip.

"Excellent job, Zach!" Sensei Haruta compliments Zach. "The technique is very similar with guns. I don't think disarming will be hard for you."

"Really? How'd I do when I snuck up to you?" Zach asks.

Sensei Haruta laughs.

"No... there were many times when I would've spotted you. But we will work on that."

Zach's grandfather starts to walk back to his backyard, and motions for Zach to follow him again.

"Come on, Zach. There is one more thing I want to introduce to you today."

****

"Honey, I'm home!"

Roger Kowalski enters his house, greeting his wife. Mrs. Kowalski speedwalks into the living room, and gives her husband a hug. Amy Kowalski has a bright smile and long, brown hair.

"You're home early," she comments.

"Yeah, the guys agreed to take over my shift," Roger replies.

"Did something happen, Roger?"

"No, Amy, it's okay," he assures her. "It's just that-"

"What is it?"

"I'm... getting old."

Roger's wife bursts out laughing.

"What do you mean?!" she asks. "You're only fifty-one!"

"Yeah, well… maybe it's about time I thought about getting a desk job."

Amy Kowalski stops laughing.

"You're serious?"

Roger nods.

"I've been thinking about it for a while," Roger admits. "I've just been unwilling to, I guess."

"What changed your mind?"

"Heh… trying to run across a field," he says with a laugh.

"Well, you shouldn't push yourself too hard, Roger," Amy replies. "You're brave... and strong... and you've protected this town for so many years. You still have a lot of strength left in you, Roger... I don't think you should give this up just yet."

"Yeah, but how am I going to help take down bad guys if I can't catch up to them?"

"Speed isn't as important as what, Roger?" his wife asks him. "Remember what you told me… all those years ago…"

"...when I married you," Roger finishes for her, gazing affectionately into her eyes. "I was telling you about getting into the police academy, wasn't I? Like my dad. He told me... that the most important part of being a police officer is to care... by protecting and serving."

"Do you think you can still do that where you are now?"

Roger just looks at her, processing this in his mind. He counts all of his recent failures and compares them with his past successes.

Yet, at this moment, the recent gang conflict comes to his mind. He considers how the Scorpions have been rising to power, above all of the other gangs in Old York.

If the Scorpions take over... all of the work I've done for this town will have been for nothing, Roger thinks.

I won't let them have Old York.

****

Zach Rylar and Kenshin Haruta stand in Kenshin's basement, facing a large weapon rack. On it are a countless number of weapons, including sais, knives, a scythe, katanas, short-swords, and many others that Zach does not recognize or much about.

"What's that one called?" Zach asks his sensei, pointing at a knife with a triangular-shaped tip and a hold beneath the handle.

"A kunai," Sensei Haruta tells him. "Sort of like a small knife, but also an excellent gardening tool."

"And the throwing stars?"

"Better known as shurikens. They're like small frisbees for ninja. Except, they are usually with more than one at a time."

"Huh. And that one?"

"That's an ax."

"Oh."

"Perfect for cutting wood."

"Yeah, I know."

Zach turns his attention to another weapon on the wall. Next to the fork-like 'Sais,' there is a small weapon with a chain and two handles.

"Those are nunchucks, right?" Zach asks.

"Yes," Sensei Haruta replies. "The nunchaku is a fascinating weapon. If used incorrectly… well, as you say… it can hurt… a lot."

Sensei Haruta takes a couple of steps back while examining the weapons.

"I guess that can be true for all of these," he adds. "Which is why we will end off the first day of your combat training by using less dangerous versions of these… training weapons."

He leads Zach to a closet in the basement and opens it to reveal wooden and plastic versions of the weapons on the wall. For the next twenty-seven minutes, Sensei Haruta shows Zach how to use each of the practice weapons, and Zach tries his best as he attacks the air with each of them.

"Try the shurikens again, Zach," Sensei Haruta instructs him, so Zach tosses a few plastic shurikens at the wall, and they bounce off of it.

"Hmm… now pick up the nunchaku."

Zach reaches down and lifts up the nunchucks. The training version is lighter than the actual weapon; its handles are made of hard plastic instead of metal and connect to a rope instead of a chain.

Zach swings it around smoothly and carefully, trying his best to avoid hitting himself.

Zach's grandfather beams.

"That's what I thought. You're a natural. Zach… I believe we just found your main weapon."

CHAPTER 6: "FIGHTING BLIND"

Over the next four weeks, Zach continues to train with Sensei Haruta almost every day. He improves physically and becomes way more skillful in ninjutsu than when he started his training. As Haruta's training sessions go on, Zach becomes quicker and stronger. Sensei Haruta even lets Zach battle him for some training sessions. While he doesn't beat his sensei, Zach gets better with every attempt. September becomes October, and Sensei Haruta puts Zach's new skills to the test.

Zach's grandfather hands him a piece of cloth.

"Is this… a blindfold?" Zach asks.

"Exactly, Zach," Sensei Haruta replies with a grin on his face. "And you'll be fighting... me."

"Well, this is going to be difficult," Zach thinks aloud.

"Use senses other than sight," the ninja master teaches him. "Focus on where my position may be and use critical thinking to determine where I will strike."

"So basically I need to smell where you are."

"Focus on what you can hear," Sensei Haruta corrects. "Pinpoint in your mind where you hear my movements, where you can hear me from your current position."

Zach nods and covers his eyes with the blindfold. He ties it to his head and then moves his pupils to look forward. All he sees is dark blue. The walls of the dojo, Sensei Haruta, and Zach's grandfather's house have all disappeared from Zach's vision.

"I won't use any weapons during this exercise," Zach hears his sensei say.

Zach turns in the direction of his voice.

"Except for my hands and feet," Kenshin clarifies, and this time his voice comes from behind Zach.

Zach turns around again and meets a blow to the chest. The ninja-in-training clutches his stomach, grunting. He then quickly punches the air around him.

"Use your other senses," Sensei Haruta reminds him.

Zach moves around, continuing to hit and kick the air around him. He considers Sensei Haruta's words and stops suddenly. *Focus,* he tells himself, just standing there breathing. Zach closes his eyes but realizes that doing so doesn't really make much of a difference in this scenario.

Zach feels a fist slam into his side. However, this time, Zach whirls around and kicks Sensei Haruta behind him.

His sensei comes in again for a serious attack. He hits Zach's right cheek, kicks his leg, and attempts to do more– only to be stopped by Zach's counterattack. Zach kicks his sensei's chest and proceeds this with two punches.

Zach Rylar and Kenshin Haruta end up getting in an intense battle, with each other punching and blocking quickly. Sensei Haruta gets out of the way and kicks Zach backward. Zach falls to the ground but immediately jumps back to his feet. Suddenly, he begins to feel blows from all sides. Kenshin is circling around Zach, continuously landing hits as Zach stands there, confused.

Zach counters this by spinning around with two arms extended, causing his arms to find precisely where Sensei Haruta is. Zach then lunges at his opponent quickly.

A blow to the chin impacts Kenshin, and the ninja master falls on the ground.

"Very good, my student," Zach's grandfather compliments him. "You may take off your blindfold now."

Zach takes off his blindfold to see his teacher getting back on his feet.

"Wait... did I actually beat you?"

"I actually went easy on you there. Also, in a real fight, you would have to make sure I stay down."

"I'm not going to be killing any Scorpions... am I?"

"Killing is not our objective. In battle, we should avoid it as much as we can," Sensei Haruta explains. "Ninja of old were master assassins. Their objective was to get in quickly and slay those they were sent to kill. I teach a different kind of ninjutsu. One meant for justice, protection, and ultimately– the greater good."

****

Roger Kowalski flips through a stack of files. He is standing in front of a desk in the Old York Police Department Headquarters, with Johnny and Richie next to him.

"Stop!" Richie exclaims. "I saw something."

Roger's friend grabs a piece of paper from the stack and examines it.

"This is what we've been looking for," Richie proclaims.

"What's the address?" Johnny asks him, and Richie shows him the paper.

Roger examines the document. It explains the details of a warehouse that was abandoned.

"You're right," he says and compares it with other papers in front of him. "It's the middle of Old York... and these charts say that Scorpion activity is very active in the area around it."

Roger Kowalski looks up from their research.

"Boys... I think we just found a Scorpion hideout."

Three police vehicles race up to a warehouse and stop in front of it. Roger Kowalski, Johnny Law, and Rifle Richie each rush out of their cars and raise their guns.

A lone door is the only thing on the front wall of the building. John Lawson bangs on it.

"OYPD! Open up!"

No response.

"We will search you! We have a warrant!"

Again, there is no response.

Roger examines the doorknob and approaches it. Stepping in front of Johnny, he turns the knob.

"It's unlocked," Roger points out, and motions for the other officers to get back.

All of a sudden, Roger pushes the door open and moves behind the nearest inside wall. When no shots are fired at him, he turns to Johnny and Richie. Roger gives a countdown with his fingers, and then advances through the doorway, with his gun still raised. His fellow officers do the same behind him, but to their surprise, they find a vast, empty room.

"It seems the abandoned warehouse has been... well, abandoned," Johnny points out.

"Maybe the Scorpions never stayed here," Richie guesses.

Roger is about to agree with him until he notices something painted on one of the walls.

"I wouldn't say that," he responds, nodding at the wall.

Johnny and Richie look up to see a large, graffitied emblem of a Scorpion.

****

A ninja runs through the streets of downtown Old York, moving from cover to cover. The ninja, wearing a gray kimono, peers up from where he is crouching. He gazes into a dark alley, where seven hooded figures are conversing. The ninja whips out a pair of actual nunchucks and rushes into the shadows. He knocks down two of these gangsters quickly and then returns to the darkness. The remaining seven turn their attention to their stunned companions. Five of them step out of the shadows, and have their guns are raised in the air. A gray blur moves in front of them and one of the gangsters is whacked down by the nunchaku. A second is pushed against a wall. Three more down. Four.

Suddenly, the ninja unsheathes a short-sword and knocks the gun out of the last gangster's hand. The ninja raises his leg, and a blow to the face sends the gangster flying against a trash can.

"I have beaten you," the ninja tells his fallen opponent.   "Now, where is Scorpio?"

The Scorpion laughs uncontrollably.

"A better question is… who is Scorpio?"

"Focus, Zach!" a voice commands.

Zach Rylar looks up, expecting to see Sensei Haruta. Instead, Zach's chemistry teacher, Mr. Earnheart, is staring right at him. Zach instantly recalls that he is in his first-period Chemistry class.

"Were you sleeping in my class, Mr. Rylar?"

"No! I was just daydreaming, sorry!" Zach spits out quickly.

"I'll ask you again... what is the rarest element on the periodic table?" Mr. Earnheart questions.

Zach has no idea. He remembers elements such as hydrogen and oxygen as he searches deep in his brain for something that sounds somewhat intelligent.

"Invinsium!"

The whole class bursts out laughing, and Mr. Earnheart joins in.

"Invinsium isn't an element... oh, Zach... I think you need to pay more attention when I talk."

"Yes, sir," Zach replies, and his teacher continues with his lecture.

Zach remembers where he got 'invinsium' from. When his sensei showed him the Gray Ninja Suit, he told Zach that the armor was made out of invinsium, one of the rarest elements on Earth.

So maybe I was right, Zach thinks with a smile.

He thinks about his daydream again and fantasizes about what it would be like to fight as a skilled ninja. Moreover, Zach ponders over the Scorpion's question in the dream.

Who is Scorpio?

****

"Are you sure they meet here?"

Roger, Johnny, and Richie are now staking out in a dark alley, in between two shops in downtown Old York, and only a few blocks from the warehouse. They have been waiting for members of the Scorpion gang to show up. They have been doing this behind a dumpster for nearly two hours, avoiding trash and bugs as best as they can.

Roger Kowalski is about to reply to John Lawson's question until Richie raises his hand to silence them. Roger notices two figures walking into the alley.

"Hey man, you ready for another meeting?" one of the figures asks the other.

"Yeah, I've been waiting to hear about our progress," the second figure replies.

"Should we move in?" Johnny mouths to Roger.

"Wait," Roger mouths back.

After several minutes, six more figures enter the alley.

"Let's see how this plays out," Roger whispers.

"I have a message…" one of the figures begins to speak. "From Master Scorpio."

Roger's heart beats faster.

"He says we have succeeded… in taking down the westerners," the Scorpion tells the others.

Some of the other Scorpions begin to cheer.

"The gang that dominated western Old York has been disbanded. Their leaders have fallen, and their members scattered. Some have even joined us."

All of the other Scorpions are now giving their approval.

"How about now?" Johnny whispers to Roger.

Roger shakes his head.

"What is our next move?" one of the Scorpions inquires to the one in charge of the meeting.

"Scorpio wants us to train, to build ourselves up. He wants us to be ready for his next commands."

"What about the cops, and the ninja?" another questions.

Roger listens closely to their words.

"What about them?" the leading Scorpion responds. "The police haven't been able to catch us yet, and that ninja only slows us down."

A ninja? Roger questions in his mind. He remembers hearing rumors that the Scorpions were being attacked by someone else, potentially a vigilante. Roger wonders if that could be this 'ninja.'

"That's all I have to mention this time," the Scorpion in charge states. "I know this meeting was shorter…"

As he continues to speak, Johnny Law and Rifle Richie both turn to Roger. Roger nods, and motions for them to stand. All of a sudden, the three police officers take out their guns and rise to their feet.

"OYPD! GET ON THE GROUND, NOW!" Johnny Law shouts.

The Scorpions take off running. Several of them fire their own guns, causing the three policemen to duck behind the dumpster. Rifle Richie fires back with his pistol, blasting a firearm out a Scorpion's hands. The other gangsters run out of the alley, while this disarmed Scorpion reaches down to grab his gun.

"Leave it!" a retreating Scorpion tells him, but he doesn't listen.

With Roger and Richie covering, Johnny Law leaps out and tackles the remaining Scorpion. Richie handcuffs the Scorpion on the ground, while Roger advances out of the alley, with his gun still raised. The other seven Scorpions are nowhere to be found.

Roger turns around and faces the handcuffed Scorpion.

"Where'd your buddies go? Where are your hideouts?" Roger questions him. "And where's Scorpio?"

The Scorpion looks Roger in the eyes, expressionless.

"That's a lot of questions. What makes you think I even know?" he responds blankly.

"Then tell us what you do know," Roger commands.

"You may think of us as just another gang, but in a lot of ways, we're just like you," the Scorpion says. "We try to keep the peace... the ninja is the real threat! If you cops should be going after anyone, you should go after him!"

"Alright, that's enough," John Lawson asserts, grabbing him by the handcuffs. "I've heard this ninja story before. It's ridiculous."

Roger turns to look at his friend.

"Whenever they fail, they use this ninja as an excuse," Johnny scoffs, and then eyes the captured Scorpion. "Come on, you're coming with us."

As Roger Kowalski and his fellow officers drive the Scorpion back to the police station and take him inside for more questioning, Roger thinks about what he has heard. *Could there really be a ninja vigilante out there?* he wonders.

He contemplates the possibility but also considers the lack of information they have surrounding the Scorpions.

After the Scorpion is in custody at the station, Roger requests to be the interrogator.

Carrying a coffee mug, Roger makes his way to the interrogation room, where the Scorpion is now being confined. Johnny Law rushes up to him from behind.

"I'll join you," he tells Roger.

"Why?" Roger asks him, sipping his coffee.

"To satisfy my curiosity, mostly," Lawson replies with a smile beneath his brown mustache. "We've been blindly pursuing these Scorpions for too long. I just want to know more about them."

Roger gives him a nod, which Johnny laughs at.

"Don't look so worried, Roger. It'll go like this... you be a good cop, and I'll be the bad cop."

"You're already a bad cop," Roger roasts.

"Hey, don't forget, I caught this guy," Johnny jokes back.

The two officers enter the interrogation room. It is a relatively small room with a gray wall. A single table with a chair is in the middle. Sitting on the chair is a Caucasian man with hair only on the very top of his head, wearing an orange jumpsuit. Roger recognizes him as the Scorpion gang member they captured.

"We're back," Johnny Law remarks, and then suddenly clears his throat. "I mean, uh..."

The mustached officer slams on the table.

"TELL US EVERYTHING YOU KNOW!" he shouts.

The Scorpion remains expressionless for a moment and then begins to crack. Except, instead of talking, the gangster explodes with laughter.

"Hey... stop laughing!" Johnny commands, but the Scorpion doesn't stop.

Roger Kowalski turns to his embarrassed friend.

"I think I'll be the bad cop now," Roger tells Johnny and turns to the Scorpion.

All of a sudden, Roger chucks his coffee mug at the wall behind the Scorpion, and it loudly shatters into a million pieces.

The prisoner jumps, and his eyes widen with shock. Roger slowly creeps towards the Scorpion, with squinched eyes beneath his blond flat-top. Second by second, Roger advances towards the prisoner, with his eyes locked with the prisoner's. Fear is written all over the Scorpion's face, as Roger leans down to him.

"He may mess around... but I don't," Roger speaks softly, with his eyes still locked.

The Scorpion gulps.

"Okay," the prisoner gives in. "I'll tell you what I know."

The Scorpion gives them a few new leads on potential Scorpion hideouts, which the policemen find to be abandoned.

However, all of the hideouts have a Scorpion symbol on one of their walls, exactly like the one Roger and his friends found a few days earlier. With the mysteries of the Scorpions and the ninja heavy on his mind, Roger Kowalski tells himself that being out in the field is where he needs to be.

Even if he's just fighting blind.

CHAPTER 7: "THE BIKE RIDE"

"Phew! That was tiring," Zach comments after a lengthy training session.

"Yes, but wasn't it worth it?" Sensei Haruta challenges him cheerfully.

"Ha, it doesn't really feel like it now… but I know you're going to say…"

Zach Rylar makes his best impression of his sensei.

"But, this effort will help you master the art of endurance in the future!" Zach imitates.

Sensei Haruta laughs.

"Well, it looks like you need training in the art of imitation!" he jokes.

"Don't tell me that's real."

"Oh, it's real," Zach's grandfather replies and does a crane pose to demonstrate.

"Animal imitation isn't the same…"

"Close enough."

"That looks more like a flamingo," Zach observes.

"No… this is a flamingo."

They both laugh at Sensei Haruta's ridiculous demonstration.

"That's great," Zach adds, laughing some more.

"What are your plans for this weekend, Zach?" Sensei Haruta inquires.

"Well, actually, some of my friends and I were talking about going on a bike trail sometime this weekend."

"Don't you have school off on Monday?"

"Oh yeah... for Columbus Day. You know, that explorer that mistook the Bahamas for India."

"He was a brave one, though. And his bravery got you a day off from school."

"That's true," Zach agrees. "I think we can still do training over the weekend, I'll just suggest Monday as a good time for the ride."

"Actually, I was going to let you have the weekend off."

"Oh, really? Thanks, Sensei!"

"A bike ride sounds fun. Mind if I tag along?" Zach's grandfather asks. "I even have a special bike mount that attaches to my car."

"Oh... um..." Zach responds.

He thinks about it for a moment. *What would Ryan, Mike, and Seth think if my grandfather went bike riding with us?* Zach wonders. *That might be kind of weird.*

Sensei Haruta looks at him and chuckles as if he is reading Zach's thoughts.

"I think I know how you feel, Zach," he states. "An eighty-year-old hanging out with your teenage friends? That seems awkward, doesn't it?"

"I'm gonna be honest... it kinda does."

"But we are friends, aren't we?"

"Yeah... yeah, you're right..." Zach realizes and then gives his answer. "Yeah, you can come along."

****

The next day, Friday, Zach sits down with his friends at lunch.

"Sup Zach?!" Mike greets.

"Not much, how are you doing?"

"Fantastic!" Mike exclaims enthusiastically. "Especially since we're doing that bike ride this weekend, right guys?!"

"Dude, do I look like I do bike trails?" Seth questions.

"Well, you are kinda scrawny," Mike comments. "Yeah... y'all need the cardio."

Zach holds back a laugh, daydreaming about his ninja training.

He has no idea!

"I used to play football," Ryan reminds them.

"Used to," Mike points out. "When was the last time you rode a bike, though?"

Ryan shrugs.

"I used to ride with Zach all the time when we were kids."

Zach nods.

"Those were the days," Zach reminisces.

"And this'll be fun, too!" Mike exclaims.

"I'm with you," Zach agrees.

"We don't have cars yet, Mike," Seth points out.

"I can just borrow my mom's car," Mike responds.

"Will she be okay with it, though?" Seth questions.

"For sure!"

"You're 100% sure?"

"You just don't want to go, do you?"

"Bruh, I'm not in shape," Seth states.

Zach remembers something Sensei Haruta told him before his first day of school.

"Seth... how can you get there?" Zach asks his friend. "How can you get in shape?"

"You gotta get gains!" Seth answers.

"Well, Seth, the path to getting gains is available. You just have to be willing to uh, bike... on it."

"Zach's right," Mike concurs. "That's how you get muscles."

"Mussels? Good idea, let's go to the ocean!" Seth declares.

"Not those mussels!" Mike replies with a sigh. "And you do realize the ocean is like, two and a half hours away from us, right?"

"How about a creek?" Ryan suggests. "There's a bike trail at the edge of town near a creek."

"Oh, yeah!" Seth exclaims. "I'll even bring my swimming trunks."

"But it's October!" Mike protests.

"Hey, I'll go if we bike to the creek," Seth offers. "That is... if we can actually get a ride..."

"I can get us a ride," Zach blurts out.

"See? We can go," Mike tells Seth.

"Okay, fine," Seth gives in. "But I'm bringing my swimming trunks."

"You're difficult," Mike says to Seth.

"Why, thank you."

****

"You're actually wearing swimming trunks," Ryan observes as Seth rides up to him.

"I came prepared," Seth replies.

The four friends decide to head out the following morning, which is a Saturday. Ryan and Zach are currently standing next to their bikes in Zach's front yard, while Mike and Seth approach on their own bikes.

"Well, we have our bikes," Mike points out and turns to Zach. "Where's our ride?"

"Oh, it'll be here," Zach assures his friend.

Zach pulls out his phone and checks the time.

Grandpa should be here by now, he thinks. *He's usually not late like this. I wonder if he's...*

Zach imagines his sensei fighting gang members in a ninja outfit. He rejects the idea, remembering how Zach's grandfather told him that he mostly fights at night.

A few minutes later, a familiar silver car pulls up in Zach's driveway. It instantly catches the attention of Zach's friends.

"Um... who's giving us a ride, Zach?" Ryan asks him. "This isn't your mom's car."

"You're right," Zach replies, grinning. "It's my grandpa's."

Zach's friends stare at him in bewilderment.

Suddenly, the driver door of the car opens, and out comes Kenshin Haruta, dressed in a blue jacket and exercise pants.

"Is he riding with us?" Seth whispers.

"Oh, yeah," Zach responds. "And he might beat you, Seth."

Seth Davis takes another look at Zach's grandfather and tries his best to hold back a laugh.

Mike elbows him and then walks up to greet the older man.

"You must be Zach's grandfather."

"That's me," Kenshin Haruta smiles while shaking Mike's hand. "What's your name, young man?"

"Mike."

"Nice to meet you, Mike."

"And I'm Seth!" Seth blurts out. "Are you, uh... riding with us, Mr...?"

"Haruta. And yes... yes, I am."

"Oh... cool!" Seth responds, faking his enthusiasm. "Just a random question... how old are you, if... I may ask?"

Mike looks at Seth crossly.

Zach's grandfather chuckles.

"How old are you, Seth?" the eighty-year-old questions.

"Uh... that's classified!" Seth answers.

Ryan snickers behind him. Kenshin turns to meet eyes with Zach's neighbor.

"Hello, Ryan," the older man greets.

"Hello," Ryan greets back quietly.

The man whom Zach knows as his sensei steps closer to the bikes and starts to examine them. He puts his index finger and thumb on his chin.

"Hmm... these bikes are impressive," the ninja master comments, as his eyes move from Ryan's camouflage bike to Zach's blue one.

He gazes intently at a purple bike beside Mike.

"Especially this one," Sensei Haruta adds.

"That's mine," Mike proudly tells him. "I've done a few modifications on it, so it's easier to shift the gears and maneuver."

"Outstanding job, young man," Sensei Haruta compliments before his attention is stolen by something behind Seth.

"What is that?"

"It's my bike," Seth replies, moving out of the way.

Seth's bike is much smaller than the other bikes and rust covers most of its red paint.

"I call it... Ol' Reliable!" Seth exclaims.

He pats it, but the kickstand gives way, causing it to tip over and fall on the ground.

Zach, Mike, and Ryan burst out laughing.

"You'd better hope it's reliable," Mike remarks.

"Maybe come up with an original name for it, too," Ryan adds.

Zach's grandfather moves over to Seth and helps him pick up the old bike.

"Thanks," Seth says to him.

"You're welcome," Kenshin replies. "I actually brought a spare bike in the trunk with me... just in case. You may use it, Seth."

Seth thanks Zach's grandfather again and agrees to use it.

Kenshin Haruta proceeds to instruct Zach and his friends how they can strap the bikes onto the bike rack, which is on the roof of his car. Zach and his friends pitch in to help Kenshin Haruta securely attach Mike and Ryan's bikes to the roof rack, next to Kenshin's, which is already on it.

"I appreciate all of your help so far," Kenshin tells them before pointing to Zach's bike. "We have one more to go. Zach, Mike, lift it up... and I'll help you both raise it onto the rack."

Mike and Zach grab opposite ends of Zach's blue bike, and with Kenshin Haruta's help, begin to mount it onto the rack.

"Seth!" Kenshin Haruta calls the brown-haired teenager. "Please pull this strap down, will you?"

"I gotchu!" Seth responds to the grandfather's request.

"Should I get the other side?" Ryan offers.

"Yes. Thank you, Ryan," Kenshin acknowledges him, and then takes a step back to analyze in their accomplishment. "Fantastic job, everyone."

He moves close to Zach and speaks softly to him.

"God has blessed you with good friends, Zach," Zach's grandfather tells him with a smile.

Yeah... God... Zach thinks but pushes the thought out of his mind.

The five friends embark on their journey. Kenshin is at the wheel, with Zach in the passenger seat, and Zach's friends in the back.

"This is a really nice car," Mike comments, as Zach watches his friend's eyes scan the gray interior of the vehicle.

"Thank you, Mike," Zach's grandfather replies.

"With some modifications, it could be even nicer," Mike adds.

"Like what?" Ryan asks, who is also into cars.

"Well... if it were black and purple-"

"What's wrong with gray?" Zach questions Mike.

"Gray is dull and bland and-"

"Boring?" Sensei Haruta offers.

"Yeah, pretty much," Mike responds.

"Gray is the color of the unknown," the secret ninja master defends. "Gray is the color of humility, and of storms. It also the color of age, and-"

"Koalas," Seth interrupts.

"And wolves," Ryan points out.

"Alpacas," Seth adds.

"Well, black is the color of the night and the color of shadows," Mike defends. "And space."

"Ninjas are black," Seth says.

"Not always," Zach's grandfather corrects him with a grin on his face. "Besides, the plural form of 'ninja' is 'ninja.'"

"You know what the best color is, though?" Ryan pipes up.

"Purple," Mike answers for him. "Perfect for school colors, too."

"No," Ryan disagrees. "*Camo.*"

"Ew, no," Mike protests. "A camouflage car would look ugly."

"No, it would look beautiful!" Ryan exclaims. "Just imagine."

"I am… with disgust," Mike says.

"How about gold?" Seth proposes. "Don't you agree, Zach?"

"I'm more a blue kind of guy myself," Zach answers.

"The color of sadness... Zach, do we need to talk?" Seth jokes.

Zach sighs, rolling his eyes.

Eventually, Kenshin Haruta stops his car on a gravel parking lot of a park, which is just barely outside of Old York. Part of the bike trail begins in the park and is surrounded by trees. The group steps out of the vehicle and get their bikes ready for the ride.

"Are you sure your grandfather can handle this?" Seth whispers to Zach as the group starts to move their bikes towards the trail.

"Definitely," Zach promises.

Seth gives him a look of disbelief.

"You'll see," Zach reassures.

"Hold on," Kenshin Haruta blurts out, and the bikers stop.

He takes a water bottle out of his cup holder.

"Let's get a drink before we start."

"Good idea," Mike agrees with him.

The five bikers take out each of their water bottles and drink from them.

"Is everybody ready to begin?" Kenshin Haruta then asks when he sees that they are finished.

Mike speaks for all five of them.

"Pretty much-"

Before Mike could finish, Seth takes off.

"SEE YOU GUYS AT THE CREEK!" he shouts from what is now 'the distance'.

"And he didn't want to come," Ryan remarks.

"He'll slow down," Zach's grandfather assures him.

Kenshin Haruta starts to ride, and the others follow him. Less than ten minutes pass before they meet up with Seth. Seth Davis quickly looks behind him, and then speeds up even more as Mike, Zach, Kenshin, and Ryan approach, in that order.

"Gotta go fast!" Seth exclaims, but Mike accelerates.

"Get passed!" Mike shouts as he zooms past his friend.

Zach and his grandfather also pass him, but Seth stays in front of Ryan.

"Are you seeing now?" Zach gloats.

"No, I'm blind!" Seth responds.

"We're not racing, though," Ryan says.

"You know, you wouldn't be saying that if you were up here!" Mike calls from in front of them.

"Don't be overconfident, Mike! Your pride wants to control you, but choose to balance your confidence instead," Sensei Haruta teaches him.

"And your pace," Zach adds.

"Do you see these legs?!" Mike jokes, motioning toward his muscular calves.

"I told you, I'm blind!" Seth answers.

"We're all in fairly good shape, actually," Ryan points out. "Well, except for Seth."

"Hey!"

Everyone but Seth laughs.

Another mile into the trail, Zach and his grandfather pass Mike.

"Look at these legs, though!" Zach tells Mike, pointing at Sensei Haruta's legs.

"Bro!" Mike exclaims and matches their speed.

Not long after, Mike and Zach slow down.

"Water break?" Ryan suggests from the back.

"I second that!" Seth agrees.

Zach looks in front of them. His grandfather is well in the lead, zipping past trees, as the bike trail has goes further into a wooded area.

"What do you think, Grandpa?" Zach asks his sensei.

While still in motion, Zach's grandfather reaches down into his bike's cupholder and grabs his water bottle. He carefully unscrews the cap and takes a drink, pedaling with no hands. Then, he screws the lid back on the bottle, sets his left hand on his handlebars, and puts the water bottle back into the cupholder.

"That was my water break," he replies.

"We'll catch up to you!" Mike tells him.

"Are you sure?" Kenshin Haruta questions. "I can wait for a moment."

"Oh, don't stop on our account," Seth tells him deceptively. "In fact, go as far as you can!"

"If you insist," Zach's grandfather responds, picking up speed.

The four teenagers brake and stop by the side of the trail for a water break.

As Zach drinks from his water, something pecks on his leg.

"Ow!" Zach exclaims and jumps.

Mike explodes with laughter, and Ryan and Seth join in.

"It's a chicken!" Ryan observes.

"Where'd he come from?!" Zach questions.

"I don't know… but that was hilarious!" Mike says, laughing even more.

"Come on… it wasn't that funny," Zach responds with a red face.

"Your face, though!" Seth blurts out.

Mike squats down.

"Hey there, little guy!" Mike says to the small, white chicken, who is pecking at his jacket. "Don't eat my jacket, please."

"What should we call him?" Ryan inquiries.

"How about Funky Fidel IV?" Seth suggests.

"No, something more simple," Zach disagrees. "Like Paul or Jon or-"

"Nick," Ryan proposes.

"I like it!" Mike states. "Nick the chicken."

The chicken walks away from them and towards the woods.

"Goodbye, Nick," Seth says to the chicken while wiping away a fake tear. "We'll miss you."

"Why are you so dramatic?" Ryan questions him.

Seth ignores him and gets on his bike.

"Zach… let's catch up to your grandfather," Seth tells him. "I'm sure he's not far off."

Ryan, Mike, and Zach also get on their bikes, and the four friends continue to ride. They seem to be riding for miles, but it seems that no matter how far they go, Sensei Haruta is nowhere to be found.

"Does he have a phone?" Mike asks Zach.

Zach nods and stops by the side of the trail to pull out his phone, as his friends stop beside him. Zach calls his grandfather and puts the phone on speaker.

"Hello!" Kenshin Haruta greets.

"Hey, Grandpa," Zach greets back. "Where are you exactly?"

"By some breathtaking scenery," his grandfather replies. "Have you finished your water break?"

"A while back, yeah."

"Oh. Did you pass the neighborhood with the treehouse?"

"Maybe... I'm not sure," Zach responds and looks to his friends. "Did we, guys?"

They all shrug.

"We don't know, Mr. Haruta," Mike answers for them.

"It's one you can't miss. So you must be in the woods still, right? By the farm?"

"I think we passed the farm," Ryan tells Zach's grandfather.

"Oh, okay! I'll head back," Kenshin Haruta decides.

"No need!" Seth says with a raised voice. "We're on our way! Just tell us... what else did you pass that's of significance?"

"Let's see... a road with a big pothole... um, a park with a pond, and there's a wooden bridge that goes over a creek," Haruta describes over the phone.

"The creek! We'll be there!" Seth declares and snatches the phone out of Zach's hands.

Seth hangs up.

"Why'd you do that?!" Zach demands.

"Dude, there's no way!" Seth tells him in disbelief. "Your grandfather is acting like he's some kind of superhuman or something!"

"He's... an interesting guy," Zach admits. "But I'm telling you... he's not lying. And he's not trying to brag about it either."

"Well... we'll see, won't we?" Seth challenges.

"Guys," Ryan interrupts. "Look at that!"

The four friends turn to where Ryan is pointing.

"What does that look like to you?" Ryan questions Seth.

Zach squints off into the distance. Behind some trees is a house, and in its yard is...

"A treehouse!" Mike points out.

As they resume their ride and advance towards the structure, it becomes more apparent to Zach. Behind the woods is a small neighborhood, and rising high above it is what Seth feared would be there.

"Now that is impressive," Mike analyzes.

"If I lived here, I would just move straight into the treehouse," Ryan adds. "Forget the house!"

"Whatever, man!" Seth grumbles. "There are three more things that we have to get to."

He fiercely picks up speed again, but Zach, Ryan, and Mike all accelerate after him. The four friends continue down the trail, encountering the park Sensei Haruta described as well as the wooden bridge. Ryan didn't miss the opportunities to point them out to Seth, either.

"Dude, I get it!" Seth tells Ryan. "I was wrong. Zach's grandfather is superhuman."

Zach can't help but laugh at his friend's response as they each brake beside the bridge.

Shortly after they stop, the four friends notice Kenshin Haruta on his bike, riding towards them in the distance.

"We made it to all of the things that you told us about Sen- I mean, Grandpa," Zach informs Sensei Haruta as he arrives.

"Except for the pothole," Ryan admits.

Zach's grandfather chuckles and gets off his bike.

"That's probably a good thing," he jokes, and then motions for Zach and his friends to follow. "Come on. Hopefully, we avoid it again on the way back."

"Way back?!" Seth questions him. "What about the creek?!"

"Wait, you're actually serious about swimming?" Ryan questions. "It's October!"

"That's like saying ice cream isn't good in the winter," Seth responds. "Which still is, by the way."

Sensei Haruta looks down the side of the trail, where a hill declines down to a sizable creek below. He pauses for a moment and then turns to Seth.

"Go... have your fun."

"Really?" Seth's asks as his face lights up.

Kenshin nods.

Seth Davis jumps off his bike and bolts down the hill. Still running, he throws off his jacket, shirt, shoes, and socks and dashes into the water. The brown-haired boy waves up at Zach and the other and puts two thumbs up. Mimicking a megaphone, he puts two hands to his mouth and yells something at them.

"I think he's saying the water's nice!" Mike informs them and proceeds to run down the hill himself.

Ryan follows Mike to the creek, so Zach turns to his grandfather.

"Enjoy these moments, Zach," Kenshin Haruta tells him while gazing into the distance. "They won't last forever."

"Are you coming too?" Zach jokes.

"I think I'd better rest," the older man answers. "Join your friends."

Zach races down the hill after Mike and Ryan. They all meet up with Seth in the water, who greets them with three big splashes. They retaliate with more splashes until Ryan unites with Seth against Zach and Mike. A great splashing-battle ensues, as the four friends continue to enjoy their day off.

CHAPTER 8: "THE EXPLOSION"

"WHAT?! HOW?!" Seth exclaims.

After Zach and his friends spent enough time in the creek, they meet back up with Zach's grandfather to head back to his car. On their last mile, they decide to make it a race.

"Ryan's gonna win!" Seth adds from behind everyone else.

Ryan passes the bike trail sign and drifts into the parking lot. Sensei Haruta rides closely behind him, with Mike in third, Zach behind Mike, and Seth in last.

Ryan brakes beside Kenshin Haruta's car.

"Bro, this guy was literally in the back the whole time," Mike remarks. "And then he just destroys us at the end!"

Zach laughs.

"Ryan, how?!" he asks his neighbor.

"It's called strategy, my guy," Ryan responds.

"Ryan demonstrated how to be confident while keeping a steady pace," Sensei Haruta teaches. "He did not become prideful but remained humble. In his humility, he did not lack confidence but saved enough energy to succeed in the end."

"He found balance," Zach recognizes.

"Exactly, Zach."

"Ha! Eg-Zach-tly, Zach!" Seth repeats Sensei's Haruta's words. "That's great!"

Sensei Haruta chuckles.

"I must say… it was fun to spend time with you all," Zach's grandson tells the four friends. "I appreciate all of you letting me come along."

"No problem, Mr. Haruta, and thank you for driving us," Mike returns the gratitude.

"Yeah, without you, we'd have to ride all the way here," Ryan points out.

A mischievous grin forms on the secret ninja master's face.

"Don't give him any ideas," Zach tells Ryan. "He'd make it a challenge."

"I'd be down," Mike accepts.

"Well… I actually have another idea," Zach's grandfather proclaims, and four pairs of eyes direct their attention to him.

"Tomorrow is Sunday, and I'd like to invite all of you to come to church with me. Do any of you have plans tomorrow morning?"

"My family has our own church that we go to, but thanks anyway," Mike answers.

"My dad and I are going to a game tomorrow," Ryan replies.

"I don't think I'd be allowed to go, sorry," Seth apologizes.

Kenshin Haruta turns to his grandson.

"Zach?"

Zach nervously looks up at him.

What do I say?! Zach thinks as sweat drips down his forehead.

His grandfather had talked to him about this kind of thing before, to which Zach declined his invitation. Zach also feels terrible that all four of them would be saying "no" to him if he did. Even though Zach doesn't believe what his grandfather believes, Zach still enjoys spending time with him and is grateful for his training.

What's the worst that can happen? Zach asks himself.

"Okay," Zach gives in. "I'll go with you."

A big smile radiates on Kenshin's face.

"I'm glad to hear it, Zach," he tells his grandson. "I'm glad to hear it."

****

Ryan Hampkins typically finds hanging out with adults that he barely knows to be awkward, but Mr. Haruta is different. He is fun and charismatic, and Ryan appreciates that the older man came along.

Ryan and the other teenagers text their parents to see if they can continue to hang out. After the teens get permission to do so, Zach's grandfather drops them off in Zach's yard, where they detach the bikes from his car.

"See you tomorrow, Zach," Mr. Haruta tells Ryan's neighbor. "It was nice meeting your friends."

"Nice meeting you, too!" Mike affirms. "I'm sure Seth will beat you next time."

"Uhh…" Seth intelligently responds next to Ryan.

Mr. Haruta and Mike both chuckle, and Mike fist bumps him. The older man begins to drive away, as Ryan, Mike, Zach, and Seth all wave goodbye to him.

There is a brief moment of silence; however, an idea comes to Ryan during it.

"Zach, you know what we should do?" he blurts out.

"What?" Zach asks him.

"Stick Dodgeball," Ryan replies.

"Dude, yes!" Zach concurs.

"What's 'Stick Dodgeball'?" Seth inquiries.

"Oh, I remember when we used to play that!" Mike exclaims and turns to Seth. "Zach came up with it. It's super fun! It's like a combination of hockey and dodgeball!"

"Huh," Seth comments.

"Would you like to explain the rules?" Zach asks Mike.

"Yeah," Mike replies. "So... Seth. Each of us is gonna get a hockey stick. Instead of a going after a puck, there's a dodgeball. And we're trying to hit other people with the ball instead of getting it into a goal."

"Each of us gets three lives," Zach adds. "If the ball touches you, you lose a life... even if it rolls over your foot."

Seth starts to nod in approval.

"Okay," he comments. "I'm liking this idea. I accept your challenge."

After Ryan gets four hockey sticks and a small ball from his garage, he and his friends move to Ryan's open backyard patio. Ryan sets the dodgeball in the middle of it.

"Okay, guys," Zach takes charge. "Everyone get in a corner, and this can be our Stick Dodgeball arena. Once we get there, I'll give a countdown, and then we can begin. Remember, keep your sticks low. If the ball gets out of this rectangle, just bring it back inside. You can still hit it from the yard, just don't run away with it. Alright. 3... 2... 1... GO!"

Ryan rushes towards the ball, with his hockey stick just slightly above the concrete. He forces himself to accelerate, but Mike gets to the ball first. Ryan and Seth try to steal the ball from Mike, but Mike maneuvers the ball around their sticks and rolls it over Seth's foot.

"Oof!" Seth exclaims.

Ryan notices that Zach is still in his corner, with his eyes focused on the ball. Ryan charges at the ball, takes it from Mike, and sends it flying towards Zach. Zach ducks and the ball bounces off of Ryan's house and lands in front of Seth. Seth tries to knock the ball into Ryan's foot, but Ryan moves away at the right moment. All of a sudden, Zach seems to come out of nowhere and fights for the ball with his stick. Ryan lets him and Seth struggle for it, watching as it ends up slamming into Mike's foot.

"Dang it!" Mike complains as he loses a life in the game.

The game starts to get intense as Zach ricochet the ball off of Ryan's leg onto Seth's knee, causing both of them to lose a life.

"Zach! Turn off the life hacks!" Seth jokes.

Mike and Zach battle for the ball. Zach loses his first life in the game when Mike slams the ball into his leg. Ryan grabs it with his stick and hurls the ball in Seth's direction. Seth dodges it, and it bounces off of Ryan's house again. To Zach's surprise, the ball hits him in the back.

"Yeah, boy!" Seth cheers and goes for the ball again.

Ryan can tell that Zach is starting to get heated, as his neighbor violently lunges for the ball. Zach and Seth both slam their sticks toward the ball at the same time, and it flies into the air. Zach then swings his high into the air, causing the ball to launch at Seth and bounce off his shoulder.

"You're out!" Zach shouts.

"Dude!" Seth protests defensively. "You almost killed me with that stick!"

"Don't forget, Zach, that's also a rule," Ryan speaks up.

"What is?!" his frustrated neighbor questions.

"You can't swing the stick higher than your waist," Ryan replies. "Or you'll lose a life."

"When did we decide that?!" Zach challenges deceitfully, while Ryan recalls that Zach came up with the rule.

"Like, the first time we played this," Ryan replies.

"Well, we didn't establish it before we started this game!"

"Okay, fine," Ryan acknowledges. "How about this... Seth stays in, and we continue from when he would've gotten out."

"Sounds good to me," Mike agrees.

"No!" Zach argues.

"Yes," Seth tells Zach. "Come on, dude, just play the game."

"Fine," Zach sighs. "So, what's the score now?"

"Mike and I both have two lives, and you and Seth have only one each," Ryan clarifies.

Ryan grabs the ball and looks at Zach.

"Countdown?"

Zach throws up his hands.

"You can do it," he murmurs.

Ryan gives a countdown and then tosses the ball in the air. After a while, Ryan almost knocks the ball into Seth but misses. As Ryan tries to recover the ball, he accidentally taps it with his foot.

"I'm down to one life," he tells his friends.

Ryan quickly examines where the ball is, and with his hockey stick, steers the sphere in Mike's direction.

All of a sudden, Ryan makes a quick decision, as he notices an opening. He rotates the stick and flings the ball straight toward Zach Rylar.

WHAM!

"Oh, and Zach's down to zero!" Seth loudly points out.

Zach slams his hockey stick down on the concrete and storms off of Ryan's patio.

"Zach, chill!" Seth tells Zach. "It's just a game!"

"Yeah, a game that I invented!" Zach shouts back.

Ryan hears something behind him but reacts too late. Mike had already hit the ball in Ryan's direction, and it barely scrapes his knee.

"Did that get you?" Mike asks.

Ryan is tempted to lie.

"I'm out," he admits.

Ryan walks off of his patio and looks at Mike and Seth.

"Good luck, guys," Ryan tells them.

As Mike and Seth face-off, Ryan turns to look at his neighbor, who has his eyes glued to the game. Zach seems absorbed in the game, as Ryan detects a fiery anger inside his best friend. Ryan turns back to the game and watches as scrawny Seth backs away from the muscular Mike, who has the ball.

"You won't," Seth taunts Mike.

Mike launches the ball towards Seth, who drops his hockey stick and dives onto the ground on all fours. Seth quickly gets back on his feet, regains his stick, and goes for the ball.

"That should be illegal!" Zach objects.

"Did you say it was before this game started?" Seth challenges.

Ryan notices that Zach makes a fist, but Ryan quickly redirects his attention back to Seth and Mike when he hears Seth cheer.

"LET'S GO!!!"

Ryan realizes that Seth just won.

Mike gives a chuckle.

"Good game, Seth," Mike replies and shakes his hand.

"GG!" Seth agrees.

Before Ryan can turn back to see how Zach is doing, his neighbor explodes.

"Okay, this shouldn't have happened!" Zach yells. "I would've won if not for that stupid rule!"

"You created it," Ryan counters.

"No, I didn't!" Zach lies again.

"Zach... it's okay. Sometimes we just... lose," Mike tells him.

"Don't give me advice!" Zach shoots back. "I'm-"

Ryan's neighbor stops himself. Ryan stares at him, wondering what Zach is preventing himself from saying.

"You're what, Zach?" Seth questions.

Zach keeps quiet, yet still unmistakably burning with rage.

"What Zach?" Seth repeats. "What makes you so special... that you can't take some simple advice?!"

Zach takes a deep breath and looks down at the concrete. A moment passes, and then Zach raises his head.

"It's nothing," he spits out. "Sorry that I overreacted."

"It happens to the best of us, man," Mike comforts him. "Hey... how about this... how about we all go get some ice cream?"

"Good idea," Seth agrees.

Mike looks at Zach.

"Zach, you in, buddy?"

Ryan and Seth also turn to Zach, who is staring at the ground again.

Zach looks up at them and nods.

****

The next morning, Zach Rylar's right elbow rests against Sensei Haruta's passenger car door, with his head mounted on his hand. He stares through the window, watching the scenery go by.

"How has your Sunday been so far, Zach?" Sensei Haruta asks after Zach doesn't talk for a while.

Zach looks up at his grandfather but doesn't initially respond. Zach thinks back to the outburst he had yesterday. He remembers how Ryan got ice cream from his house and how his friends socialized as they ate their ice cream. Zach didn't talk much after the Stick Dodgeball name and went to bed early that night. He just wanted that day to be over.

"Fine so far," he replies.

"Something wrong, Zach?"

Zach sighs.

"I guess if I can't tell you... who can I tell?" he asks rhetorically. "I mean, it's not really a big deal, but I just got triggered over a game yesterday... with Ryan and the others."

"Triggered?" Zach's grandfather inquires.

"Oh, it means getting really mad about something," Zach explains. "I kind of just… exploded at them."

For once, Zach's wise sensei doesn't respond. Zach turns to him, watching the older man's concentration seems to be on the road. Yet something is off, as he appears to be lost in his thoughts.

"Do you have any advice about that, Sensei?"

"What made you mad at them, Zach?"

"It was my fault… I cheated."

"Are you just saying that, or did they cheat you?"

Zach is confused.

"What are you trying to say, Sensei?" he questions.

"Nevermind," Kenshin Haruta responds. "It's just that... I once had many friends. But in the end, they all let me down. Only God will never let you down, Zach."

"But they're still my friends, even though I didn't agree with them," Zach replies.

Zach's grandfather doesn't say anything for a while, so Zach asks him another question.

"Who did let you down, Sensei?"

Kenshin Haruta takes a deep breath.

"Before I moved to Old York, many decades ago..." he starts to narrate to Zach. "...I grew up in Japan. My friends and I discovered and studied the ancient teachings of ninjutsu, aiming to become ninja ourselves. We were the best of friends, and the more we trained, the more we realized how we wanted to form our own ninja team."

"So... what happened?"

"One day, a rock fell from the sky above our village."

"Like a meteorite?"

"Yes," the older man replies. "I found the meteorite in an underground cave and called for my friends to come over and look at it. This meteorite... it was not made up of rock... but a unique, extremely durable... metal."

"Invinsium."

"Exactly, Zach. And inside of it... was water. Water that we would realize could heal our wounds. Water... of Purification."

Anger and sadness overcome the older man, as he recounts the rest of his past.

"My friends wanted to give it away to the people, but I insisted that we keep it, examine it, and figure out if there was more around or a way to replicate it."

His expression becomes a stern one.

"My friends went behind my back to give it to the village, and that is when I realized something. I could not just let them waste it so quickly. I desired to put it to better use, to make the water last as long as it could. We had forged armor out of the invinsium, which I used to fight them and reclaim the Water of Purification."

"You... fought your friends?"

"There are things from my past I am not proud of, Zach... but they turned against me, and turned the whole village against me. I escaped with the armor, some weapons, and all of the Water of Purification. I went to a place where they would not suspect I would go: a country they had recently been at war with, a country that dropped bombs on them."

Zach is about to interrupt him again, but Sensei Haruta doesn't give him a chance.

"I came here... to Old York," the older man continues. "I devoted my life to research, to figure out more about the Water of Purification. Along the way, I even met a woman that would become... your grandmother."

"What happened to her?" Zach demands to know. "I couldn't even walk before she died."

"Unfortunately Zach, not all love stories have a happy ending. I came to realize that I could not trust her either... and chose... to part ways with her."

His expression becomes even more stern.

"Five years ago, I turned my life over to God. Not long after, I came to realize that only He is completely trustworthy... and that I cannot trust anyone *else*!" he raises his voice.

"Because of Scorpio, right?" Zach guesses. "You tried to team up with him in that gang war you were telling me about, and it didn't work out?"

Zach's grandfather exhales deeply.

"That is right," he responds. "He betrayed me and started a gang of his own... the Scorpions. Zach... I am sorry that I just let anger get the best of me. Anger is a harmful, deceptive poison and deceives people into believing that it gives them strength when it really… only lets them down in the end."

Zach considers something for a moment. While he feels insecure about bringing it up, he asks his grandfather anyway.

"Grandpa?"

"Yes, Zach?"

"Do you trust... *me*?"

Sensei Haruta takes a few seconds to respond but then replies to his grandson.

"Why... yes, Zach. If I did not trust you, I would not have told you that I am a ninja, and would not be training you," he explains. "I also trust that you will be the one to help me defeat Scorpio and his gang."

Zach ponders his sensei's words but simply nods in reply.

****

Zach and his grandfather eventually arrive at a church in downtown Old York. Zach follows Kenshin Haruta out of his car and into a side door of the building. Zach watches as the people inside of the building greet each other, but the ninja master stealthily slips by them. Zach and his grandfather approach the entrance of the church's sanctuary, where another older man is standing and passing out bulletins.

"Welcome!" the man greets.

Kenshin Haruta fakes a smile.

"Hi," he replies and grabs a bulletin.

He and Zach enter the sanctuary, where there are many rows of seats. Kenshin Haruta leads his grandson to the very back row.

"Did you know that guy?" Zach asks him, but Zach's grandfather doesn't respond.

The church service begins. As Zach sits through it, he doesn't really pay attention, and only pretends to be singing during the worship. At one point in the service, a young man walks up to the stage facing the seats. He appears to be in his 20s and has dark brown hair that is pushed back on his head. He walks up to the pulpit with a book and begins to speak. He starts off by clarifying that he is the church's youth minister and that he is substituting for the pastor, whose wife just had a new baby.

"We'll be continuing our study in first John in chapter four. I'll be reading from verses seven through ten," he announces, with the book in his hands.

Zach realizes that it is the Bible and watches as his grandfather opens his own Bible beside Zach.

"Dear friends," the youth minister reads. "Let us love one another, for love comes from God. Everyone who loves has been born of God and knows God. Whoever does not love does not know God, because God is love. This is how God showed his love among us: He sent His one and only Son into the world that we might live through Him. This is love: not that we loved God, but that He loved us and sent His Son as an atoning sacrifice for our sins."

The speaker looks up from his Bible and directs his attention to the congregation.

"How can we show love to one another?" he questions rhetorically. "Well, there are many ways we can do this. We can show others respect, choose to be kind to other people, forgive those who may wrong us... the list goes on and on. In fact, the Bible includes so many ways of how we can demonstrate God's love to other people. And if you're a Christian, you have been called by God to love others. Not to hate. Not to judge. But to... love."

Zach's eyes move over to his grandfather, who looks back at him. Zach's gaze reverts back to the preacher.

116

"Even if you are not a Christian, these things still seem like they're the right things to do, don't they? But what happens? We mess up. We can't get everything right all the time," the minister continues. "It seems near impossible to be 'nice' to everyone 24/7, to be following 'the rules' all day, every day. My friends... that's not the point. If we could live like that all the time, we would be perfect, and Jesus wouldn't have to die. But He did die. Even though we're sinners, even though we betray God all the time by disobeying Him, God still *chooses* to love us. In fact, God loves us so much that He sent His Son to be a sacrifice for us. His perfect Son, who has never sinned, took on every sin that was *ever* committed throughout time... and *suffered* for it. He was beaten up, whipped, and while injured, carried a heavy cross a mile... and was nailed to it! And then He died, very slowly and excruciatingly while a crowd of people ridiculed Him."

Zach considers listening further, but a temptation to think about other things enters his mind.

"I am blown away by what Jesus did next," he hears the minister admit. "Jesus– even though he was literally *suffering* and *dying*– prays to God in Luke 23:34 saying, 'Father... forgive them'! Why should God forgive them?! They are killing His Son! But God chooses to forgive anyone who believes in Him. As John writes in these verses, He showed His love among us through Jesus's sacrifice. God has presented a Way for anyone. Anyone who confesses with their mouth that Jesus is Lord and believes in their heart that God raised him from the dead will be... saved! God does not desire for anyone to perish, but for all to be *rescued* from sin and find new, *eternal* life in Jesus."

Zach has given in to the temptation to zone out. He becomes distracted by all sorts of things, ranging from worry over a presentation he has to do in class tomorrow to pride over how well he is improving with his ninja training.

However, when the youth minister mentions how God is love, Zach questions it in his heart. He knows that he isn't a Christian, but wonders if this is something that he should be thinking about. Zach tells himself in his mind that he doesn't need to be following this. *Sure, this may help others, but so many other things help me,* Zach thinks. *I've felt so inferior for so long. But... now that I'm becoming a ninja, I'm starting to be on top of things! This church stuff isn't for me.*

"You may be thinking... why should I do this?" the speaker predicts, getting Zach's attention again. "Why should I follow God, and stop just doing whatever I want? I'm free! No... without God, you are a slave to sin. But if you let God in, and earnestly seek Him, He will help you to grow and mature. That is what God really wants from you... not to follow simply follow some set of rules or believe in some religion. But to grow in a relationship with the One who created you and loves You more than you can comprehend."

Zach holds back a sigh. He wishes for the service to be over, as he waits impatiently in his seat. Zach looks over at his grandfather, expecting his typical, pleasant smile. Instead, a peculiar expression lies on Kenshin Haruta's face.

The older man's eyes are transfixed forward as he is immersed in the message. Then, he looks down, as if he is contemplating something in his mind.

CHAPTER 9: "ILLUSION"

Zach Rylar and Kenshin Haruta don't say much to each other on the way to Kenshin's dojo.

They both left the church service just right before it ended. Zach guessed it was because his grandfather wanted to slip out before anyone could notice and talk to him.

He really is a ninja, Zach thought at the time.

Sensei Haruta told Zach that they would go to his place for lunch, where he starts to make ham and cheese sandwiches for them.

"So," Zach's grandfather says as he puts ham on bread. "What did you think?"

"I think I'd rather have the honey ham, please," Zach replies.

"I meant about the service," Sensei Haruta clarifies, yet still switches out the hams.

"It was good, I guess."

"Come on, Zach. You can be honest with me," his grandfather tells him, tossing him a sandwich.

Zach takes a bite. As he chews, he thinks about what the minister said, yet also considering his grandfather's behavior.

"Well," Zach replies after a swallow. "I remember how he talked about how Christians should love others, and I thought about what you said earlier. About how there is no one you can trust."

"That's reality, Zach," his grandfather responds. "I really wish people could be more trustworthy, but even though they aren't, that doesn't mean I don't show love to them."

"What do you mean? How do you love people that you don't trust?"

"I protect Old York. I hold the Scorpions back from becoming a bigger threat. I love people by saving them. And that's what Jesus does too, Zach."

"I guess," Zach replies, taking another bite out of his sandwich.

Sensei Haruta finishes his own sandwich, and also starts to eat it.

"There's something else, though," Zach blurts out.

His grandfather looks up at him.

"What is it, Zach?"

Zach thinks about how to form his train of thought and then tries to voice it the best he can.

"You're not like other people," he enunciates. "You seem to isolate yourself off from the rest of society. You live a quiet, retired life, on the edge of town. And when you go to church, you stay out of sight and don't talk to anyone, do you?"

"As I've said… I've tried making friends, Zach. It's better this way."

"What about my mom? And what about me?"

"That's different, Zach," Sensei Haruta says with a smile. "You both are family."

"What about Mike, Ryan, and Seth?"

120

"They're more-so your friends, Zach. I didn't get close to any of them, just entertained them as your grandfather."

"So you don't care about them?!" Zach questions, as frustration builds inside of him.

"No... I do, just... from a distance."

"Okay. Here's a question. If you're really a Christian, what do you think the other Christians would think about this? And what does your God think about all of this?!"

"Those are two questions."

"Then answer them both," Zach firmly demands.

Kenshin Haruta looks at him sternly.

"You will come to realize, Zach, the decisions you will have to make as a ninja can be very difficult. Sometimes... the options you have are more gray than black and white."

****

The Old York Police Department gathers inside their meeting room in the police station the following Tuesday. Tables are lined up to face a podium, with several police officers at each of them. Roger Kowalski sits by John Lawson and Richard Thompson, and they wait for their police chief to enter.

A couple minutes later, the door opens. A tall, older African-American man– with gray hair and small glasses– walks into the room. He is wearing the uniform of a police chief, and Roger recognizes him as OYPD Police Chief Vincent Mulberry.

"Over the past several months, gang violence has increased exponentially. Homes are being broken into, people here are getting hurt now more than ever before. This is a historic time for Old York, and it's up to us to make sure this town survives," Chief Mulberry addresses the police force.

He moves closer to the podium in the front of the room and leans against it.

"From now on… our main priority should be to put the Scorpions away," he continues. "This extremist group declares that they are fighting for peace, that they are fighting for justice… but they are only fighting for the ambitions of their selfish leader, Bill Williams, or as they call him… Scorpio. Have there been any new leads on his whereabouts?"

One of the police officers in front of Roger speaks up.

"Sir, the Scorpions move from place to place quickly, and we're trying to figure out a pattern based on where they move and how often they move."

"Good work, Sergeant," Chief Mulberry tells him, and then looks to the rest of the officers. "Anyone else?"

"Some members have been caught and imprisoned," a female police officer speaks up. "But we haven't been able to find out much concerning the leaders. All we know is that Scorpio is on top, he has a second-in-command, and there is at least one other leader under him."

"How about the gang war?" Chief Mulberry questions. "What enemies does Scorpio have?"

Roger remembers the conversation between the Scorpions in the alley.

The Scorpions said a ninja was fighting them, he thinks. He wants to speak up about it but remembers how Johnny said it was just an excuse for when the Scorpions got captured.

"Most of the other gangs in Old York and the surrounding areas are under the control of the Scorpions," an officer in the back declares. "I've had sources that have said that the Scorpions came in, conquered, and put their own people in place to lead. Now the Scorpions reign over nearly all of their rival gangs' and their territories."

"Anyone else?"

Roger Kowalski feels as though he has to speak up. *What if it's real?* he asks himself. *I can't just keep this information to myself.*

"My team and I have found something," Roger declares.

Everyone in the room stares at Roger Kowalski and his friends. Chief Mulberry looks attentively at him.

"The Scorpions have an enemy," Roger informs them. "A vigilante that uses martial arts and melee weapons to slow down Scorpion activity."

"You mean the superhero ninja?" one officer taunts him.

Other officers laugh.

"We shouldn't just eliminate the possibility," Roger defends. "There may be a ninja vigilante out there, and if so… we need to determine if he's a friend or a foe."

"Vigilantism is against the law, Officer Kowalski," Chief Mulberry sternly commands. "If we see someone dressed up as a ninja fighting other people, we must take them in."

Roger is about to disagree with him, but the police chief cuts him off.

"Some consider the Scorpions to be vigilantes, as they take out other gangs to promote their own code of peace," the police chief states. "This ninja… if he does exist… could be just as dangerous as Scorpio. If any of you spot him… bring him in."

****

"Today, we will put all that you have learned so far to the test."

Sensei Haruta has set up a long obstacle course that Tuesday, similar to the one Zach did during his 'Speed Training.' At the start of the course is a pull-up bar, where Sensei Haruta instructed Zach to do fifteen pull-ups. Then, Zach will have to run through the obstacle course until he makes it to Sensei Haruta at the end.

"Are you ready, Zach?"

Zach nods.

"PROCEED!"

Zach rushes to the pull-up bar, jumps up to grab onto it, and raises his body. The ninja-in-training fights through the exercise, while demanding his muscles to keep working. All of the practice Zach has done since he was taught the six core elements pays off. Zach successfully performs all fifteen reps and lands on the ground.

Although the reps may have weakened him, the ninja-in-training charges through the obstacle course, knocking down trash cans and recycling bins on the way to a balance beam. Zach maintains his balance as he hurries down the beam. Then, after leaping off the end of the beam and letting his feet slide on the dirt, he completes the course.

Zach faces his sensei, who is standing several yards from him.

"How was that?" Zach questions.

All of a sudden, the ninja master pulls a shiny, silver star-like object out of his kimono and flings it at Zach. Zach quickly moves out of the way, and the projectile sticks to the wall behind him. Zach gapes at the sharp shuriken in shock.

"Sensei!"

"As I said... today, all that you have learned so far will be put to the test," Sensei Haruta repeats.

Zach's eyes open wide as his heart beats faster.

"But you could kill me!" he exclaims in fear.

"Don't forget, Zach… I have been training for most of my life," the ninja master defends. "I am skilled enough to know where not to hit you."

"Or, just don't throw them at me!" Zach protests. "You know how painful those things can be?!"

"When you face the Scorpions, you will have to deal with their guns. This lesson is crucial to your training," the ninja master explains.

Sensei Haruta looks straight at Zach.

"Do not let the idea of pain stop you. Pain is an obstacle that tries to prevent you from carrying out your mission. The enemy of pain, its weakness… is endurance, which I believe to be the most vital of the six core elements. Let pain be reduced to a mere illusion. Because for a ninja… pain… is an illusion!"

Sensei Haruta pulls three more shurikens out of his kimono.

"Complete the course again, in reverse!" he commands.

Zach steps onto the balance beam. Suddenly, a shuriken flies towards Zach. Zach jumps out of the way of the shuriken, but slips on the beam and falls to the ground.

"Balance, Zach!"

Zach picks himself up and tries to advance down the beam. Another projectile sails past Zach's ear, barely missing him.

"Sensei!"

"Guns are quicker, Zach! You must be swift to survive!"

Zach picks up speed and moves on to the rest of the course. He dashes past the fallen trash cans and recycling bins, as multiple shurikens fly all around him. A stinging pain shoots into his arm, as the sharp tip of a shuriken sticks to his arm.

"OW!" Zach yells, without noticing the lowered pull-up bar he is approaching.

"DOINK!" goes Zach's forehead as it hits the hard, metal bar.

Zach falls to the ground. Sensei Haruta walks up to him slowly.

"You gave in to pain and lost focus," the ninja master says. "You did not endure... you did not let pain be an illusion."

"How can pain be an illusion?!" Zach argues. "Besides, you're not the one with a shuriken in his arm and a bruise on his head!"

"I know very well what it is like to be 'in pain,' Zach," Sensei Haruta sternly reacts. "And I am telling you, pain can be defeated if you persevere through it. Discipline your mind, Zach. Do not let your feelings deceive you into giving up. Press on... and reduce pain to an illusion."

Zach pulls the shuriken out of his arm and then grunts loudly in discomfort. He frustratingly tosses it aside.

"Don't you have like, training shurikens you can use or something?!"

"Actually, the shurikens I use on missions do not have sharp tips."

"Then why are you using these?!"

Sensei Haruta sighs.

"Zach... as a ninja, if you do not react quickly or stealthily enough, you will be shot at. This lesson is meant to help you deal with the pain, to endure through it long enough to use the Water of Purification when the time is right."

The pain in Zach's head and arm seem to stab into him, but the ninja-in-training resists the urge to complain.

"NOW!" Sensei Haruta exclaims. "WE WILL CONTINUE!"

The ninja master immediately tosses more shurikens at Zach, who quickly ducks and dodges them.

"Think quickly, Zach!" he instructs. "Where should you go?!"

"To find cover!"

"Excellent, Zach! You're thinking like a ninja!"

Zach sprints over to the railing on Sensei Haruta's porch, and with one hand on it for support, he leaps to the other side. Zach ducks again as another shuriken sails above his head.

All of a sudden, Zach gets an idea. He grabs the shuriken and examines it.

Wait a minute... I can use this, he determines.

Zach looks through the gaps on the railing to see his sensei approaching. He watches as Sensei Haruta picks up his shurikens, and grips them.

Zach hastily gets up and tosses his shuriken at Sensei Haruta's hand. The other shurikens escape the ninja master's grip, and Zach realizes that he needs to act fast before his sensei can get them back.

Zach dives over the railing and lunges at Sensei Haruta. He forces the older man to the ground, but the ninja master grabs his arms and flips Zach over. Sensei Haruta pins Zach to the ground.

Zach groans as his back aches with pain.

"Endure, Zach! Or you will not be able to fight any of the Scorpions!"

Instantly, Zach's grandfather's words slam into Zach.

Any?! Zach questions in his mind, as rage builds up inside of him.

He thinks you're inferior, says a voice in his mind.

Zach pushes the thought away and focuses all of his strength into his arms. He pushes Sensei Haruta back and rises to his feet. Zach Rylar's fingers form fists, as his grandfather faces him.

"Very good, Zach," Kenshin Haruta compliments him. "But let your strength result from your endurance, not from anger."

Zach unclenches his fists and lowers his hands.

"Sorry about that, Sensei," he apologizes.

"That's alright, Zach. Temptation is inevitable. You just have to learn how to deal with it. Now come... let's take care of your injuries."

****

A worn-out Zach walks up to his neighbor, Ryan, at the bus stop the next day.

"Hi, Zach," Ryan greets. "How are you?"

"Tired," Zach admits.

"From lack of sleep?" Ryan Hampkins questions.

"No," Zach replies. "I did some really intense running and stuff yesterday."

"Oh, I didn't know you ran," Ryan comments. "I'd be willing to run with you sometime."

As much as Zach would probably enjoy running with his best friend, his thoughts dwell on his training. He tries to think of an excuse but is saved by the bus arriving at their stop before he can respond.

As the two friends get on, Zach realizes there are no open seats, and decides to sit next to a sleeping person in a hoodie. Ryan sits next to a bored girl across from him and turns back to Zach.

"Did you get my text?" Ryan asks him. "I called after that too... did you... listen to the voicemail?"

"I got it," Zach answers, remembering that Ryan had sent him one day before.

Sensei Haruta has kept Zach off of his phone during training, while Ryan has been trying to call Zach numerous times over the past month. Zach didn't answer most of his calls or even reply to him when he got home. Yesterday, Ryan asked Zach what he usually asks over the text and the voicemail; if Zach could hang out.

"I forgot to reply," Zach lies.

"I've tried knocking on your door," Ryan tells Zach. "Every time, you're not home."

"I'm at my grandfather's house a lot," Zach responds.

"Why?" Ryan asks.

"Uh… he uh, needs a lot of help."

"I'm sorry, I didn't know. He seemed fine during that bike ride."

"Biking for a long time doesn't affect his condition," Zach continues deceitfully. "But he's gotten worse. That's why I'm over there just about every day."

"Dude, can I help in any way?" Ryan offers. "I could rake his leaves or cut his grass or something."

"No, that's okay," Zach insists.

"Well… if you ever need a friend to hang out with, I'll always be here," Ryan tells him. "You know… in my house... all the time."

"Thanks, man," Zach replies. "Sorry about missing all of those calls... I'll try to get back to you next time."

The bus stops at another stop, and more teens get on. Mike and Seth are among them.

"Ryan, Zach... what's up, guys?!" Mike Alford greets as he sits by them.

"Not much," Zach replies.

"Hi," Ryan greets back softly.

Seth Davis, who is wearing his neon green hoodie, approaches Zach.

"Zach, my guy! How's it going!" he exclaims and scoots into the same seat that Zach is sitting in. This causes Zach to be pushed into the sleeping guy next to him, who jumps up abruptly.

"Why'd you do that?!" he shouts at Zach, and Zach realizes who it is.

It is the same guy in the hoodie who threatened to beat him up on the bus in August.

This time, I can take him! Zach tells himself.

"Well, I'm sorry, dude, but it's not my fault!" Zach snaps back and looks at Seth.

"Oops," Seth cheerfully replies, shrugging. "That's my bad."

"HEY, SWEATSHIRT!" the bus driver yells at the teenager in the hoodie. "NO THREE PEOPLE TO A SEAT!"

"Get out of my seat... BOTH OF YOU!" Sweatshirt Guy orders Seth and Zach.

"Okay!" Seth gives in immediately and moves to a different spot on the bus.

"You too, Messy Hair!" Sweatshirt Guy tells Zach. Zach clenches his fists.

"Hey, Zach, dude... it's not worth it," Ryan whispers from behind him.

Zach desperately wants to punch this guy across the face, but he knows that his sensei would not approve. So Zach stands up and heads to a different seat. With anger still burning inside of him, he sits down on the opposite side of where Seth moved.

"Why'd you have to do that, Seth?" Zach questions him.

"Do what?" Seth asks innocently.

"Sit next to me and wake that guy up!" Zach exclaims.

"I'm sorry, dude," Seth replies. "I was just having a little fun..."

"Yeah, Zach. Don't make a big deal about it," Mike adds.

When the bus arrives at Lennwood, Ryan gets off the bus behind Zach and walks with him to their first-period Chemistry class.

"If it makes you feel any better, I don't think it was your fault, either," Ryan tells Zach as they approach the building the class is in.

"Yeah... it doesn't matter," Zach responds. "Thanks anyway, though."

"Hey, uh... if you're not busy... wanna come over to my house after school today?" Ryan asks him.

Zach sighs. He halts next to the doorway of Mr. Earnheart's room, and Ryan stops with him.

"Ryan... dude... besides at school... I don't think I'll be able to hang out with you that much anymore."

"What? Why not?"

"It's just that... I've been really busy lately with helping my grandfather and a lot of homework and... yeah."

Ryan just stares at Zach, devastated. Zach turns away from him and enters the classroom. Zach notices that Ryan waits a few seconds but then also enters the room. They both sit in their usual seats as Mr. Earnheart starts to take attendance; however, the two friends avoid eye contact with each other for most of the class period. Even as they leave the classroom after the bell rings, the neighbors don't walk out together. Zach feels guilt over his deception yet is swayed by another feeling.

This is alright... a voice says in his mind. *Think about how you're getting better.*

Pride overtakes Zach all throughout the school day, as he convinces himself that this is the path he should be on. Sensei Haruta unknowingly escalates Zach's overconfidence later that day.

"You've improved so much over the past two months, Zach," Zach's grandfather tells him. "I believe you are almost ready to go on your first mission," Sensei Haruta announces.

"Wait, really?! When are we going?!" he questions in excitement and anticipation.

"Very soon," Sensei Haruta responds with a smile. "However, there is one more thing that we must go over."

At this moment, Zach realizes that his grandfather is not driving towards his dojo.

"I think you took a wrong turn," Zach points out.

Kenshin Haruta shakes his head.

"Then... where are we going?"

"Into the heart of Scorpion territory," his sensei replies.

Zach winces.

"Are you sure I'm ready for this, Sensei? I mean, without my ninja outfit on?"

"Oh, we won't be fighting any Scorpions today. Just... driving."

Sensei Haruta pulls the car into the parking lot of a fast-food restaurant.

"This is the heart of Scorpion territory? A burger joint?!"

"No, Zach," Sensei Haruta laughs and unbuckles his seat belt. "Switch with me."

"You want me to drive your car?"

"Exactly, Zach."

"You do know how to drive, right, Zach?" Sensei Haruta asks Zach after the two relatives switch places.

"Yes, I passed my driver's training course," Zach jokes and proceeds to put the car in drive.

Once Zach maneuvers the car out of the parking lot, Sensei Haruta directs him to move into the downtown area.

"Are you familiar with this part of town?" he asks.

"Yeah," Zach replies. "I've lived in Old York my entire life."

"Okay… where are we right now?"

Zach looks around.

The silver car has driven by a countless number of restaurants, and they just passed a movie theater. Zach recognizes a sporting goods store, as well as a dance studio.

"Well, there's going to be a gym up ahead. Then a clothing store. And that place sells mattresses," Zach points out.

"What else?"

"Um… more restaurants… a public library… there's a church over there…"

"What about the alleys?" Kenshin suggests.

Zach glances in between some of the buildings.

"What about them?" Zach inquires.

"Some of them are Scorpion hangout areas," Sensei Haruta teaches him. "And not all of those buildings are what they appear to be. Some of them have actually been Scorpion hideouts."

Zach stops the car at a stoplight.

"I could tell you to keep driving around, and point out which parts of Old York belong to which gang," Sensei Haruta continues. "But that time has passed. There is now only one major force of crime in Old York, and that is the Scorpions."

Sensei Haruta then instructs Zach to drive to the outskirts of Old York to his dojo. As the car passes by neighborhoods and different subdivisions, Zach wonders about what his sensei has told him. Even though Zach doesn't see anything suspicious now in broad daylight, he realizes that he has been oblivious to the things that happen while he is asleep. He knew Old York had a problem with crime, but now it is more real to him than ever before.

****

Roger Kowalski returns to the police station after a long day. He heads to the locker room, preparing to dress out of his uniform, but is stopped by Johnny and Richie.

"Rodge!" Johnny exclaims as he and Richie rush up to Roger.

"What is it? I just finished my shift," Roger replies.

"You might want to do double shift this time," Richie tells him.

"Why?"

"It's Scorpio," Johnny Law says. "We found him."

134

CHAPTER 10: "THE FIRST MISSION"

"It is time," Sensei Haruta declares.

After Zach and Sensei Haruta return to the dojo, Sensei Haruta led Zach to something in his basement. The Gray Ninja Suit rests on an armor stand in front of them.

The Suit consists of a gray and dark blue ninja kimono with chest armor underneath it, along with other armor pieces that attach to the Ninja Suit. Every armor piece is made of invinsium, the durable metal that can withstand bullets. There are wrist guards for blocking, knee and elbow pads, a karate belt, a sword holder, weapon pouches, and even a place to hold a bottle of Water of Purification. On top of the Suit is the Gray Ninja Helmet, which is silver and resembles a ninja hood.

"Wait, I get to wear that?!" Zach questions in awe.

"Exactly, Zach," Sensei Haruta replies, while starting to walk over to the basement stairs.

"Where are you going?"

"I'm going to change into my own. I expect you to put your Suit on quickly. You are going to have to slip it on with speed as you transform from being Zach Rylar into becoming the next Gray Ninja."

After Sensei Haruta leaves the room, Zach Rylar looks around the basement to recognize the Water of Purification pool and the weapons rack. Zach turns back to the armor stand, but his eyes meet up with the closet next to it. Zach curiously opens it to find three other Gray Ninja Suits. Zach smiles, remembering how Sensei Haruta told him that he made some spares.

Zach closes the closet and starts to take the Gray Ninja Suit off of the stand. Zach initially struggles to put on the Suit, but eventually manages to slip it on over his clothes. He grabs a pair of training nunchucks and attaches them to the Suit. Finally, with two hands, Zach Rylar raises the Gray Ninja helmet and puts it on over his head.

Zach makes his way up the basement stairs and enters the hallway above. Sensei Haruta steps out of his kitchen, wearing his own Gray Ninja suit and holding an identical ninja helmet.

"So... this is what you fight the Scorpions in?" Zach asks.

"Yes, and it is what you will be using from now on," his sensei tells him. "If... you are ready."

"I'm ready," Zach claims.

"That will be decided tonight," Haruta replies and then raises his head. "We have less than an hour before nightfall. Until then, we will train."

Zach takes out his training nunchucks, but Sensei Haruta stops him.

"No, Zach," the ninja master says with a smile. "With real nunchucks."

****

Sensei Haruta leads Zach back to the basement and directs his student's attention to the weapons rack. He motions towards the nunchaku on the wall before looking back at Zach.

"They are yours," Sensei Haruta announces. "Take them."

Zach stares at his grandfather with astonishment, and then at the nunchucks. Zach slowly reaches for the weapon and grabs onto it. He starts to lift it off of its placeholder, as excitement fills him.

Suddenly, the weight of the weapons pulls Zach's hand down like an anchor, and the nunchucks hit the floor.

"Zach!" Kenshin Haruta snaps at him.

"Sorry, Sensei!" Zach apologizes. "It's just heavier than the training one."

"Well… nunchucks are made of metal, Zach."

Zach picks the nunchucks off of the ground. This time, he raises them with ease, letting himself adjust to the weight of his new ninja weapon.

For the next half-hour, Zach Rylar and Kenshin Haruta train in the compound. They practice fighting each other, with Zach using his new nunchucks, and Kenshin wielding his staff. Sensei Haruta seems like he always gets the best of Zach, but Zach has become a formidable opponent. Zach blocks and dodges many of his sensei's moves, even getting some good blows in of his own. All of the combat training Sensei Haruta taught Zach has built him up to be a skilled fighter.

"Nice job, my student," Zach's sensei compliments him once they are done training. "Your fighting skills have improved exponentially."

"Thank you, Sensei," Zach responds, and bows out of respect.

"I have told you before… you don't need to bow to me. You're my grandson."

"Just take it as a thank you… for everything you've taught me," Zach insists with gratitude.

Kenshin Haruta beams.

"That means a lot, Zach," the older man responds, and then motions for Zach to follow. "Come. I believe… you are ready."

Kenshin Haruta's silver car approaches downtown Old York, with Kenshin driving and Zach in the passenger seat. They changed out of their Gray Ninja suits after training, planning to change back into them when they arrived.

"So someone doesn't look in the windows and see two ninja in my car," Sensei Haruta explains to Zach on the way there. "That would bring about too much attention."

"You know what this car needs?" Zach asks rhetorically. "A disguise of its own."

"What do you have in mind?" his grandfather inquires.

"Well… you could tint the windows, change the license plate, and maybe just… the overall design of the car could transform."

"That is an interesting idea, Zach… but I'm a ninja, not a mechanic," Sensei Haruta remarks with a chuckle.

He pulls the silver car into an alley, and the two relatives get out of the vehicle. They are carrying backpacks, which contain their Ninja Suits.

"Where do we change?" Zach whispers to his grandfather.

Kenshin Haruta points behind the car.

"In the shadows. Always in a place where you are unseen," the ninja master recommends.

"But what if someone-"

"There is no one around here," Zach's grandfather tells him with confidence. "I just checked. Now… as we discussed… change with lightning speed."

Zach hurries behind the car and takes his Suit out of his backpack. Before Zach is done changing, a figure appears in his peripheral vision. Zach turns around and jumps.

"AH!" Zach cries, before realizing that it is his sensei in his own Ninja Suit. "How'd you change so fast? And where did you-?"

"I'm a ninja. It's what I do."

Zach sighs.

"Now finish changing quickly," Zach's grandfather commands quietly yet sternly. "Master the element of Speed."

Zach Rylar hastily slips on the rest of his disguise, along with his weapons. Then, he steps out of the shadows as the Gray Ninja.

Suddenly, the older Gray Ninja jumps onto a fire escape attached to a nearby building and climbs onto its roof.

"Uhh… we didn't cover this in training!" Zach informs him rather loudly.

Kenshin Haruta puts his index finger in front of the lower part of his ninja helmet– where his mouth would be– before motioning for Zach to follow.

Zach walks over to the fire escape and starts to climb up it. At this moment, Zach's mind brings his thoughts back to the speed training course. Zach recalls scaling the dojo's tall wall-like fence and uses the experience to his advantage.

The younger Gray Ninja reaches the top of the fire escape, jumps into the air, and grasps the edge of the roof. He remembers the pull-up bar on the course and proceeds to lift his entire body up and over the edge.

"Very good," Sensei Haruta softly compliments him. "But… don't forget the rules of stealth and disguise. Talk quietly, or say no words at all. Hand motions are also a good idea and-"

"I'm sorry, Grand-"

"Stop. You will address me as 'Master' or 'Sensei' when you are disguised, and I will address you only as 'Student.'"

"Okay."

"Now, Student… look around you. Tell me what you see."

Zach's eyes move from the roof of the building and scan the dark town around him.

"Buildings… some homes… some stores… many closing for the night."

"What else? Remember what I taught you earlier."

"I see… dark alleys, and… some people walking past them. Plus, cars. Cars passing them and... parked cars. Oh, and one just parked next to that old building. A few guys are getting out of the car. They're approaching the building..."

"Do they look like Scorpions?"

"Well… I haven't met one before. I mean… I've seen scorpions at the zoo, but not… not the… not the gangsters… yeah."

"Fewer words better when disguised."

"K," Zach replies mischievously.

"Follow. Let's figure out who they are."

The older Gray Ninja makes his way down the fire escape with Zach following closely behind him. The two ninja advance through the alley before stopping to crouch beside the corner of a building.

Zach notices a two-lane street in front of them, with cars driving down it every so often.

"How will we cross? We're gonna be seen!"

"For open areas, a ninja relies on speed to achieve stealth," Sensei Haruta explains. "However… sometimes the best disguise is to blend in."

"How will we do that?"

Sensei Haruta walks back into the shadows and takes off his helmet.

"No," Zach protests.

"Yes."

"You're telling me… that I have to take this off… put it in the backpack… and then put it back on *again* once we cross the street?!"

"With lightning speed."

Zach attempts to facepalm but hits his ninja helmet. Reluctantly, he obeys his sensei and moves into the darkness to take off his Suit.

After the two Gray Ninja change into their regular clothes, Zach and his grandfather walk out of the alley with their Gray Ninja backpacks.

"Talk to me," Zach's grandfather tells Zach as the two relatives stroll down the sidewalk. "Make it look like we're talking."

Zach nods.

"So… um… Grandpa?"

"Yes, my grandson?"

Zach searches frantically through his thoughts to find a conversation starter.

"Uh…"

"How about when you went to the zoo?" Kenshin offers. "What was that like?"

"Oh yeah… I mean… it was fun and all… I went once on a field trip, but other than that, my mom didn't really take me many places ever since Dad died."

"Oh… I'm sorry to hear that."

"Yeah… I sort of just learned how to entertain myself and hung out with a few neighborhood friends a lot," Zach reveals. "I haven't been that close to her."

"I never knew that… I'm-"

"I mean… it's fine, like… she's provided food and stuff for me… and we talk sometimes, and we live in the same house… but she's gone a lot with work, and I've kind of learned how to be more independent."

"But you're a teenager, Zach… you need some sort of parental figure in your life… and soon you'll be away from your mom… don't just take for granted the time you could spend with her."

Zach stops walking and stares at him. Frustration starts to build up inside him.

"What about you?!" Zach questions sternly. "Where have you been all these years?!"

Kenshin Haruta is taken aback by Zach's remark.

"Well… your mother and I… had our differences... and I've had my own... adventures... throughout my lifetime," Zach's grandfather tries to explain to him. "I'm here now, aren't I?"

After looking both ways and seeing no close cars, Kenshin Haruta uses the crosswalk on the street in front of them to get to the other side of the road.

"Yeah, but why?" Zach inquires while walking behind his grandfather. "Do you really care about me, or are you just using me to accomplish a plan of your own?!"

"What are you saying, Zach... focus, remember?" the secret ninja master whispers to him.

Zach takes a deep breath, hoping to slow down his racing heartbeat.

"Oh yeah. Sorry, Sen- I mean- Grandpa. That was uh... that was all part of the act," he lies.

The two relatives scan the area around them for eavesdroppers before moving behind a large dumpster in a nearby alley.

Zach ignores the stench of the garbage to concentrate on changing back into the Gray Ninja quickly. In only a couple minutes, Zach and his grandfather are ready for battle.

On the left side of the alley is a clothing shop, and on the right is a sporting goods store. The older Gray Ninja takes the lead, running stealthily through the alley to get behind the stores. On Kenshin's left, adjacent to the backside of the clothing store, is a parking lot, residing next to a tall, elegant, older-looking building.

Zach runs up behind his sensei. The two ninja are now crouching from behind a corner, gazing upon the structure.

"It's the library," Zach recognizes.

Sensei Haruta nods.

"This is a Scorpion hideout?"

"No, my student," Haruta replies. "And the people back there were not Scorpions. Look beyond the library."

Zach squints and picks up a dull brick structure, a few buildings down from the library. A black van and a dark gray truck are parked in front of the ordinary structure. The door to the building opens, and a figure in a black hoodie steps out of the doorway.

"That person is," Sensei Haruta tells Zach, before rushing towards the building.

Zach tries to keep up with his sensei, as they both find cover behind anything in their path. As the two ninja run from cover to cover, they move their feet quietly, like Sensei Haruta taught Zach during the Stealth training lesson.

Finally, they reach the black van and crouch behind it. A minute later, two more figures in black walk out of the building, each carrying something that alarms Zach.

"They have guns!" the teen whispers to his grandfather.

"Remember all I have taught you," Sensei Haruta instructs him quietly. "And imitate what I do."

Suddenly, Sensei Haruta whips three shurikens out of his ninja outfit and raises his arm above the hood of the van. His wrist extends, and he tosses a shuriken at one of the figures in black. The shuriken hits the Scorpion's armed hand with great force, causing the Scorpion's gun to fall to the ground. Sensei Haruta tosses a second shuriken at the Scorpion beside the disarmed Scorpion, disarming him as well.

The third Scorpion dodges the last shuriken, but a gray blur lunges out from behind the car. Kenshin Haruta unsheathes a katana, and slashes at the Scorpion's gun, sending it flying out of his hands. Then, he hits the Scorpion in the head with the hilt of his sword, knocking the ninja's opponent down. The other two Scorpions try to pick up their guns; at the same time, Sensei Haruta unsheathes his katana and reaches for his staff.

Before they know what hit them, the Scorpions and their guns fall to the ground, defeated.

Zach steps out from behind the black van, his eyes filled with wonder.

"That... was... AWESOME, Sensei!" he exclaims.

"The fight is not over yet," Sensei Haruta sternly responds. "Follow!"

The ninja master charges into the building with Zach obediently accompanying him. The building is mostly empty, except for some stone pillars that act as supports for the roof. Both of the ninja rush over to the supports and take cover behind them. Zach peers out from his and notices five figures in black on the other side of the building.

"Hey! Who's over there?!" one of them demands.

The Scorpion pulls out a gun and approaches the pillars. Zach's heart beats faster as the hooded figure advances up to him. When he is several yards away from Zach, Zach tosses a shuriken at his weapon.

Zach misses.

"What?!" the Scorpion questions, bending down to look at the shuriken.

Kenshin nods at Zach to make his move, and Zach redirects his attention to the distracted Scorpion. Zach leaps out from behind the pillar and bolts over to the Scorpion.

The armed opponent's attention is quickly brought back to Zach, and he raises his weapon at Zach. Zach immediately moves his right elbow in front of his chest, and a bullet repels off of his invinsium wrist-armor. Zach firmly grabs onto the Scorpion's gun and remembering Sensei Haruta's training, twists the weapon out of the Scorpion's hands.

Zach's opponent looks up at him with surprise as the Gray Ninja chucks the gun away from them. Then, the Gray Ninja punches the Scorpion across the face, knocking him to the ground.

"Very good, my student," Zach hears Kenshin Haruta say. "Now, double back."

Zach looks up to see four more figures in black on the other side of the building, unsheathing knives and running towards him. Instead of doing what his sensei told him, Zach whips out his nunchucks.

"Student! Remember the element of stealth!" Zach hears from behind as he charges towards the gangsters. Zach jumps behind a pillar while the Scorpions approach. One runs up to him, but Zach leaps out and swings his nunchucks at the Scorpion, hitting the gangster in the head. Zach's opponent falls over as two others race over to Zach, one on his left and the other on his right.

The Gray Ninja knocks the knife of the Scorpion on his left with his nunchucks, but the Scorpion wielding the weapon maintains his grip. The Scorpion on his right lunges at Zach with his knife, attempting to stab him, but Zach blocks the attack with his wrist guard. The Gray Ninja swings his nunchucks at him, and a powerful kick sends the right Scorpion to fall to the ground. The left Scorpion raises his knife again, and Zach grasps his nunchucks. Out of his peripheral vision, he notices a fourth Scorpion charging at him, so Zach throws his nunchucks at the running Scorpion. Zach misses again as the nunchucks fly past the charging Scorpion, but quickly disarms the one in front of him, twisting the knife out of his hand with lightning speed. The Gray Ninja then kicks that disarmed Scorpion in the stomach and punches him down.

Zach instantly realizes that he has two ninjatō, or ninja short-swords, on the sword holder on his back, and unsheathes one of them. The remaining Scorpion, who Zach tries to throw his nunchucks at, leaps at him with the knife. Zach dodges the attack and swings his Ninjatō at the standing Scorpion. The Scorpion also dodges Zach's move and goes in for another assault. This time, his knife cuts Zach on his right arm, and a slight burning sensation impacts Zach.

Pain is an illusion, Zach thinks with a grunt, and uses the hilt of his Ninjatō to hit the Scorpion on the head, as he saw his sensei do minutes before.

The last Scorpion falls to the ground, unconscious.

"You should have listened to me," a familiar voice booms.

Zach spins around to face his Gray Ninja counterpart.

"Aw come on, Sensei... I did it!" Zach protests. "I just beat five Scorpions... aren't you proud of me?"

"Pride is a distraction," Sensei Haruta replies. "And you.. are bleeding."

Zach looks at his right sleeve and notices the red cut. He reaches down to grab the Water of Purification bottle attached to his Suit, but an arm stops him.

"Only for emergencies, remember?" Sensei Haruta reminds him. "That is a minor cut. We can wrap up that wound."

Zach exhales.

"Right... pain is an illusion... pain is an illusion," Zach repeats to himself while taking deep breaths.

It seems to Zach to be of no help. Zach's arm still hurts.

Zach quickly snatches the Water of Purification bottle out of its holder and pours a drop on his arm.

"Student!" Sensei Haruta reacts crossly.

"Pain's no illusion, Sensei!" Zach shoots back. "You may want it to be, but it is definitely real!"

"Even if it is... you let it get to you," Haruta replies. "I will let that slide for now, but for future reference, you should listen-"

Sensei Haruta suddenly stops his train of thought and redirects his attention to something behind Zach. Zach turns around. He notices that his sensei is starting to walk to where the Scorpions were standing when the ninja entered. Zach follows his sensei's gaze to a table on the other end of the room.

"What?" Zach asks. "What is it?"

Zach follows the older Gray Ninja to the table, and the two of them stare at it. On top of the table, is a cell phone.

"Listen," Sensei Haruta softly commands.

Zach's ears pick up the sound of a voice on the other end of the phone. He picks up the phone off of the table and taps on the speaker button.

"Hello?! Are you guys coming?!" shouts a voice on the other end. "We need backup! We're at our base in Midridge Apartments! The police have arrived, but Master Scorpio is here!"

****

On the other side of downtown Old York, police cars are lined up outside of an apartment complex. Five officers are pinned down behind their vehicles, taking fire.

Roger Kowalski's squad car and Johnny Law's police SUV approach the scene. Roger gets out of his vehicle while Johnny and Richie get out of Johnny's SUV. All three officers take out and raise their guns, duck as they make their way to the other officers, and then crouch beside them.

"Johnny Law has arrived!" Johnny announces.

"What's been happening?" Roger questions the five officers who were already there.

"There are at least six armed hostiles in the building!" a female officer replies.

Roger peers around the stationary police car quick enough to get a good glance. He notices that the apartments are old, torn up structures, and detects several armed figures dressed in black.

Bullets fly above the police car as a few of the law enforcement officers fire back. Roger Kowalski realizes that he has entered a battlefield as his ears are filled with the roaring sounds of gunshots.

"Anyone else inside the building?" Roger asks the female officer.

"Not that we know of so far!" she answers.

Next to them, Rifle Richie has been setting up his sniper rifle and is looking through the scope.

"I'll let y'all know if I see any!" he informs them.

The highest-ranking officer there, a police captain, takes charge of the situation.

"Officer Thompson, stay back with these two," he orders Richie while pointing at two officers behind him. "Officers Kowalski and Lawson, you're with the rest of us."

"Yes, sir!" Roger and Johnny say at the same time.

"Move in!"

After the police captain's shout, five policemen start to advance towards the building, while Richie and the other two stay behind. The advancing policemen duck as they run, and find any kind of cover they can. They use it to stop and fire back on the Scorpions, and slowly approach the front of the apartment. A bullet whizzes past Roger and hits an officer behind him. He looks back at the wounded man for just a second, before-

BOOM!

Roger and the others are knocked back from the explosion, and Roger Kowalski struggles to see what caused the violent impact. Suddenly, figures dressed in black surround Roger and the other officers around him, with guns raised at them.

Roger looks around with shock as the police captain and female police officer put their guns down. The wounded officer already has his firearm on the ground, but Roger can't see Johnny. He spins his head around frantically to search for his mustached friend, and his eyes pick up his fallen body several yards behind the Scorpions. Roger also notices that other armed Scorpions have surrounded Rifle Richie and the other two officers, who drop their weapons.

"PUT YOUR WEAPON DOWN!" one of the armed Scorpions shouts at Roger.

Roger quickly turns at the police captain, searching for an answer.

"Drop it, Roger," the police captain tells him with sorrow in his tone.

Roger Kowalski lets his firearm slip out of his hands, and it hits the ground. All of a sudden, Roger sees a figure emerge through the flames.

Roger recognizes him from pictures and videos he had seen in the police station. However, Roger had never before seen the legendary master in person.

Knives are strapped to the gang leader's chest, and two pistol holsters are connected to his belt. He is dressed in black and dark gray, with a round black beard around his smirking lips. And on his bald, brown head lies a scar across his face. It seems to have cut through his right eye, as an eyepatch lies over it.

It is Scorpio, the infamous leader of the Scorpions, and the most wanted criminal in the entire town of Old York.

CHAPTER 11: "RUN"

Roger Kowalski breathes heavily.

"Cuff em'," Scorpio tells the other Scorpions.

The armed gangsters take the police officers' handcuffs and begin to handcuff each of them.

"What are you going to do with us?" the female officer questions, with a hint of fear in her tone.

Scorpio turns his head and looks at her.

"I haven't decided yet," he replies as he walks up to her with his hands folded behind his back. "I could kill you... or torture all of you for information. Then again, that would go against what I stand for."

"And what's that?!" the police captain demands. "Shooting at officers of the law?"

"You invaded our territory," the gang leader responds. "We were defending our brothers and sisters!"

"Whatever!" the captain shouts. "You're a murderer, Scorpio!"

"Am I?" Scorpio questions him. "I have to admit... your little 'police force' has been a thorn in my side for a long time. I really wish that all of you would stop what you're doing... and stop fighting the wrong enemy!"

Roger watches as Scorpio throws up his hands before speaking again.

"I could kill all of you... but that would solve nothing."

Scorpio pauses to examine the scene in front of him. Roger follows his gaze and realizes that the Scorpions now have both of his friends, Johnny and Richie, in handcuffs.

"It didn't have to be this way," the gang leader continues. "I remember when the government wasn't so corrupt... and when violence didn't pollute the streets. But my group did everything in our power to stop the gang war... and you repay us by coming here with guns?!"

Scorpio stops to take a deep breath.

"Put them in the vans," he orders his men, and the Scorpions begin to grab the policemen.

I have to stop this, Roger thinks.

Roger Kowalski scans the area for a means of escape. He notices that the ground beside Scorpio is soaked with gasoline, and concludes that one of the Scorpions must have lit a match to cause the explosion. Roger looks down at his duty belt and takes into account what he still has on it.

A taser, he observes and hastily forms a plan.

Seconds later, a Scorpion grabs Roger's handcuffs and is about to cuff him as well, until Roger pushes the gangster's hands out of the way. The other Scorpions turn to them, but not fast enough. Roger Kowalski has already pulled out his taser and aims it at the flames behind Scorpio.

FOOM!!!

The fire ignites, towering over the gangsters. Scorpio shields his eyes with his hands and steps away from the blaze. As the Scorpions' attention is redirected to the fire, Roger shouts something to the other policemen.

"RUN!"

Roger Kowalski bolts out of the scene. His fifty-one-year-old legs maneuver past the Scorpions, the police cars, and down the sidewalk. He looks back to see if the others escaped too, but no one is following him. Tears build up in his eyes as he remembers Johnny and Richie, but he keeps running.

****

"What do you usually do next?" Zach inquires.

Zach and his sensei are still in the Scorpion hideout, in their Gray Ninja Suits. Sensei Haruta takes the phone from Zach and looks at it.

"I usually dial 911," the ninja master replies. "However... this time, there seems to be a greater threat."

He starts to rush out of the building, and Zach races after him. As they move in between the stone pillars of the brick structure, Zach notices that some of the Scorpions are-

"They're getting up!" Zach exclaims.

"Quickly, my student!"

The two ninja stealthily sprint back the way they came until they make it back to the road. Kenshin Haruta stops Zach in an alley, and they look back at the dull building. The Scorpions they had fought outside of it are starting to stand to their feet.

"Change back, and FAST!" Kenshin Haruta orders, and retreats into the shadows.

He and Zach take off their helmets and quickly change out of their ninja suits. They shove the outfits into their oversized backpacks, which they placed behind their sword holders. Then, Zach and Kenshin grab their stuffed backpacks and cross the street.

"Whew!" Zach exclaims when they are back in Kenshin Haruta's silver car. "That was crazy!"

His grandfather drives the car out of the alley and down the street.

"Is that all you do... beat up some guys and then take off?" Zach asks him.

"There is more to it than that," Sensei Haruta answers. "And this time was different. We could have stopped them again to make sure the police arrest them... but we have a more pressing concern."

Zach realizes that Kenshin is driving in the opposite direction of Lennwood High, Zach's neighborhood, and his dojo.

"We're going to those apartments, aren't we?"

"I am. You are staying in the car."

"Oh, come on, sensei! Were you not watching me before? I defeated not *one,* not *two*... but *five* Scorpions!"

"I'm glad you can count."

Zach frowns.

"If Scorpio really is like this big bad leader guy... then you can use all the help you can get. And I'm willing to help you!" Zach offers.

"I understand that, Zach... and I am grateful," Zach's sensei tells him. "I just don't think you are ready to face Scorpio yet... and I'm still deciding whether or not you are ready to be out here anyway."

"Wasn't that last fight proof enough, though?" Zach questions.

"SILENCE!" Sensei Haruta shouts. "A student should always show his sensei respect. Do not question me, Zach. I know what I am doing."

"And I don't?"

Sensei Haruta looks sternly at Zach.

Zach sighs.

"Sorry..." he spits out.

"Thank you," Kenshin Haruta responds, as he pulls the car into a parking lot. "Now… while you are in here…"

Zach looks up at him.

"What?"

"Master the element of patience."

Sensei Haruta grabs his backpack and exits the car. Zach slumps in his seat, sighing again. He then turns to look out of the driver window and sees a gray blur run through an alley.

Zach weighs his options before redirecting his gaze to his own backpack, which is sitting in the back seat. He unzips it, starting at the Gray Ninja Suit inside of it before driving his attention forward.

No, he forces in his mind.

But then he turns to look at the Suit again.

****

Kenshin Haruta, in his own Gray Ninja Suit, runs through a small wooded area. The backside of the Midridge Apartments is up ahead, and the older Gray Ninja maneuvers from tree to tree until he reaches the building.

"... and you repay us by coming here with guns?!" Kenshin Haruta hears faintly and recognizes Scorpio's voice. "Put them in the vans."

Kenshin moves along the outside wall of one of the apartment buildings. Flashes of orange brighten in his peripheral vision. The elderly vigilante moves forward to watch as a police officer with a blond flat-top takes off running.

"RUN!" the blonde policeman shouts.

However, he is the only one capable of retreating.

Kenshin spots multiple armed Scorpions in front of the apartments, each of them surrounding the other police officers. Scorpio is closest to the ninja master, with his back to Kenshin.

A few of the Scorpions raise their guns at the escaping policeman. However, Scorpio orders them to instead concentrate on restraining the other officers.

Kenshin Haruta studies the area around him for places of cover, only to find a burning tree and several dark vans on the pavement in front of the apartment. As the Scorpions begin to force the officers into the vehicles, the ninja master recognizes that his time to act is now. Even with little cover in front of him, Kenshin Haruta knows what to do.

The old Gray Ninja extracts a shuriken from one of his Ninja Suit pouches and thrusts the projectile on the ground in front of Scorpio.

The leader of the Scorpions' diverts his attention to the ground and immediately looks up. Scorpio spins around, just in time to see the ninja master lunging at him with his staff. Scorpio ducks beneath the weapon and takes out one of his pistols. He fires it at the ninja, but Kenshin dodges the blast and whacks Scorpio's arm with his staff. Scorpio is knocked back, as the weapon flies out of his arm.

The other Scorpions aim their guns at Kenshin Haruta, who runs behind one of their parked vans. They begin to shoot at the vehicle, although the ninja already has good cover. He takes out more shurikens and tosses them over the hood of the van. Each of the projectiles precisely hit a gun out of a Scorpion's hand.

Kenshin glances above the hood of the van, counting eleven Scorpions in total, including Scorpio. Some of them enter the other vans, while the others advance toward the ninja. Kenshin takes out four more shurikens and sends them flying across the other side of the vehicle at two Scorpions, who dodge them.

The Scorpions now surround the van Kenshin is behind. Consequently, the ninja master unsheathes a pair of fork-like hand weapons known as sais. One Scorpion appears from the front of the van with a knife, but Kenshin blocks the attack with his sais.

The sais force the Scorpion's blade into the door of the vehicle. The Scorpion tries to pull it out, yet Kenshin hits him in the face with the hilt of one of his sais, launching the gangster backward.

More Scorpions come around from the back, while Haruta opens the driver's door of the van. One of the gangsters has the same idea, entering through the passenger door. Kenshin slams both of sai's handles against the Scorpion, knocking him out.

Suddenly, muscular arms grab the eighty-year-old's back and yanks him out of the van. The old Gray Ninja tumbles onto the ground, as Scorpio towers above him.

"Get out of here with them!" Scorpio orders the Scorpion next to him, and the Scorpion gets into the driver's seat. "I'll take care of the ninja."

Kenshin Haruta gets to his feet to view all of the Scorpion vans driving away, with the captured police officers inside. Scorpio aims his remaining pistol at Kenshin Haruta, who instantly pushes it out of the way and twists it out of his hand. Two other Scorpions remain standing on the scene that also aim their guns at the ninja master.

All of a sudden, shurikens fly past the Scorpions from behind, completely missing them. All four of the fighters turn to see a second Gray Ninja racing towards them, swinging his nunchucks.

"I told you to stay back!" Kenshin strictly tells his student.

The younger Gray Ninja swings his nunchucks at the two Scorpion henchmen, knocking them both out.

"You looked like you were in trouble," Zach replies.

"So… you finally got someone on your side," Scorpio remarks from behind Kenshin.

Both Gray Ninja face him. Kenshin Haruta raises his sais, while Zach grips his nunchucks with both of hands.

"I have an entire army, while you have one student," Scorpio taunts.

"Your men are defeated," Kenshin points out.

"But I have more men… and women, all for one common goal. You cannot stop what we're accomplishing, Gray Ninja."

"And what are you trying to accomplish, Mr. Big Bad Leader Guy?" Zach questions him.

A devious-looking smile unfolds on Scorpio's face as he turns to the younger Gray Ninja, amused.

"I don't believe we've met before… what's your name?" Scorpio asks the teenager.

"The Gray Ninja," Zach answers.

"How original," Scorpio sarcastically comments. "My name... is Bill Williams. People call me Scorpio... because I am the leader of a family. A family that is trying to accomplish something good in this corrupt town!"

Suddenly, Kenshin Haruta lunges at Scorpio with his sais. Scorpio blocks one of the sais with his hands, but the other penetrates through Scorpio's shoulder. Grunting in pain, he rips it out and flings it on the ground. Sensei Haruta unsheathes a ninjatō and aims the sword at Scorpio's throat. The Scorpion leader kicks Kenshin back, forcing him to the ground. Scorpio starts to retreat but stops to look at Kenshin's grandson.

"You're on the wrong side, boy!" Scorpio tells Zach and points at Sensei Haruta. "This man fights only for himself!"

As Sensei Haruta gets up, the Scorpion leader slips behind the apartments. Realizing that Scorpio has escaped, Kenshin turns to Zach.

"You should not have followed me," he sternly says to his student. "You could have been killed!"

"Stop underestimating me, Sensei!" Zach responds defiantly. "I just saved your life!"

"*I* had it under control," Sensei Haruta replies. "*You* obviously do not! A real ninja would think before questioning his sensei!"

"What are you saying?!"

"I'm saying you're not ready for this!"

****

Zach looks into his grandfather's angry eyes with a fiery rage of his own.

"I've been training hard every day for two months, and you're telling me that I'm not ready?!" Zach shoots back.

"Have patience, Zach! You just need a bit more training! Then... you will hopefully be ready for more of this," Sensei Haruta sternly promises.

Zach is about to argue with him further, but the sounds of sirens start to fill his ears. Kenshin Haruta lifts his head up as if he is trying to focus on the noise.

"Firetrucks... and more police cars," the older man evaluates, and then turns back to Zach. "Return to the car!"

Sensei Haruta and Zach hastily pick up their fallen weapons and flee from the scene. The two vigilantes dash through the open area, passing rising Scorpions. They maneuver in between apartment buildings and through the woods behind them. They eventually reach an alley nearby Kenshin's car in the downtown area. When they make sure the coast is clear, the two Gray Ninja transform back into Kenshin Haruta and Zach Rylar and get into the car.

"Are we going back to the dojo?" Zach asks as his grandfather starts the car.

"I am taking you back to your house," Sensei Haruta replies. "And I'm keeping your suit."

"What?!" Zach protests. "But-!"

"*Until* you are ready," his sensei finishes.

"How will we know when I'm ready?" Zach questions, calmer this time.

Kenshin Haruta ignores his question.

"We will go through some more advanced lessons. On Monday, I will teach you how to fight on a roof... but before then, I am giving you some time to think," he says.

Zach holds back a sigh. He knows that arguing with his sensei on the matter will just make things worse for him, so he keeps his argumentative thoughts to himself.

"Yes, Sensei."

****

Later that night, Roger Kowalski finds himself in his police chief's office. The office appears as a standard office, with a desk and chairs, and even potted plants. Chief Mulberry looks sympathetically at Roger through his glasses.

"What happened out there, Officer Kowalski?" the police chief asks him.

Images flash in Roger's mind. He remembers all of the gunfire and then seeing Scorpio for the first time. He remembers being surrounded by guns and then seeing his friends being handcuffed and put into the backs of vans.

"We... uh... failed, sir," Roger tells his commanding officer.

"Don't think of it as a failure. Just tell me what happened."

"Scorpio was there... and an ambush. They surrounded us... and then..."

"And then what?"

"They took them hostage," Roger voices, as tears form in his eyes. "Officers... Lawson and Thompson... and a few others..."

He wipes the tears from his eyes and clears his throat.

"Was I the only one to escape?"

Chief Mulberry nods.

"Yes... several officers investigated the scene shortly after you left it... the Scorpions managed to get away before they got there," he explains. "They tried looking into the security footage, but it was damaged. We suspect on purpose. But... we did find something."

The police chief opens a drawer of his desk and pulls out a small bag labeled, "EVIDENCE."

He slides the bag over to Roger.

"Open it," Mulberry insists.

Roger Kowalski opens the evidence bag to pull out a silver object with triangular-shaped edges.

"It's a... throwing star?"

"Ninja shuriken," Chief Mulberry corrects. "The rumors may have been true after all. There may actually be some lunatic pretending to be a ninja who's helping these guys."

"Wait. What do you mean by... 'helping'?" Roger asks him. "I didn't see any ninjas with Scorpio."

"Judging by how quickly the Scorpions covered their tracks, I'm willing to bet that this ninja vigilante was assisting them. You may not have seen him because he could have appeared after you escaped."

Roger Kowalski's thoughts bring him back to his friends. He remembers Johnny's unconscious body, and then the Scorpions' weapons being aimed at Richie.

"What about the others?" Roger demands.

Chief Mulberry looks into his eyes sorrowfully.

"The other officers who didn't make it out of there!" Roger clarifies. "Do we have any leads on where they were taken or...?!"

The police chief takes off his glasses, folds them, and looks back up at Roger.

"I'm... sorry, Roger. I know they mean a lot to you... and I really appreciate that. I wish more people in this town would care as much as you do," Chief Mulberry says, and then breathes a sigh. "I really wish we knew... but... we don't."

Roger's stomach sinks at the police chief's next words.

"We have no idea where they are now."

CHAPTER 12: "THE ASSEMBLY"

Instead of going to his first-period Chemistry class with Mr. Earnheart the next day, Zach Rylar heads to the gymnasium. Over the past few days, Lennwood High's students had been told to go there for a school-wide assembly.

When Zach enters the gym, he meets up with Mike and Seth.

"Sup," Mike greets him with a nod, and Zach nods back.

"Do you guys know what this assembly's going to be about?" Zach asks them.

"It's something sports-related, I believe," Mike replies.

"Lol Zach, do you even listen?" Seth teases him and then asks him a question Zach had been avoiding. "Where's Ryan?"

"I don't know," Zach responds honestly.

"I thought you and Ryan usually walked to your chemistry class together," Mike comments.

"Maybe he's sick today," Zach suggests, ignoring the fact that he and Ryan had been talking less since their conversation yesterday morning.

"I saw him on the bus earlier," Seth recalls. "Unless he has a twin."

"Yeah," Zach replies. "I'm sure-"

"He has a twin?!" Seth exclaims.

"No, I just mean... I'm sure he'll turn up."

Mike and Seth stare at Zach, but he continues to walk into the gymnasium. Mike and Seth follow Zach through a sea of people, and the three friends squeeze through the enormous crowd to reach an open seat on the bleachers.

"Oh shoot, dude... I almost forgot," Seth randomly blurts out, and unzips his backpack.

Seth takes out a binder, turns to a folder in it, and flips through its papers.

"What are you doing?" Mike questions him.

"This math worksheet," Seth replies, showing him a piece of paper.

"Oh wait, I didn't do that either!" Mike exclaims and starts to look through his own binder.

As Mike gets his worksheet out, he also extracts a mechanical pencil and an advanced graphing calculator from his pencil case. Seth simply goes with a thin, cheap calculator and a discolored pencil that is missing an eraser.

While they get started on their soon-to-be-due homework, Zach directs his attention forward to the basketball court.

Lennwood High's athletic director steps onto the court and faces the students on the bleachers.

"Good morning, and happy Thursday!" she greets, and almost no one responds. "Please stand for the Pledge of Allegiance."

Some of the students start to get up, and then more students stand up and put their hands on their hearts, including Zach and his friends.

As the collective group recites the words, Zach sees a familiar camouflage jacket out of the corner of his eye. A few rows down from him, he sees Ryan standing by himself.

I should call him over, Zach thinks, but decides that it would be too disruptive.

All of the students sit down, and Zach soon realizes that Mike is right: the assembly is sports-related. Each of Lennwood High's sports teams dash onto the court. After the athletic director introduces each of them, an awards ceremony commences.

At one point in the assembly, a couple of coaches wheel out a cart with a sheet covering it. Zach curiously wonders what is underneath.

"Guys, are you watching?" he says to Mike and Seth, who aren't listening to him.

"Did you figure out how to get the answer to number 12?" Seth asks Mike.

"Yeah, you just have to divide that, and then..." Zach looks back at the sports teams gathered along the basketball court. The two coaches with the cart wheel it in front of the teams. They leave it there and start to walk off of the court.

"And before we give out this last trophy, a quick word from one of our faculty," the athletic director proclaims through the mic.

Zach looks to the bottom row of the bleachers to see a row of teachers sitting there, with Mr. Earnheart among them. With a notecard in his left hand, the orange-haired Chemistry teacher stands up and walks over to the athletic director. She hands him the mic, and Mr. Earnheart speaks into it.

"Uh, for those of you that don't know me, I'm Mr. Earn-heart... and I've been asked to present-"

Mr. Earnheart points at the sheet with both of his hands.

"The greatest trophy of all time!" he shouts enthusiastically, a little too close to the mic. "Why is it the greatest trophy, you may ask? Well, I'm a science teacher, which means I know *science*! And this thing... is *extraordinary*!"

He puts his notecard in his pocket and moves over to the cart with the sheet over it. Mr. Earnheart grabs the sheet before quickly lifting it into the air. A large, shiny gold and silver trophy stands confidently on the cart, and on the top of the award rests a glimmering, red object.

"May I present to you... The Knight's Jewel!" the chemistry teacher exclaims. "Originally found in a meteorite underneath this very school...this jewel was placed on this spectacular trophy! Now, it is an incentive for all of our sports teams to give their best effort! From this moment on, every year, we will award the sports team that worked the hardest with this special trophy... and this year, this winner is...!"

Zach's chemistry teacher stretches out the last syllable before he reveals the winner.

Zach watches as the football team gets hyped with anticipation, and notices that Ryan inches up to look at them.

That was Ryan's old team, Zach realizes, remembering that Ryan used to play football.

"The girls' basketball team!"

The girls on the basketball team jump up and cheer, as Mr. Earnheart hands the trophy to their coach. The guys on the football team get frustrated, as many of them groan, and one of them even punches a wall. The students on the bleachers start to get up from their seats, as the assembly concludes. Zach keeps his eyes on Ryan, watching as his neighbor goes over to his old team and high-fives them.

Zach then turns to the spectacular trophy on the cart, which is being wheeled off of the basketball court and to the athletic director's office. Zach imagines himself holding the priceless jewel but then forces the thought out of his mind.

That'll never happen, he assures himself.

After the assembly is over, Zach, Mike, and Seth have some free time before their next period, so they decide to hang out in the lunchroom. They sit down at the same table they habitually sit at every day during lunch, with each one of them in their usual spots: Mike and Seth on one end, and Zach across from Mike.

Suddenly, Zach's ears pick up footsteps behind him, and Ryan Hampkins suddenly sits down next to Zach, facing Seth.

"Hey guys," Zach's neighbor greets the group.

"Ryan! What's up, dude?!" Mike greets him back, and fist bumps him.

"Hey, man!" Seth also greets, while Zach doesn't say anything.

"So, what did you guys think about that assembly?" Ryan asks them.

"We weren't even really paying attention, to be honest," Seth admits.

"Yeah, our homework took precedence," Mike adds.

"What do you mean 'presidents'?" Seth questions him.

"No... press-uh-dense," Mike clarifies. "It means it's more of a priority for us."

"WOW! That's a BIG WORD!" Seth jokes.

Mike starts to laugh, while Ryan turns to Zach.

"How about you, Zach?"

"Huh?"

"What did you think about the assembly?"

"It was alright."

There is silence for a moment, and then Ryan speaks up again.

"Is there a team that you think should have won that last trophy, or were you fine with the results?"

"I don't know," Zach simply responds. "They probably deserved it. I mean all that training, it can really take a lot, you know?"

"Yeah," Ryan says. "Remember when we played basketball together when we were younger? Like, it was just us and some other guys in the neighborhood? Heh... we had like our own little tournament and everything."

"Oh yeah."

"That was so much fun, wasn't it?"

"Yeah, it was."

"What if we did something like that again?"

Zach wants to tell his friend that he would love to but remembers what Sensei Haruta told him last night.

I have to focus on training if I want to wear the suit again, Zach tells himself.

"Maybe," Zach responds. "Probably not anytime soon, though."

"Oh... okay," Ryan says, lowering his head.

"I'd be down for something like that," Mike blurts out.

"Yeah, same here," Seth agrees.

Ryan smiles, thanking them, and Zach's friends start to develop the idea.

Zach doesn't say much, as his thoughts dwell on his training and Sensei Haruta. *How can I get him to believe in me?* Zach questions in his mind. *How can I prove to him that I'm good enough... that I'm ready?!*

After all of Zach's classes are over, he heads to the parking lot, expecting Sensei Haruta to pick him up. When Zach doesn't see his grandfather or the silver car, Zach pulls out his phone to call him. When he looks at his phone, he sees a text message from his grandfather.

"No training until tomorrow," it reads. "Rest is often necessary for improvement."

Fine, Zach thinks to himself as he gets onto his bus. *I guess I could use a break as I figure out how to get the suit back.*

He sits close to the back and puts in his headphones. He closes his eyes as the music plays.

"Hi, Zach," says a voice behind him.

Aw man, Zach thinks. *I really don't want to talk to anyone right now.*

Zach pretends to jam to his music as if he's super into it and can't hear a word the person next to him is saying.

"Zach?"

Zach half-recognizes the person's voice but still jams to the beat.

All of a sudden, the music stops abruptly as Zach's headphones are ripped out of his ears. Zach instantly turns to see Ryan holding them in his hands.

"Why'd you do that?!" Zach exclaims angrily.

"Why have you been ignoring me?" Ryan questions. "At first, I thought you were just busy, but now it seems like you don't like to hang out with me anymore. What's going on, Zach? You're not usually like this..."

"I just... need some time to myself," Zach says.

"Yeah? How much time?"

"Until I'm ready, okay?!" Zach responds rather loudly, thinking of Sensei Haruta's words in his mind.

"Ready for what?" Ryan asks with a soft voice, with no idea that Zach's frustration is actually directed at his grandfather. "Ready to be my best friend again?"

"We... are still best friends, Ryan... I just need some time alone right now... okay?" Zach tells him.

Ryan gets up from the seat.

"I understand. See you later, Zach," he gives in and heads to the front of the bus.

"Ryan... Ryan, wait! I'm sorry, I-" Zach tries to say, but Ryan keeps walking.

Zach watches as Ryan sits by Mike and Seth, and joins in on their conversation.

Whatever. I don't need them right now, he determines in his mind with a sigh. *I can figure this out on my own.*

Zach puts his headphones back in and tries to think about his training. As Zach pushes away thoughts of his friends, his attitude begins to change.

****

Roger Kowalski wakes up the next day to a ray of sunshine slapping him in the face. He turns, expecting to see his wife beside him, but she is not there.

Roger moves over to his alarm clock to and gapes at the time.

"9:23 A.M," it reads.

"Good... you're awake," Roger hears and quickly looks up to see that his wife has entered the bedroom.

"Amy... why didn't you wake me up?" Roger questions, taking off the bedsheet. "I have to get to the department, and-"

"Stop," his wife tells him. "I called in… and told them you need a little time off."

"Why'd you do that?" Roger protests.

He starts to get out of bed, but Amy Kowalski stops him.

"Stay in bed… and get comfortable," Roger's wife orders. "I made you breakfast. Hold on. I'll be right back."

Roger Kowalski's eyebrows raise as his wife exits the room. She returns a few minutes later with a plate containing golden-yellow scrambled eggs and tan biscuits drenched in white gravy.

Roger's heart skips a beat as he smells the pleasing aroma of good food.

"Wow," Roger marvels after taking a bite of one of the biscuits. "This is delicious! Amy… you didn't have to do this."

"Yeah, well… I wanted to," she simply replies. "I thought you could use something like this after what you've been going through."

A lump starts to form in Roger's throat as he remembers Johnny Law and Rifle Richie, and them being forced in the vans. He slowly chews the biscuit as he blinks rapidly, fighting back the tears forming in his eyes.

His wife sits on the bed and looks into his eyes.

"Roger… yesterday, you were so distant. You went off to work as usual, but you didn't seem like yourself. You came back so quiet, and you stayed awake for so long," she tells him. "So... I had to do it."

Roger swallows his bite.

"Do what?"

Amy smiles at him, mischievously.

"I sabotaged your alarm clock."

Roger starts to laugh and then gives his wife a hug as she laughs back.

"Thank you for this," he tells her, looking back into her eyes.

"I pray for you all the time, Roger," she says abruptly. "I apologize if I don't show it as much as I should, but I really love you, Roger."

"Oh, you show it to me even when I don't deserve it," Roger replies.

His wife beams.

"That's what God does, too, you know."

"Amy, you know I'm a Christian… you don't have to bring God into this."

"That's kind of the point, though," Amy tells him. "I've been thinking about this a lot recently… I know we go to church on Sundays, but I've been thinking... maybe we should take our faith a little more seriously."

"What do you mean?"

"Well... I was reading my Bible the other day… and I realized how much I've been living for myself, and how I could be doing more… by helping you, for one thing. And when you seemed so down after coming home the past two days… I knew something was wrong, and I felt like the Lord was urging me to serve you somehow."

"Wow… that's…" Roger responds with a chuckle. "That's… really something."

Amy Kowalski puts her elbows on the bed and lets her head rest in her hands, grinning at her husband.

"Tell me your story again," she insists. "Please."

"Which story?"

"Everything. The one where you told me everything that led to you becoming an officer... do it for me."

"Why...?"

His wife mischievously grabs his plate.

"Heh… okay, okay! Fine!" Roger jokingly gives in, and she hands him back the plate.

Roger takes a moment to think about what to say before recalling his past.

"Well, my dad was a police officer, and I looked up to him. Heh, I wanted to be like him someday. He was a good Christian man... but one day he... he was killed. I was fifteen at the time... and I got so mad at God. I prayed, 'Why God, why did you take my father away from me?!'"

Roger breathes a sigh.

"I was headed down a dark path... and only did what I wanted to do, but then one day... I found my dad's Bible... and realized how much he was devoted to God. I found this one verse... to 'live is Christ, to die is gain. 'I had to know what it meant. I had to know why my dad was so committed to this. I searched through the pages to try and figure out some meaning to all of this..."

"And then what happened?"

"I realized that I had it all wrong. God isn't some heartless deity who likes to kill people... No... I realized how much He loves my dad... and how much... He loves me."

"And no offense, but it's more than I love you," Amy remarks with a laugh.

"Heh, yeah," Roger responds before continuing to tell his story. "That's when I let Jesus in. From that moment, I could feel Him calling me to follow in my dad's footsteps, to protect and serve the people of Old York," Roger continues. "Oh yeah, and then I met some beautiful lady, and we got married... but I can skip that part."

Amy snatches Roger's plate from him.

"I regret making you breakfast!" she jokes.

"Seriously, though, dear... this is... incredible," he tells his wife, gratefully. "This means so much, Amy."

"Oh, we're not done yet!" his wife exclaims. "This day's only just begun!"

Roger's smile widens as he takes another bite of
his breakfast. His happiness wavers, however, as his
friends reenter his mind, with armed Scorpions surrounding
them.

Johnny... Richie...

****

"JOHNNY!"

John Lawson awakes at the sound of his fellow
officer's voice. He looks up to see the dirty face of Richard
Thompson and his hurt eyes staring down at Johnny.

"Richie... what..."

An unpleasant smell, resembling rotten eggs and
old shoes, fills his nostrils.

Johnny's eyes move around the cold, stone room
they are kept in. Richie and four other prisoners stare at
Johnny as the mustached police officer sits up. John
Lawson instantly remembers being captured by the
Scorpions. He tries to move his hands, but a rope tied
around them prevents him from doing so.

"Why'd you wake me?" he asks Richie.

Richie nods his head towards a Scorpion guard,
who is standing above them.

"You have a visitor," the guard tells the prisoners.

Johnny notices that the guard is armed, and two
other armed guards are standing outside of the door.
Johnny's heart beats faster as another figure in black
enters the room, which Johnny has never seen before.
This gangster appears to be wearing Scorpion getup,
except for dark gray sleeves and a unique black hood over
his head.

A ninja hood?! Johnny analyzes.

"You shouldn't have tried to escape that other room," the Scorpion remarks. "Now look where Scorpio's keeping you."

He scoffs.

"If I had my way... you six wouldn't be treated so *nicely*."

"Who are you?" Johnny voices. "A ninja?"

The ninja-like figure lowers his eyebrows as Johnny detects a burning hatred in his eyes.

CHAPTER 13: "BATTLE ON THE ROOFTOP"

"I've really enjoyed today," Roger Kowalski tells his wife.

Roger and Amy have spent the entire day together; they watched a movie, went out to lunch, played mini-golf, and are now in the park for an afternoon walk.

"Yeah?" she questions, smiling back at him.

"Yeah," Roger Kowalski says. "And I've thought about what you've said… about our faith and everything."

The air seems colder, seeming to crawl on his skin as he thinks back to the night when his friends were captured.

"RUN!" he hears himself shouting as the events replay in his mind.

"I can't get Johnny and Richie off my mind…" he continues. "I don't think God wants me to give up. I think God wants me to move forward and keep searching for them."

"Do you have any clues about where they were taken?" his wife asks.

"No," Roger answers. "The gang that took them move around a lot. We don't know where many of their hideouts are."

"Is there anything that could help you in your search?"

Roger recalls the shuriken that had been found on the scene. An idea forms in his mind as he fights to remember what he saw during his escape. He knows that he looked back at one point but can't seem to recount a ninja being with the Scorpions.

What if that ninja did show up? Roger wonders. *And what if he wasn't helping the Scorpions?*

"So... is there?"

Roger looks back at Amy.

"Maybe... maybe there's not... not something," Roger stammers. "But... *someone.*"

Roger informs her of the possibility of a ninja vigilante.

"Interesting," she simply responds. "What if he's not friendly, though? Ninjas did start out as assassins, after all."

"That's what I keep hearing," Roger says. "But what if this ninja is actually *against* the Scorpions? If he really was on the Scorpions' side, wouldn't we have encountered him by now?"

"Hmm..."

"Yeah, I can't recall an instance when any of our officers encountered this ninja, let alone fought him," Roger adds. "Although... the Scorpions themselves have said things like, 'this ninja's the real enemy,' and have seemed to use him as a reason for getting caught."

"If you can find this ninja," Amy Kowalski replies. "You may have an ally in this fight... one that could help you to find your friends."

****

Zach Rylar spent that Friday afternoon resuming his training with Sensei Haruta. Instead of a new lesson, Sensei Haruta decided that they should practice some basic skills, such as shuriken throwing.

Shortly after Zach's grandfather dropped Zach off at his house, Zach's phone rang.

"I forgot to ask you," Kenshin Haruta tells Zach over the phone. "This Sunday... would like to go to church with me again?"

Zach thinks back to last Sunday, and the events are succeeding it. *He's kind of a hypocrite,* Zach thinks about his grandfather in his mind. *He wants me to trust in this God of his, while he doesn't trust other people.*

All of a sudden, the ninja-in-training is brought back to their encounter with Scorpio in his thoughts.

"You're on the wrong side, boy! This man fights only for himself!" Zach remembers the gang leader's words.

"Zach? Are you still there?"

"Yeah, yeah... I'm here," Zach replies to his grandfather over the phone.

"I asked if you would be okay with going to church with me on Sunday."

"Um..." Zach starts to respond.

What do I say?! he thinks frantically in his mind. *This stuff makes me so uncomfortable, and I don't want to go back to feeling inferior because of this!*

"I don't think it's for me," Zach concludes.

"Oh, but it can be, Zach," Sensei Haruta tells him. "The Bible says that anyone who believes in Jesus won't perish but will have eternal life."

"And yet these people still die," Zach debates. "How is that 'eternal'?"

"Eternal life means spending your life after your earthly death with Jesus forever."

"Like in heaven?" Zach questions with a snicker. "What if I don't want to be with Jesus?"

"It would give me great sadness if that were the case, my grandson…" Zach's grandfather continues over the phone with sorrow in his tone. "I don't like to think about you facing the alternative… but just know that, even if you don't want to be with Jesus… Jesus still wants to be with you."

Zach struggles to come up with his next words. He just wants this conservation to be over, for the awkwardness to end.

"Cool," he simply responds. "Well… I guess I'll see you Monday… Sensei."

Zach Rylar hangs up.

****

"Zach? Are you still there? Zach?!"

Kenshin Haruta is inside his bedroom, with his phone to his ear. The phone makes a beeping sound, indicating that Zach has ended the call.

The grandfather sets the phone down on his desk and pushes his hair back with his hands.

"Oh…" he prays out loud, folding his hands together. "What should I do, God? Zach's so lost… and he needs you… please, show him the way!"

He gets down on his knees as emotions overtake him. Considering what Zach had said over the phone, the older man imagines what it would be like if Zach kept rejecting God.

"Please, God… I ask for your wisdom in this… I pray that I won't lean on my own understanding… but on yours. Please… give me the right things to say... and help me to endure."

When thinking about endurance, a passage in Scripture comes to him, so Kenshin reaches for his Bible. He takes it off of his desk, and flips to the book of Hebrews, and starts to read chapter 12.

"Therefore, since we are surrounded by so great a cloud of witnesses," Kenshin begins to read from the first verse. "...let us also lay aside every weight, and sin which clings so closely."

His eyes move down the page.
"And let us run the race with endurance that is set before us, looking to Jesus, the founder and perfecter of our faith."

Kenshin Haruta starts to realize how the writer uses Jesus as an example of endurance, and that Jesus endured so much hostility against him.

The secret ninja master eventually gets into verse seven, "it is for discipline that you have to endure" and smirks with confidence. Kenshin starts to feel prideful of his accomplishments, as he considers what he has endured through and how much self-discipline he has achieved.

Suddenly, when he gets to verse fourteen, he realizes that he was not really reading the other verses, but merely going over them in his mind. Kenshin Haruta feels a conviction as he whispers verse fourteen aloud to himself.

"Strive for peace with everyone..."

He looks up from his Bible, recalling the last time he encountered Scorpio, and how Kenshin had stabbed his enemy with a sai. All of his fights with the Scorpions come back to him, and he recounts how he disregarded their way of thinking. Immediately, some famous words of Jesus come to his mind:

"Love your enemies."

No, Kenshin Haruta tells God. *I'm doing the right thing. I'm stopping the Scorpions from committing crimes, from hurting people! They just kidnapped police officers, and you want me to love them?! The Scorpions must be brought to justice, and while I won't kill them, I won't just let them go either!*

Sensei Haruta recognizes that he has been wrestling with this for some time, yet still does not give in to this conviction. He thinks back to his life before fighting the Scorpions, his life before he became a vigilante in the gang war. He thinks back to a time when Old York was a more peaceful place. Kenshin then remembers how he and Scorpio fought side-by-side, but recalls the disagreement they had.

Scorpio wanted to stop the gangs by starting a gang. I reacted harshly, the ninja master reflects. *We fought, and I-*

Kenshin Haruta forces the thought away in his mind, trying to forget what he did to Scorpio. But as he pictures the gang leader as he is now in his mind, Kenshin cannot ignore it.

"What have I done..." Kenshin Haruta laments aloud. "If I had reacted differently... if I had sought you more, God, I..."

He sniffs.

"I might've been able to stop the Scorpions from ever rising up."

More events replay in the older man's mind as he recalls an attempt of his to fix it on his own. A ninja-like Scorpion appears in his mind.

Kenshin tried to push him out of his mind for a long time, but the familiar figure still sticks with him. The grandfather thinks about his grandson and desperately begs God that the teenager will not go down the same path.

Lord, PLEASE! Kenshin cries out. *I already failed with one student... please don't let me fail with Zach! I jogged by his house for so long, waiting for the opportunity to ask to train him... and I thank you so much for the time we've spent together since then! Please... be with him. Guide Zach to turn to You, to not fight his own way, but how You want him to, Lord.*

Realizing that he needs to pray this for himself as well, Kenshin Haruta finally gives in.

"Okay, God," he prays out loud. "Help me to love my enemies… and strive for peace with them. You made me realize that I've been wrong in many ways, so show me... what is right."

****

Tick tock. Tick tock.

Ugh. Monday, Zach thinks with a sigh.

His eyes follow the hands of the clock, longing for them to speed up. He redirects his pupils to the front of the classroom to observe the moving lips of his math teacher. Zach wishes to be anywhere but here; anywhere in his Gray Ninja Suit, that is. He imagines himself battling Scorpions in the Suit before pushing the thought away, reminding himself that Sensei Haruta took it back.

Maybe today's the day I'll get it back, Zach hopes.

After the final bell rings, the teen practically runs out of the school. He is halfway down the steps to the parking lot when-

SLAM!

A guy in a hoodie falls to the ground. Zach pauses, realizing that he bumped into someone.

"Hey!" the guy shouts. "What'd you do that for?!"

Zach tries to apologize until the guy in the hooded sweatshirt shoves him back.

Immediately, Zach recognizes him as the Sweatshirt Guy on the bus. A rage overtakes Zach, igniting his desire to get 'even.'

Now I can take him, Zach thinks pridefully, cracking his knuckles.

"You don't know who you're messing with!" the ninja-in-training taunts his rival.

Sweatshirt Guy scoffs.

"You don't either!" he counters and pushes Zach again.

Zach raises his fists, about to slam his right knuckle into Sweatshirt Guy's face.

Suddenly, another force grabs Zach's right arm before he can serve the blow. Someone behind Zach yanks his hood and spins him around.

"Grandson! What have I taught you about anger?!"

****

Kenshin Haruta looks down sternly at his grandson.

"Grandpa, you don't understand!" Zach protests. "This guy has been giving me a hard time on this bus, and this time he pushed me down on the ground!"

"A hard time?" Sweatshirt Guy scoffs. "I was just tryna sleep, bro!"

Kenshin turns sympathetically to the teen in the hoodie. He glances up quickly and scans the area around him. Other students are starting to leave the building and head down the steps.

The older man pulls out his wallet and hands the guy in the hoodie a $20 bill.

"Here," the secret ninja master insists. "I apologize for my grandson's actions. We were never here."

"Aw, sweet!" Sweatshirt Guy exclaims.

He examines the money and then looks up at Kenshin. The teenager in the hoodie pockets the cash and pretends to zip his lips.

"My lips are sealed."

"Did you just bribe him?!" Zach whispers to Sensei Haruta as the two relatives walk to the older man's car.

Sensei Haruta ignores him and studies the surrounding area a second time. He unlocks the car, and the two relatives get in.

"What I should have done is reported you to the principal!" Zach's grandfather strictly responds once they are inside. "I have taught you to not let your anger consume you, for it could lead to consequences that could simply be avoided by PEACE!"

Kenshin Haruta takes a few deep breaths before continuing to speak. He then starts the car and pulls out of the parking lot.

"I'm sorry, Zach... I also need to watch my temper," he admits. "But know this, Zach... I care so much about you... and you know that I want what's best for you... so please, take my words to heart."

Zach's expression of frustration changes.

"Okay, Grandpa... I will," Zach replies. "I won't do this again."

Kenshin Haruta smiles.

"I forgive you, Zach. Now... why don't we do some *real* fighting?"

Shortly after, Kenshin Haruta and his grandson step out onto the courtyard of the dojo, dressed in their training kimonos. Zach asks his grandfather what the lesson is for today.

"It involves climbing to high heights," Kenshin replies. "Like on top of my house."

Kenshin detects anxiety in Zach from the teen's sudden expression of shock.

"I have to climb on the roof of your house?" Zach questions, appearing concerned.

"Zach... this is an essential part of your training. To be a ninja, you have to be able to master your surroundings. In Old York, rooftops are likely to be your battle locations."

"Yeah... I guess that's true," Zach simply responds. There is some silence, as Kenshin Haruta studies his grandson's nervous appearance.

"Are you afraid of heights?" Sensei Haruta asks bluntly.

"Whaaat...no... I just didn't know what you meant, exactly, that's all."

"Zach... it's okay to tell me about these things. In fact, I believe that it will greatly benefit your training if we are completely honest with each other."

Zach gives him a peculiar look.

"Okay, before you said you didn't want me to question your judgment, and that was me being honest. So now you're saying it's okay?"

"Zach..."

"Alright, fine. I honestly think that after today, I should get the Suit back."

Frustration builds up inside Kenshin Haruta, but he takes a deep breath. *Focus, Kenshin,* he tells himself in his mind, while silently praying to keep his cool.

"I think you know what I mean, Zach," the ninja master replies. "And if you ever feel any fear or pain... don't hesitate to let me know."

"But pain is an illusion," Zach shoots back defiantly. "It's a lie, an obstacle that's holding me back from becoming The Gray Ninja."

Kenshin Haruta pauses, realizing that Zach is quoting his teachings. A thought comes to him to check and see if it is in line with the Bible, but the ninja master pushes the idea away to agree with his own thinking.

"Yes, and don't let your fear stop you, either, Zach. Don't deny it, but accept that it is there and fight it. Turn it into an illusion as well."

Zach keeps his mouth shut this time, and simply nods instead of continuing to argue.

"Good. Now... let us get into today's lesson," Sensei Haruta proclaims before commanding Zach to climb on top of his roof.

"Wait... but how am I supposed to get there?" Zach asks.

"Throughout your entire training, you have been developing 'ninja instincts.' Use them," Haruta replies and then smiles mischievously. "And... I know you can figure it out."

Sensei Haruta watches as his student looks at his wall-like fence, and runs over to it.

He's doing it, Kenshin thinks, with pride for his student.

Zach climbs up the fence and stands on the top of it. Next, the ninja-in-training parkours onto the roof of Haruta's house.

"Oh... this actually isn't that high up," Zach comments.

"While my house is only a one-story building, many of the others you will have to climb will be higher."

Sensei Haruta looks down at his own gray training kimono and pulls out three shurikens. He raises them up for Zach to see.

"Oh, no! Not this again!" Zach exclaims.

"There will be times when you will be attacked on the rooftop, which can include being shot at from the

186

ground," the sensei tells his student. "Would you rather want me to bring out a shotgun?"

"Do you even have a shotgun?"

"No… but I have a crossbow."

"Okay… let's just stick to the shurikens."

Sensei Haruta prepares to throw the first shurikens into the air but realizes that Zach is sitting down.

"STAND UP!" he shouts, and his student obeys.

A silver and dark blue shuriken is released from Sensei Haruta's grasp, soaring straight for Zach. Zach instantly moves out of the way.

"Your reflexes have been greatly improving," Kenshin compliments. "But let us see how well they do against multiple projectiles!"

Immediately, Sensei Haruta tosses three shurikens up to Zach, although, the ninja-in-training ducks beneath all of them. Kenshin reaches into his kimono again to pull out four more shiny, silver shurikens. With lightning speed, he hurls the first one at Zach.

Zach dodges it.

However, while Zach is moving, Kenshin throws the second, and then the third. Zach moves his head sideways as the second shuriken flies past his face. The third shuriken comes in low, and Zach jumps over it.

"Very good, my student!" Sensei Haruta exclaims while holding the fourth shuriken behind his back.

"Thanks, Sensei! Wow, that was-!"

All of a sudden, Sensei Haruta hurls the last of the shurikens in Zach's direction, and it sails straight towards him.

With lightning speed, Zach Rylar leaps out of the way, and it flies past him.

"Never forget, Zach… a ninja must always be ready for anything. For in life, we never truly know what to expect."

Kenshin Haruta grins, believing that Zach won't expect what he is about to say.

"Now... go to the basement and get in your Suit. In five minutes, return to the roof."

****

Zach Rylar beams beneath his ninja helmet. He is excited to be back in the Gray Ninja suit, yet is also curious as to what his grandfather has in mind.

When Zach makes it onto the roof, he feels as though he is looking into a mirror. Sensei Haruta is also there, in his identical Gray Ninja Suit.

Oh, I know what we're going to-

Zach train of thought is interrupted by the distance to the ground. Zach gulps.

"I don't know about this, Sensei," Zach blurts out wearily. "What if we fall off?"

"Well... you did want the Suit back," Kenshin Haruta remarks. "So... you may have it for this fight."

Zach thinks for a moment.

"How about this... if I beat you, I get to keep the Suit," Zach challenges.

His sensei laughs.

"Just be patient, Zach... I'll give you the Suit when you're ready for it," Sensei Haruta assures him. "Although... if you beat me... I'll be more likely to consider it."

"Fine," Zach responds and grips his nunchucks. "Let's go!"

Suddenly, Sensei Haruta kicks Zach Rylar's legs from under him. Zach loses his balance and topples down. Zach's nunchucks fall out of his hands and down to the ground below. The teenager starts to roll down the roof, but his grandfather grabs his arm.

"What?! Is it over already?!" Zach questions.

Sensei Haruta helps him up.

"Yes, Zach. An opponent can kill you in no time at all."

Sensei Haruta backs up.

"And now… we will go again!"

Sensei Haruta sends a fist towards Zach, which Zach blocks. Zach then tries to karate kick his sensei, but Sensei Haruta dodges his attack. Sensei Haruta moves in closer and pushes Zach back. Zach blocks another attack to lunge at his sensei with his fist. However, Sensei Haruta blocks the attack with his wrist guard.

"Ow!" Zach exclaims and shakes his fist.

Kenshin Haruta sweeps the leg once again, and Zach falls onto the roof shingles. Zach jumps back to his feet to meet a blow to the shoulder. Zach attempts multiple attacks against his temporary opponent, which the ninja master mostly dodges and blocks. Finally, Sensei Haruta unsheathes a ninjatō and raises it at Zach.

"Defend yourself!" he commands, swinging the sword at Zach.

Zach blocks the attack with a wrist guard and then pushes on the blade hard with one of them. The sword is knocked back, but Sensei Haruta maintains his grip. Zach spins toward Kenshin and grabs his hands. The ninja-in-training then quickly twists his sensei's grip and disarms him.

Zach obtains the ninjatō and aims it at his temporary opponent.

"You are defeated," Zach declares.

A great force pushes Zach's legs out from under him again, and Zach once again loses his balance. The ninjatō falls from the roof, as Zach starts to fall with it. This time, however, Zach grabs onto the roof tiles, and his feet dangle in the air.

"You have a ways to go... but I think you're getting the hang of it," Sensei Haruta teases.

Zach raises his eyebrows and chuckles nervously. "Uh... can you help me up... please?"

****

For the next two weeks, Zach continues his training with Sensei Haruta. As his sensei teaches him new lessons, and they redo old ones, Zach becomes even more skilled as a ninja. However, his relationship with his friends does not improve, as he and Ryan talk even less. They still sit at the same lunch table, but Zach contributes less to the conversations. His mind becomes way more focused on his ninja abilities, as his determination to fight the Scorpions in the Gray Ninja Suit increases much more.

Kenshin Haruta tries to talk to Zach about his faith a few times, but Zach doesn't consider his words.

October becomes November, and on the second day of this penultimate month, Sensei Haruta has something to tell Zach. After training, the ninja master leads Zach into his basement.

"You are almost ready to go out again," Sensei Haruta announces.

"For real this time?" Zach questions in disbelief.

"Yes... 'for real,'" Sensei Haruta replies with a chuckle. "I have decided to give you the Suit back."

"Yes!" Zach cheers, raising up his fist and then pulling his arm halfway down.

"But-!" Sensei Haruta interrupts his celebration. "It is only to study it... to get more of a feel for it. Since we have mainly been using the training kimonos, I will let you take your Ninja Suit home with you to... *study*. Don't leave your house with it, except to bring it back here to train in."

190

Sensei Haruta hands him what appears to be a big, white poster board. Zach opens it up to realize that it is a diagram of the Gray Ninja Suit. For each of the various armor pieces, Sensei Haruta has labeled them with different moves and attack strategies.

"I apologize that I didn't think of this before," Sensei Haruta tells Zach. "But now that you are becoming more equipped to keep it, I will let you do the studying on your own."

I don't even care if my grandpa just gave me homework, Zach thinks to himself. *I'm just glad to get this thing back!*

That night, Zach lies on his bed, watching a YouTube video on his phone. The Gray Ninja Suit is stuffed in a large backpack in the corner of the room, with the poster board beside it. Zach's eyes meet up with the backpack, and he pauses the video.

As he stares, he remembers how Sensei Haruta told him not to leave the house with it.

But I'm ready to use it, Zach assures himself.

A temptation rolls over Zach, as he debates in his mind whether or not to obey his sensei's command.

Zach Rylar gets off of his bed and walks over to the backpack.

Sensei Haruta thinks you're inferior, too, says a voice in his mind. *Prove him wrong.*

Zach unzips his backpack and lifts up the Gray Ninja helmet.

CHAPTER 14: "REBELLION"

Zach sets the helmet down. *No, I shouldn't use it yet,* he thinks. But Zach remembers beating the Scorpions before, and how Sensei Haruta had described that they were everywhere. *They're criminals... they need to be stopped,* he tells himself. *And I can stop them.*

Zach opens his door and tip-toes over to his mother's bedroom. He opens it slightly and peers inside the dark room.

"Mom?"

A loud snoring sound is her reply.

Zach Rylar quietly closes the door and tip-toes back into his room. He takes the helmet out of the backpack, starting to take out the entire outfit.

A moment later, Zach is standing in his bedroom wearing the full Gray Ninja Suit, weapons and all. He looks down at the poster board and kicks it aside.

I don't need this, he thinks pridefully before heading over to his window.

On the wall, above Zach's bed, is a window, which Zach decides to go through. The Gray Ninja jumps onto the mattress, opens the window, squeezes his body through it, and lands on the ground below. Next, he rolls over to some bushes in front of his house and hides behind them.

How am I going to get to the Scorpions? Zach wonders.

This is something that Zach had forgotten to consider, but fortunately, he has an idea. His scooter is in the backyard, so he tip-toe runs through his side-yard, jumps his fence, and grabs the scooter. The Gray Ninja folds it up and holds it in his right hand. He leaps over the fence again and runs back behind the bushes.

Dang, Zach thinks. *If I go there on my scooter, I'll be out in the open.*

He realizes he has to make a decision fast, so he's not seen in the Suit in front of his house. Unfolding his scooter, the Gray Ninja hastily decides to go through with this. He runs over to the sidewalk, gets on it, and hurries down the concrete path. Zach rides speedily down sidewalks for a couple of miles, avoiding the busier streets to remain unseen. Whenever he hears a car approaching, he hides behind any cover he can find.

As he approaches downtown Old York, he scans the area for crime. He doesn't notice many cars or people but does spot a person walking down the sidewalk across from Zach. The Gray Ninja moves into an alley and unfolds his scooter. He peers around the corner to stare at the person walking from a distance.

It's just some older guy walking his dog, Zach analyzes.

Suddenly, the dog looks in the ninja's direction and starts barking loudly. Zach moves closer into the shadows as the middle-aged man tries to calm down the dog.

Zach's eyes move around the alley before shifting upward. Zach recalls the roof training lesson he had with Sensei Haruta, and how he and his sensei climbed a roof to get a better view the last time he was out here in his Suit.

The Gray Ninja climbs up the fire escape on the side of one of the buildings and makes it up to the roof. The building only consists of two stories, yet Zach can still see plenty around him. The ninja-in-training's eyes move throughout downtown Old York, examining every structure, car, or person around him. After several minutes of searching, Zach's eyes finally stop at what appears to be a warehouse a block away from him. He decides to check it out and proceeds to makes his way down to it.

The Gray Ninja runs over to the side of this building, which is in a different alley. He advances through the darkness and quietly sets his scooter behind a dumpster. The Gray Ninja's eyes pick up a window, which he approaches stealthily.

He looks into it to see several armed figures dressed in black moving about the warehouse. And on the back wall, Zach notices a giant, graffitied symbol of a scorpion.

Zach pats his invinsium helmet, hoping that it is as strong as Sensei Haruta said it was. He rushes forward and crashes through the glass with the helmet.

Surprisingly, Zach is unphased by the impact.

This invinsium stuff is great, Zach thinks to himself.

The Gray Ninja crawls through the hole he made and enters the warehouse. A Scorpion in front of him turns, but the ninja quickly moves behind some boxes.

Fortunately for Zach, in this Scorpion hideout, there is plenty of cover. Not only are there tall pillars holding the roof up, but also dozens of rows of large boxes and crates.

The Scorpion walks in Zach's direction.

"Jimmy? Is that you?"

The Gray Ninja takes out his nunchucks.

The Scorpion approaches the boxes and starts to move behind them.

WHACK!

As soon the Scorpion moved close enough, Zach whacked him in the head with his nunchucks.

The Gray Ninja briefly puts his nunchucks away to pull the defeated body behind the boxes. He then crouch-runs with his arms behind him towards more boxes and hides behind them. The ninja detects two more Scorpions with guns close by, standing between him and more cover. Zach remembers the stealth training lesson that he completed with his sensei and recreates it. He rushes toward one of the Scorpions and takes him out with a powerful punch.

The other one whirls around, confused, but the Gray Ninja is too fast. He jumps behind the boxes on the other side before leaping back out to face the second Scorpion. Zach whips out one of his ninja short-swords out of his sword holder and knocks the gun out of the Scorpion's right hand.

The Gray Ninja then kicks him in the face, knocking him off of his feet. The gangster falls in front of the first Scorpion, as Zach runs stealthily out of sight. Another Scorpion walks up to the fallen Scorpions a moment later to find them half-unconscious.

"Get up! I know that it's late, but you mustn't sleep!" he hollers, nudging them.

Zach can't hold back a snicker, and the Scorpion's attention is drawn to the crates that Zach is crouching behind. The Scorpion raises his gun, but The Gray Ninja hurls a shuriken at it and lunges out from his hiding place.

The gun slides across the floor.

Zach raises his sword as the Scorpion pulls out a knife. Zach quickly strikes the blade out of the Scorpion's hands, sending that weapon landing beside the gun.

The gangster curses right before Zach knocks him out with the hilt of his sword.

With him down, The Gray Ninja dashes towards another pile of boxes and crouches behind them. Three more Scorpions gather around the scene of the previous fight. As soon as they see the defeated Scorpions on the ground, they raise their guns.

"It's that old man ninja!" one of the Scorpions tells the others. "Search the area!"

The Gray Ninja sheathes his ninjatō and takes out a pair of sais. He throws one of the sais at the furthest Scorpion's gun and then charges at the two in front of him. Zach kicks the leg of the first Scorpion, knocking him over, and punches the second one in the face with his the hilt of his sai. The furthest Scorpion tries to pick up his gun, but Zach sprints over to him and shoves him down. The Scorpion tries to get up, but Zach quickly takes out his nunchucks and smacks him in the face with them. The other two Scorpions also start to rise to their feet, but Zach beats them both with his nunchucks.

By this moment, Zach feels pretty proud of himself for taking out so many Scorpions so far. *What was Sensei Haruta even talking about?* Zach thinks. *I've been ready for this for a while, probably! He just underestimated me.*

"Stop right there!" Zach hears from behind him.

The Gray Ninja does a 180°.

A man dressed in black has his gun pointed at Zach. This Scorpion isn't wearing a hood or mask, but has the weirdest mustache Zach has ever seen; it is quite oversized. To add to that, the Scorpion has thick, black sideburns and hair in a tiny man-bun on the back of his head.

"Well, well, well," the Scorpion says with a heavy Southern accent. "The student... we finally meet."

"Who are you supposed to be?!" Zach questions.

"Name's Bartholomew Mustachio," he replies, with the gun still pointed at the Gray Ninja. "And I can mess you up if you come any closer."

Zach looks beyond Mustachio and notices a heavy, fortified door on the back wall, with heavily armed Scorpions guarding it.

Are they hiding something here? Zach wonders. *What could it be... Drugs? Money? Weapons?*

"Fine. I won't hurt you..." Zach assures him. "If you tell me what you guys are hiding here."

"Heh, don't you already know?" is the mustached Scorpion's response. "Your old man has been searching for this place."

Suddenly, more Scorpions approach the scene. Zach looks around and realizes they are all around him, with their guns raised.

"We knew you'd come here eventually, Gray Ninja," Mustachio remarks with a laugh. "You fell right into our trap!"

"What are you going to do with me?" Zach asks as fear sweeps over him.

"That's for Master Scorpio to decide. Fortunately for you, he gave us strict orders to leave you unharmed until he arrives... unless you try to move."

Bartholomew Mustachio turns to another Scorpion.

"Call Master Scorpio," he commands. "Tell him... we have the student."

****

For the past two weeks, Roger Kowalski has been trying to figure as much as he can about the ninja vigilante and the Scorpions. He has spent a lot of time on missions with the OYPD to search potential Scorpion hideouts for the missing officers. Many of them were vacant, but a few were occupied, and the police force brought a few Scorpions in for questioning.

Roger sits with one of them in an interrogation room, who appears to be in his early twenties.

"Tell me everything you know about the ninja vigilante," Roger tells him.

"Will you reduce my sentence?"

"You know what… I'm in a good mood today. If you tell me who he is… I'll let you go."

"I don't know who he is!" the Scorpion protests. "No one does!"

"Then tell me about him. What's he like?"

"Well… he wears this big suit, with armor and stuff… It's like… um, gray and dark blue, with all these weapons, like ninja swords, shurikens… that kind of stuff. Oh, and instead of a hood, he has a metal helmet shaped like one."

Roger Kowalski has been taking notes with a pen and notebook in his hands.

"Okay… metal helmet… got it," Roger says, and looks back up at the Scorpion. "What else?"

"He's really fast… and hurts. But he doesn't kill us, just knocks us out."

Roger scribbles that down on his notebook.

"How old would you say this guy is… if you had a guess? Or… is he not a guy?"

"I've never fought him up close," the Scorpion admits. "A buddy of mine did, though, and he said that when he looked at his eyes… he looked like an old man."

"This buddy of yours… do you think he knows more than you about this ninja?"

"Probably."

"Where can I find him?"

"OYPD! On the ground!" Roger Kowalski shouts as the police officer in front of him busts down a door.

Roger Kowalski and his team of officers got a warrant to get into someone's home, and they arrest the man living there. Later that day, the man is put into an interrogation room, with Roger questioning him.

"It's pretty obvious that you're a Scorpion," Roger tells him plainly. "We found your outfit in your house, with multiple guns and knives. And we also captured some of your friends."

"Did they snitch on me?!" the prisoner questions angrily.

"I can actually read minds," Roger replies sarcastically. "Yes, they 'snitched' on you. And you're gonna have to 'snitch' on some other friends of yours because I'm determined to find out where your 'master' TOOK MY FRIENDS!"

The Scorpion snickers.

"You think I know where your cop friends are? That's where you're wrong, dude. Only a select group of us know where they're hidden, and I don't even know who they are."

Roger thinks for a moment.

"Well… Scorpio knows where they are, doesn't he?"

"I don't know… probably."

"So wouldn't that mean he would tell those closest to him?" Roger guesses.

The officer moves closer to the guy he is interrogating.

"Who's his second-in-command?!" Roger questions.

"Man… I don't even know him," the Scorpion responds. "The guy's like a ghost. Apparently, he's some former military sniper that's really skilled in martial arts and tech and stuff. I've seen him once... he was wearing this black ninja hood."

"A ninja hood? Is he related to the ninja that's supposedly fighting you guys?"

"Now the ninja I can talk about. That old guy always beats up my buddies, and interferes with anything we're trying to do!" he complains. "This one time, we tried to rob this one-"

The Scorpion looks up at Roger and then stops talking.

"Go on," Roger insists.

"It's not important," the guy replies. "We didn't try to rob a store or anything. We were actually trying to buy some stuff, and then the ninja just came in and beat us up!"

"Tell me more about the ninja. Where did he come from? What's he like?"

The Scorpion doesn't give him any new information, so Roger decides to steer the conversation back to the Scorpion hierarchy.

"So about this 'second-in-command'... does he have anyone close to him that you know of?"

"Dude, he's just about as secretive as the ninja," the Scorpion informs Roger. "The only two guys he's probably close to are Scorpio and Number Three."

"Number Three? Who's Number Three?"

"Uhh... I've said too much! That's all you get to know!"

"By number three, do you mean third-in-command?" Roger inquires.

"You'll know him by his mustache, that's all I'll say!" the Scorpion responds and refuses to reveal anything further.

****

Zach Rylar waits nervously as the Scorpions keep their weapons aimed at him. He can't help but stare at Bartholomew Mustachio's ridiculous-looking oversized mustache.

All of a sudden, the front door to the warehouse bursts open. The Gray Ninja redirects his attention to the door and watches as an eyepatched man enters the room. As he approaches, Zach recognizes the gang leader.

"Lower your weapons," Scorpio orders.

Bartholomew Mustachio looks at him with surprise. "But Master Scorpio-"

Scorpio raises his hand, and the mustached gangster stops talking. Mustachio then nods to the other Scorpions, and all of the gangsters lower their guns and knives.

Scorpio motions for the Gray Ninja to follow him.

"Come with me," he tells Zach, but Zach just looks back at him blankly through his helmet.

Scorpio moves a few steps until he notices that Zach is not walking with him.

"I'm not going to harm you," Scorpio assures him. "I just want to talk."

Zach realizes that he isn't in a better place– having a bunch of armed gangsters surrounding him– so Zach does what he says.

Scorpio leads him into a back room. Although it isn't the one with the fortified door, Zach still keeps that mystery on his mind.

Once they enter the back room, Zach realizes how nice this room actually looks. It has carpet, painted walls, paintings on the walls, a table and chairs, a mini-fridge, and even a couple of couches facing each other in the middle of the room.

Scorpio stands over one of the couches, and motions for the Gray Ninja to sit on the other.

"Ease up a little bit," Scorpio suggests. "Get comfortable… maybe take off that helmet of yours. I'm sure it's making your head sweaty."

"I'm not taking it off," Zach sternly tells him.

"Fine… fine, your loss," Scorpio says, and walks over to the mini-fridge.

The older man opens it and grabs a soda can.

"Can I offer you anything?" he asks Zach.

The Gray Ninja looks down at his outfit and lifts up a bottle of Water of Purification.

"Built-in water bottles," Scorpio comments. "That's interesting."

Scorpio opens his soda can and proceeds to take a drink from it. Then, he walks back over to the couch and sits down on it.

"I'm not going to tell you anything until you remove your weapons," the Gray Ninja demands.

Scorpio looks down at his gear, noticing that he has a few knives and his pistols on him. His eyes move over to the Gray Ninja Suit, and all of the weapons on it.

"You first."

"Make me."

"I could…" Scorpio says. "But I don't think it's necessary."

"Why are you keeping me here?" Zach questions.

"I told you… to talk," Scorpio replies. "You can go after we've had our conversation."

Zach gives him a puzzled look through the helmet, which Scorpio ignores.

"Tell me, Gray Ninja… why are you here?" he inquires, and then takes a sip of his soda.

"Well… you're criminals, doing criminal things. Old York used to be a good town, but this gang of yours… is messing it up."

"Ouch," Scorpio responds. "I can see that sensei of yours has been putting his ideas into your head. You're right… Old York used to be a good town, but then… something happened."

Zach stares at him.

"I grew up in Old York. I've experienced injustice firsthand, but all around, Old York was a decent place. It had good leaders, and a good, small police department. But over time, everything changed. These honorable leaders were replaced by corrupt ones, who do anything for money. Old York became a town of crime. Gangs rose up in the streets, and I knew… that someone… had to put a stop to it."

Scorpio takes another drink of his soda before setting it back down on the table and continuing to speak.

"The corrupt Chief Mulberry called me 'The Scorpion'," he narrates. "I was a vigilante to him, a vigilante who went around trying to put an end to those gangs as I took out their evil leaders. Along the way, I encountered an ally in the war… another crime fighter known as 'The Gray Ninja.' He didn't tell me his name, and I could tell there was a conflict inside of him. He trusted no one, but still had a moral code, as he refused to kill his enemies. I admired this about him, but it also became his weakness. He has this one-sided view that held him back from eliminating crime for good."

"What do you mean?" Zach asks.

"Well… I had a solution… a solution to end crime in Old York," Scorpio explains. "During the gang war, I realized that many of the gangsters that were recruited were only teenagers, and I didn't want them wasting their lives… so I formed a group of my own… that they could join instead of their misguided organizations."

"So… you formed a gang to end the other gangs?"

"A gang… a gang… I hate that word. I see us more as… a family."

"A 'family' that dresses in black carrying weapons?" Zach counters.

"You know who else does that?" Scorpio responds. "The police… and you and your sensei aren't so different. We carry our weapons as a means of self-defense, just as you do. And while some of our members disobey me, and steal cars and rob stores… the majority of us aren't about that."

"Then what are you about?"

"Restoring peace. Putting an end to the evil gangs and recruiting as many as we can to our cause."

"This… this is just going to bring more violence to Old York," Zach responds.

"Says 'The Gray Ninja'!" Scorpio remarks, and then sighs. "Look… I can tell that you've been taught a lot from that sensei of yours. But you don't know what he's done."

"What has he done?"

"When he found out that I was starting the Scorpions… he tried to stop me. I tried to reason with him, but he didn't listen. He fought me, and in the process, I lost my eye."

Scorpio touches his eyepatch.

"He's hurt me, and so many people around him. And he insists that hurt… that pain… is just an illusion. No… pain is *very* real… and this world is full of it," Scorpio says. "And so much of the pain in this town is caused by the corruption. You can help us, Gray Ninja… you can help us to put an end to crime in this town."

Zach takes a moment to wrap his head around this whole thing. Scorpio's argument is convincing, but Zach still doesn't trust him or the gang. He has known his sensei as his grandfather, a fatherly figure, and a best friend. Yet Zach also remembers how Kenshin Haruta wasn't there for Zach during his childhood. Zach realizes that the first time his grandfather really seemed to show up in his life was when he missed the bus on his first day of school.

The day Grandpa that first asked if he could train me, Zach thinks.

"I know what you're thinking," Scorpio continues. "You just met me... and you've known your... *sensei*... for much longer."

The leader of the Scorpions chuckles.

"It may seem as though I'm holding you hostage in here with my 'army' outside this door with a bunch of weapons," he adds. "But I can assure you... that isn't the case."

Scorpio walks up from the couch and makes his way to the door. He opens it, and stands by it, holding it open.

"You may go," he tells Zach. "But please... stop beating up my sons and daughters, and my brothers and sisters... imagine if you were in my position, and someone went after your family. Trust me, it's never a good feeling to know that someone's hurting people you care about."

Zach gets up from the couch.

"However, I'm more than willing to look past our previous disagreements," Scorpio promises. "Please... consider all that I've told you. I'll give you some time to think about this, Gray Ninja, and when you've reached your decision, return here and tell Mustachio to contact me. I'll... be waiting."

CHAPTER 15: "SEEN AND UNSEEN"

"Have you seen the news?"

Zach looks up at Seth. He realizes that he has been thinking about Scorpio's offer the whole school day. It is now lunchtime, and Zach is sitting at his lunch table with Mike, Ryan, and Seth. Seth just asked him a question, and now all three of Zach's friends are staring at him.

"What?" Zach asks.

"The news," Seth repeats. "About the ninja?"

At this moment, Zach's heart starts to beat. *Oh no,* he thinks. *Did someone see me?*

"Look at this," Mike tells Zach and pulls up a video on his phone. He moves the phone over to Zach, while Ryan and Seth turn so they can also watch it.

"This is NNN, Narrating News Network," a male reporter proclaims in the video. "Late last night, in the town of Old York, this man was walking his dog-"

There is a picture of a man shown on the screen, and Zach immediately remembers him and the dog from last night. *But that guy didn't see me,* Zach assures himself.

"Saw a mysterious figure riding down a sidewalk on a scooter," the reporter continues. "And to prove he's not crazy… he shot this video."

Zach's heart races and eyes widen as the video cuts to the next clip. He watches in horror as he sees himself in the Gray Ninja suit, weapons and all, riding down a sidewalk on his scooter.

He must've recorded this on my way back home! Zach anxiously concludes.

"They called him 'The Silver Warrior,'" Seth tells Zach in awe. "And I'm pretty sure he's a ninja… just look at his outfit."

"Wow," Zach comments, trying to play it cool. "That's insane. But are you guys sure it's real?"

"I think it's real," Mike replies. "I have some friends who live in the downtown area who say that they've seen him before."

"I don't know, dude… that video's probably fake," Zach responds.

"Aw come on, Zach," Seth says to him. "Wouldn't it be awesome, though?! To have a ninja in Old York?!"

"Is he friendly, though?" Ryan wonders aloud.

"I think he is," Zach blurts out. "I mean… if he actually exists."

"I'm not sure yet about that... he is carrying weapons, after all," Mike points out. "And he's getting away fast like he did something wrong."

"Or he just saved someone's life!" Seth suggests. "He could be a superhero!"

"I read an article that said the police chief labeled him as a vigilante," Ryan adds.

Zach looks up the article on his phone, and sure enough, Old York Police Chief Vincent Mulberry has done just that.

This is the guy Scorpio said is corrupt, Zach recalls.

"We have reason to believe that this 'ninja vigilante' has been working with the gangs here in Old York, most notably the Scorpions," the police chief describes in the article.

Frustration builds up inside of Zach.

I'm not working with gangs! he tells himself in his mind.

Nevertheless, the secret ninja's thoughts bring him back to Scorpio's offer. *What if Scorpio's right?* Zach thinks. *What if the Scorpions aren't gangsters… and what if Scorpio's solution will work?*

Zach ponders the question in his mind but still doesn't trust Scorpio.

Later that day, Zach's grandfather picks him up from school. Zach expects his sensei's typical cheerful mood but is instead confronted with hostility.

"I trusted you, Zach!" Sensei Haruta says to him when Zach approaches.

"What are you-?"

"We'll talk about it in the car!"

Zach gets in the passenger seat of Sensei Haruta's silver car, while Kenshin gets in the driver seat. As they start to drive away from the school, Zach tries to explain his actions.

"Look, Sensei… I know what you said, but-"

"No! Sit on this with your 'but,' Zach!" Sensei Haruta responds sternly. "I told you that you weren't ready, that you shouldn't take the Suit out of your house and fight with it yet. And the *day* that I give it back, you immediately go out and disobey me! And to top it all off, you're *seen*! Ninja are masters of *stealth*, Zach! We are supposed to be *unseen*!"

"You're still saying I'm not ready?!" Zach argues, ignoring everything else his sensei said. "You've been looking down on me, underestimating me this whole time... and I realize it now."

A lump starts to form in Zach's throat as his emotions take over.

"You think I'm inferior, just like everyone else..." Zach continues, fighting back tears. "Well, guess what? You're wrong! I went out and took down so many Scorpions and got further than you ever have. In fact, I even faced Scorpio and survived!"

"YOU WHAT?!" Sensei Haruta exclaims angrily and pulls the car over.

"That's right!" Zach replies. "I fought a whole warehouse full of Scorpions, beat all of them, and they had to call their daddy scorpion to help them-!"

"Scorpio is a dangerous man, Zach! You could have been killed!"

"Oh yeah?! Well, guess what?! He didn't fight me!" Zach tells him. "He didn't even want to fight me! Instead, he told me all about you... how you guys were friends, how you guys fought crime together, and then when he tried to find a solution, you slashed his eye out!"

Sensei Haruta doesn't respond.

"He wants peace too, but he has a different solution," Zach continues. "And you... you're unwilling to work with him! You're so stuck up with your Bible verses and your catchy sayings..."

"Zach..." Kenshin Haruta starts to say, lowering his head. "I'm sorry if I hurt you, and I hope you know that I care about you-"

"NO! No, Sensei... you can't hurt me! Because hurt doesn't exist, DOES IT? Pain is an illusion, as you say! BUT IT'S NOT, AND YOU KNOW IT'S NOT!" Zach shouts. "You just deny it, but I WON'T DENY IT, BECAUSE I

KNOW IT'S THERE! I THOUGHT YOU COULD BE LIKE THE FATHER I LOST..."

Zach sniffs.

"But you don't care about me... you've just been using me just to help you in your little *feud* with Scorpio... when all this time... I didn't know what the Scorpions were really like. YOU HAVE NO TRUST FOR ANYONE...NOT FOR SCORPIO... AND NOT EVEN FOR ME!"

"Zach... listen to me..." Zach's grandfather tries to tell him calmly. "Scorpio may believe what he's doing is right... but his solution won't save anyone. Fighting against the law, trying to form his own law... it's just going to make things worse..."

"Why should I believe anything you say?!"

"If you don't believe me, Zach, then believe the police officers he's captured!"

Zach stops.

"What?"

"At the apartments... before you arrived... Scorpio captured several police officers, and they haven't been seen since."

Zach just stares at him.

"I've been searching for them, but I haven't been able to find them," the ninja master admits.

Zach's thinks back to his encounter with Bartholomew Mustachio at the warehouse and seeing the guarded door behind him. *Is that what they're hiding?* Zach wonders. *Prisoners?!*

"Now, Zach... please... let's go back to the dojo and get this all sorted out..."

Suddenly, Zach's anger overtakes him again.

"No! I'm done with this!" he shouts and opens the car door.

Zach seizes his backpack and jumps out of the parked car.

"I can at least drive you back to your house!" his grandfather offers.

"I can get there on my own!" Zach insists. "I don't need you anymore, Sensei… and I don't want to talk to you EVER AGAIN!"

Zach slams the door. He starts to make his way down the sidewalk, in the direction of his house. As Zach walks, his thoughts bring him back to his first day of school. He remembers when he and his grandfather jogged to school instead of driving. He remembers when his grandfather saw potential in him, and when Sensei Haruta started to teach him ninjutsu.

Zach Rylar starts to run… run away, far away from his sensei's silver car. He doesn't look back, as he doesn't want to think about it anymore. But he can't help but remember all the time he has spent with his grandfather, and how much Zach has gotten to know him. He feels a pull to turn back and make things right.

Zach looks back, only to realize that his sensei has already driven away.

I don't need him, Zach tells himself while fighting back tears. *I can do this on my own.*

Zach Rylar runs all the way to his house, as he battles conflicting thoughts in his mind.

****

Despite his talk with Scorpio, Zach goes out again that night in his Gray Ninja Suit, intending to go after the Scorpions. He still has anger in his heart towards his sensei but suspects that what he was saying about the captured police officers was true.

I need to figure out if the Scorpions are holding them behind that door, Zach determines, as he rides back to the Scorpion warehouse on his scooter.

This time, Zach is even more careful, stopping and hiding at any sound that could be a person walking or a car. After it seems like hours have passed, the Gray Ninja finally gets close to the warehouse, but then realizes that he has to go through a parking lot to get to it.

Zach quietly sets his scooter down in an alley before advancing towards the parking lot. As he approaches, Zach observes several dark figures in familiar getup heading in the dark to the warehouse. They are all dressed in black, with hoods and masks to cover up their faces.

The Gray Ninja runs stealthily up to a parked car and crouches behind it. He peers around the car, counting five Scorpions.

"You guys go on ahead, I'll catch up to you," one of the Scorpions tells the others.

Zach recognizes that this is his chance to attack. He waits for the other four Scorpions to walk out of sight, and then directs his attention to the remaining Scorpion, who is typing something on his phone.

The Gray Ninja lunges out from behind the car, swinging his nunchucks. However, the Scorpion reacts quicker than Zach expects. Zach's opponent immediately puts his phone in his pocket and dodges the nunchucks. The Scorpion grabs Zach's hand, disarms him, and starts to attack Zach with his own nunchucks. Zach raises his wrists to block the attacks with his armor before kicking the Scorpion back.

The Gray Ninja then takes out his non-sharp shurikens and tosses them at the Scorpion. The Scorpion tries to cover his face with his arms but is hit a couple times.

The gang member loses his grip, and the nunchucks fall out of his hands. Zach then unsheathes two of his ninja short-swords while the Scorpion pulls out a dagger.

The Gray Ninja aims the swords at the Scorpion.

"Surrender," Zach commands from beneath his ninja helmet.

The Scorpion doesn't listen and moves forward for a low attack. The Scorpion's dagger slices through the durable fabric on Zach's leg, and then the ninja's opponent kicks one of the ninjatō out of Zach's grip. Zach grasps the remaining short-sword with both of his hands and swings the weapon at the Scorpion. Zach's opponent dodges the attack before hitting the dagger against the sword. Their blades clash until the Gray Ninja smacks the dagger out of the Scorpion's hands.

But this Scorpion doesn't give up. He grabs Zach's right hand with his left and punches it with his right with great force. The ninjatō flies out of Zach's hand, but the Gray Ninja quickly whips his sais. The Scorpion grabs the short-sword in midair and charges back at Zach. The Gray Ninja slams his sais into the sword, and the two fighters move their weapons back and forth, trying to get the best of one another. The Scorpion uses the hilt of Zach's sword to hit Zach's right hand again, knocking the sai out of his hand. Zach holds up the remaining sai and lunges at the Scorpion, but the Scorpion blocks the attack with the ninjatō.

Suddenly, Zach hears a shout from a distance.

"IT'S THE NINJA!"

Zach turns to see the four Scorpions from before. Wielding knives, they rush over to Zach and his opponent.

WHAM!

The Scorpion fighting Zach took advantage of the distraction. He grabbed the hilt of the sai and slammed it into Zach's helmet. The attack should have dazed Zach, but the invinsium pulled through.

"Huh?" the Scorpion questions, realizing that his opponent was unaffected.

The Gray Ninja tries to break free of the Scorpion's hold, but the Scorpion fights back harder and disarms Zach.

Zach's opponent aims the short-sword at the ninja's throat as the other four Scorpions approach with knives raised.

All of a sudden, an unmarked black car drives into the parking lot and brakes next to the fight. The driver's door of the car bursts open.

"OYPD! Put your weapons down!"

A police officer with a blond flattop rushes out of the car with his gun raised. The Scorpions divert their attention to him, so Zach seizes the opportunity. He grabs the hilt of the sword pointed at him and twists it out of the Scorpion's grip. Then, with great force, the Gray Ninja karate-kicks the first Scorpion back, sending him flying into a parked car. The Scorpion slams into the car door and lands on the ground.

The other four gangsters lunge at Zach, but Zach swings the ninjatō around, forcing them to step back.

"I said... PUT YOUR WEAPONS DOWN!" the police officer yells again as he starts to move towards the fighters.

Zach slams the hilt of his sword into the first Scorpion's face, and he falls to the ground. The second lunges at him with his knife, but Zach grabs his arm and kicks him in the stomach. The Gray Ninja then pushes the Scorpion back to block an attack from the third Scorpion with his sword. He knocks the third Scorpion's legs down with his own leg, and the Scorpion loses his balance. Zach punches him down to the ground, while the fourth Scorpion attempts to stab him.

ZAP!

Zach turns around to see that the police officer has tased the fourth Scorpion. The gangster's knife slides out of his hand, and he falls to the ground.

The Gray Ninja just stands there, with a ninja sword in hand, staring at the police officer.

"You aren't with them, are you?" the police officer asks, lowering his taser.

The Gray Ninja shakes his head.

"I've been looking for you," the officer tells him as he puts the taser away. "I'm Roger Kowalski... and I think we have a common goal, ninja."

"What's that?" Zach inquires.

"To stop the Scorpions," Roger replies. "And for the past three weeks, they've been holding some friends of mine hostage."

"Are they other police officers?"

"Yeah, have you seen them?"

"No," Zach admits. "But I think I know where they are."

"In this building?" Roger questions while pointing at the warehouse behind Zach.

The Gray Ninja nods.

Suddenly, Roger Kowalski's handheld radio beeps.

"Officer Kowalski, come in!" commands a voice from it.

The blonde police officer raises it up to his mouth.

"10-4, Chief," he replies.

"I told you to tell me first if you find out anything about the ninja and the Scorpions, and I've just been told that you went after them yourself?!"

"It was urgent, sir, I didn't want this opportunity to pass on by," Roger responds.

"Wait for backup, Roger! I repeat, wait for backup, and don't engage!" the police chief sternly instructs him.

"With all due respect, Chief Mulberry, sir, I have all the help I need right here."

"Don't tell me you're working with that vigilante! I could decommission you for this!"

"I'm sorry, sir, but if we attempt an all-out attack, the Scorpions will see us coming and get away! I need to do this now!"

"If you really care about your career, you will stay right where you are, officer, and bring that vigilante in!" Chief Malberry yells over the radio.

"I care…" Roger starts to say. "…about my *friends*! Saving them is more important than this job!"

Roger Kowalski tosses the handheld radio away from him.

"Why'd you do that?" Zach questions, dumbfounded.

"I did it for my friends," Roger replies, looking up at him. "Wouldn't you for the people you care about?"

Zach thinks about his grandfather, Ryan, Mike, and Seth for a moment, but then pushes them away in his mind, telling himself to focus on the mission.

He picks up the weapons of his on the ground and quickly reattaches them to his Suit.

"Come on," he tells his new ally and motions for Roger to follow. "It won't be long until the Scorpions find out they're missing these guys."

"Good point," the officer agrees with him. "Lead the way, Gray Ninja."

Roger Kowalski accompanies Zach to the side of the building. Zach crouches in front of the window he had broken with his helmet and peers through the window.

"They've doubled since the last time I was here," Zach informs Roger in a whisper.

"You've been here before?" Roger questions.

216

"Yeah, yesterday," the Gray Ninja replies. "But I was overpowered."

"Well, hopefully, I can be of some help," Roger comments with a smile.

The Gray Ninja turns to the police officer.

"How'd you find me?"

"An informant of mine sent me a message. He figured out that they're hiding something here," Roger explains. "I figured this is where they're keeping my friends, so I came here immediately. I was expecting to see a Scorpion when I arrived... but I'm surprised it was you the whole time."

Zach remembers the Scorpion that told the others to go on ahead without him; the one was texting on his phone.

"Yeah, um... I'm not your informant," the Gray Ninja admits nervously. "I think I beat him up... accidentally."

"Accidentally?"

"Yeah... sorry about that."

Roger rubs his eyes.

"Well... at least I don't have to fight my way through this place alone," he says. "Speaking of which... how do you suggest we do this?"

Zach thinks for a moment.

"The way I see it... there's only one way we can do this."

"And how's that?"

"The ninja way."

****

Roger Kowalski looks back at the Gray Ninja. When he first met the vigilante, he expected him to be different. Contrary to what the Scorpion he questioned told Roger, this ninja appears to be much younger. Still, the police officer is confused by the ninja's statement.

"I'm afraid I don't know what you mean," Roger admits.

"The element of stealth is our ally in this," the ninja tries to explain. "There are probably too many of them for us to take all at once."

"Hmm..."

"But if we can get past them without being seen... we'll be more likely to get to where your friends are being kept."

"And if they see us?"

"Then... I'll hold them off while you get your friends," the Gray Ninja tells Roger.

Roger Kowalski smiles, as the thought of seeing Johnny and Richie again appears in his mind.

"Thank you," he says to the ninja.

"You're welcome."

"And hey, is there something I can call you?"

"Just 'Gray Ninja' is fine, Officer."

"Okay, and if this works out, you can call me Roger," the police officer jokes.

Roger Kowalski follows the Gray Ninja into the warehouse through the broken window. The armored ninja runs over to a pile of boxes, and ducks behind them. Roger carefully does the same.

The ninja moves stealthily behind rows of crates and boxes as Roger follows closely behind him. Scorpions patrol the rows, but the duo advances before the gangsters have a chance to see them.

Roger Kowalski and the Gray Ninja continue this process until they are almost to the back of the warehouse. The Gray Ninja stops behind some crates, and Roger realizes that there is no more cover in front of them. He peers over the ninja's shoulder and observes that they are yards away from a big metal door. Two Scorpions with machine guns are standing in front of it, guarding the metal door.

The Gray Ninja takes out two non-lethal shurikens and aims one at the guard on the left. Roger's ally swiftly throws the shuriken, and it hits the guard on the head. The guard falls to the ground, unconscious. The second guard looks at his accomplice, while the Gray Ninja throws the second shuriken at him.

He misses.

The second guard raises his machine gun and starts to fire the thunderous weapon at the crates Roger and the ninja are behind. The two allies instantly move further behind them, as bullets fly next to them. Roger's heart rate accelerates as his adrenaline increases. He watches the ninja breathe in and out slowly while telling himself to focus.

The Gray Ninja starts to throw more shurikens at the firing guard but misses every time. He even throws both of his sais at him, but the Scorpion dodges them.

"We're pinned down!" Roger exclaims.

Zach Rylar recognizes the sound of multiple footsteps heading their way.

"I think we got everyone's attention!" the ninja adds.

"Any ideas?" Roger asks him.

"Just one."

The Gray Ninja stands up. He unsheathes one of his ninja swords, raises it high, and waves it in the air.

"WAIT!" the ninja shouts. "I'M WITH SCORPIO!"

The guard stops firing.

"SCORPIO OFFERED FOR ME TO JOIN YOU, AND THAT'S WHY I'M HERE!"

"What are you doing?" Roger whispers, but the Gray Ninja ignores him and carefully peers out from behind the crates.

****

Zach's heart races as he watches as the huge, muscular Scorpion has his massive firearm aimed at him.

"Scorpio offered that I can join your cause!" Zach calls out from behind the crates.

"I know! He told me about you!" the guard replies and then points down at his fallen associate. "But you threw weapons at us!"

"That's my bad!" Zach replies. "It's a force of habit, I guess!"

"Come out of there!" the intimidating gangster orders.

Fear overwhelms Zach as he realizes that he is out of shurikens. He knows what to do, but isn't sure if he has the courage to do it.

Okay, Zach tells himself. *If I get shot, I need to get to cover and pour on some Water of Purification as fast as I can.*

With his heart pounding practically out of his chest, Zach Rylar steps out from behind the crates.

"I'm with Scorpio!" Zach repeats and then sheathes his ninjatō. "You can lower your weapon."

To Zach's relief, the Scorpion lowers his firearm.

"Why did you throw weapons at us?" the guard questions again.

"I was… testing you," the Gray Ninja answers deceptively. "We're going to be fighting alongside each other now, don't you realize? So I wanted to see how strong you are! And you, my man, are like the strongest Scorpion I've met!"

Zach offers him a handshake.

The big guard snickers pridefully, and goes in for the handshake.

With lightning speed, Zach moves over the guard's right hand as it reaches down and grabs the machine gun. The Gray Ninja knees the guard in between his legs and quickly rips the machine gun out of his grip.

"Oof!" the guard exclaims, and the Gray Ninja proceeds to hit down back with the giant gun.

The muscular guard falls to the ground.

All of a sudden, Zach notices multiple Scorpions headed their way. Zach throws the massive gun aside and hastily picks up his weapons.

Roger Kowalski moves out from behind the crates and over to the Gray Ninja.

All of a sudden, the metal door bursts open, and an armed gangster aims his gun at Roger.

ZAP!

The police officer's reflexes are quicker. Roger tases him instantly, and the Scorpion falls to the ground.

As the Scorpions get closer, Zach pulls out the shurikens he had thrown and picked up before. He starts to toss them at the approaching hostiles, and two of them are knocked back from the impact. Zach knocks each of the Scorpions down with his nunchucks as bullets fly past him.

Suddenly, a sharp pain stings Zach's side. Zach shoves the remaining Scorpion against some crates, but the impact of the gunshot causes Zach to stumble.

"Gray Ninja!" Roger Kowalski exclaims. "You've been shot!"

"Get your friends out of here," Zach weakly tells his ally. "I'll hold off the others."

"But you'll die!" Roger sharply replies. "We're not leaving you!"

Zach considers the bottle of Water of Purification attached to his Suit. He is confident in its ability to heal his wounds, yet a chilling thought creeps over him. *What if I really will die?* he thinks. *What am I doing?*

Zach pushes the thought away and quickly grabs the bottle of Water of Purification. He unscrews the bottle and pours some of it on his wound. Roger watches in amazement as the bullet falls on the ground and the wound closes.

The Gray Ninja reattaches the bottle to his Suit and looks up at Roger.

"More Scorpions are coming! I have to lure them away!"

Roger gives him a look of confidence.

"I know. Be careful, Gray Ninja, and... thank you."

****

Roger Kowalski crouches behind the door, watching as The Gray Ninja charges towards two approaching Scorpions, and beats them both down with his nunchucks. Several more Scorpions advance towards the ninja, but the ninja retreats in the opposite direction of the door with the gangsters pursuing him.

When Roger notices that the area around him is clear, he quickly advances through the open doorway.

Roger instantly detects a foul stench. The room he enters is cold and seemingly empty, with a stone floor and dirty walls.

Six figures are sitting in the corner of the room, all tied up and gagged. Roger rushes over to them, identifying them as to be the officers who were taken. He immediately recognizes his friends, Johnny and Richie, among them.

"Guys!" he exclaims and proceeds to ungag them.

"Rodge!" Johnny replies happily.

After Roger unties his friends, he, Johnny, and Richie untie the others.

"Now, quick! We have to get out of here before the other Scorpions come!" Roger exclaims.

****

Zach Rylar dashes through the aisles of the warehouse, taking out Scorpions with his nunchucks and dodging their gunfire.

He realizes that three of them are currently pursuing him from behind, so he tosses multiple shurikens in their direction. One of them falls down while the other two push through the projectiles. Zach notices an opening to his left, so he jumps into it and waits for them to catch up to him.

As soon as the Scorpions are close enough to him, Zach lunges out from his cover, swinging his nunchucks. After a few good hits, both of the Scorpions fall to the ground.

Zach hears a gunshot to the right of him and realizes that the Scorpion he knocked down with his shurikens has gotten up.

The Gray Ninja retreats through the opening, only to find more Scorpions coming at him with guns raised.

Zach swings his nunchucks around at each of the Scorpions, knocking them down one by one. However, some Scorpions fire their guns at the ninja, and bullets repel off of his armor.

BANG!

Another bullet enters Zach's side. Zach loses his balance again, and this time, the teenager falls to the ground.

Zach counts five Scorpions towering above him, with their guns pointed at him. Red bleeds through Zach's

Ninja Suit as he hastily reaches for his bottle of Water of Purification.

The bottle slips out of his fingers and rolls across the floor.

Chapter 16: "Trust"

"This way!" Roger Kowalski exclaims as he leads the captives to the broken window. "Through here!"

One by one, the captured policemen crawl through the window to exit the warehouse. John Lawson is last in line. Roger watches as his best friend looks up at him.

"I have to go back for him," Roger tells Johnny.

"I'll go with-"

"No, Johnny. You guys need time to recover. Besides, I don't want to lose you again."

"I don't want to lose you, either, Rodge!"

Roger Kowalski spots some flashing red and blue lights through the window.

"Backup has arrived. Don't worry about me, just get to them as fast as you can!" Roger commands.

Johnny gives in with a nod and crawls through the window.

Roger Kowalski raises his gun and advances through the warehouse. Many Scorpions are already on the ground, beaten. He carefully moves past them, following the sound of gunfire on the other end of the warehouse.

****

Zach fights through the pain to get back to his feet. He rolls behind some boxes as bullets fly around him. Another stinging pain shoots into Zach's other side, as the Gray Ninja realizes that he has been shot again. He reaches for his Water of Purification on the floor, but the five Scorpions advance towards him. Zach battles fear in his mind, and the excruciating pain doesn't help at all.

As the Scorpions get closer, Zach rapidly takes out and tosses multiple shurikens at the approaching hostiles. Two of them are knocked back from the projectiles, and Zach lunges at the remaining three. The Gray Ninja hits the first one in the head with his nunchucks, disarms the second, but the third is quicker than Zach.

BANG!

The third Scorpion fires his gun at the Gray Ninja, but the bullet repels off of the ninja's invinsium helmet. However, the impact still makes Zach feel like he had been slapped in the head. He stumbles, struggling to maintain his balance, but endures through the blow enough to push the Scorpion on the floor. The disarmed Scorpion tries to pick up his gun, but the Gray Ninja karate kicks him back into the third.

As intense pain overloads Zach's body, the Gray Ninja collapses on the floor. A thought reenters his mind.

What if I'm going to die?

Zach battles the pain and reaches for the Water of Purification on the floor. He stretches out his arm as far as he can and grabs onto the Water of Purification. He moves it over to his other hand, unscrews the cap, and pours it over his wounds.

A soothing sensation flows through his body as the bullets fall onto the concrete floor.

The Gray Ninja rises to his feet, as his strength is rejuvenated. The two Scorpions he karate kicked lunge at him, but Zach quickly and easily takes them both down.

"What's that supposed to be, some sort of healing water?!" a voice questions behind him in a southern accent.

Zach Rylar spins around and quickly hurls a shuriken at Bartholomew Mustachio's pistol. The gun flies out of his hands, and Mustachio watches in disbelief as his weapon slides across the hard floor.

Zach unsheathes one of his ninjatō and aims it at the mustached number three.

"I have a message for Scorpio," the Gray Ninja declares. "Tell him... I'm declining his offer. The Gray Ninja doesn't work with kidnappers."

****

Roger Kowalski moves through the building, searching for the Gray Ninja. Occasionally, he detects Scorpions nearby but can tell that they are in retreat.

"Are they safe?"

Roger rotates around to figure out where the voice is coming from. He activates his police flashlight and squints around the dimly lit area around him. Unfortunately, he only makes out stacks of boxes and crates.

"The policemen who were captured... are they safe?" the familiar voice repeats.

"Because of your bravery, yes. Don't worry, Gray Ninja, I'm not going to arrest you," Roger assures him.

There is silence for a moment. Roger continues to search the area around him until he picks up a gray blur.

"I know you won't," the young vigilante replies from the shadows. "See you around... Roger."

All of a sudden, Roger hears faint footsteps from behind him. He raises his gun, only to recognize the familiar gray hair and glasses of his superior officer.

"Where's the ninja?!" Chief Mulberry demands, with three other armed officers behind him.

"Sir... he's a hero," Roger firmly counters.

"Hero or not, he's still breaking the law," Chief Mulberry responds. "I appreciate his efforts, but we still need to question him."

"I'm... sorry, sir. He left right before you got here."

"How convenient. Well, Officer Kowalski, we'll discuss this further back at headquarters. Right now, my teams moving in to capture this base."

"Allow me to assist, sir," Roger offers.

"You've done enough, Roger. You saved some good people today, and for that, I am grateful," Mulberry thanks him. "Now go... spend time with your friends."

****

The Gray Ninja observes from the shadows as Roger exits the warehouse and embraces a couple of the police officers outside. The three friends instantly reconnect and start to laugh. Zach grabs his scooter, gets on it, and rides away from the scene even more stealthily than before.

Once Zach reaches his house, he changes out of the Gray Ninja suit and sneaks back through his unlocked window into his bedroom. Yet as Zach prepares to go to sleep that night, he can't seem to stop thinking of Roger Kowalski's actions. How the police officer was willing to sacrifice his job— and his life— for his friends. Guilt overtakes Zach, as he considers how he has been ignoring

Ryan and recounts the argument he had with his grandfather.

Then, Zach's thoughts seem to bring him back to when he got shot. He remembers falling on the ground, wondering if he was going to die. Zach now realizes, in that moment, he was also thinking about his grandfather and neighbor.

"I should try to fix this," Zach says aloud to himself. "Ryan and I have been friends for so long... and Grandpa and I have spent so much time together recently."

Zach tries to go sleep, but all of this is too heavy on his mind. He rises out of bed and puts the Gray Ninja suit back on.

****

"Master Scorpio!"

Bill Williams turns around, recognizing the southern accent of his third-in-command. The gang leader is in his planning room at his home base, and he looks up from a map of Old York. Bartholomew Mustachio rushes into the room, sweating and out of breath.

"What is it, Bartholomew?" Bill asks him.

"It's our warehouse, sir!" his mustached third-in-command says quickly. "It's been taken!"

"Slow down," the gang leader commands. "How did this happen?"

"Well you see, sir... there was uh, an attack," he stammers. "By this one policeman..."

"Wait a minute," Scorpio interrupts him. "You're saying the base got taken by ONE POLICEMAN?!"

"No, sir... he had help."

"From who?"

"The Gray Ninja," Bartholomew Mustachio replies. "The younger one, though. He and that one cop freed all of the other cops! And then more cops came, and then they copped the entire warehouse! Only I and a few others escaped."

The leader of the Scorpions puts a hand on his chin, pausing to think.

"Are you saying… he didn't have his sensei with him?"

"Yeah," the mustached gangster nods.

"The student's getting stronger," Scorpio evaluates before giving a sigh. "I tried to reason with him... I tried to make him realize the truth... but just like the old man... he didn't listen."

Scorpio looks back up at Bartholomew Mustachio.

"Bring Stinger in," he commands.

Mustachio leaves the room, closing the door. Minutes later, the door reopens, and Scorpio watches as a muscular figure enters. This man is wearing a military-style black suit, with dark-gray sleeves, and a black ninja hood. He has a longsword strapped to his back, as well as a gun and knife attached to his belt.

"Stinger," Scorpio greets him, and the mysterious figure bows. "Do you know why I've called you here?"

"It's my old mentor, isn't it?" the ninja-like figure replies.

"Not just him," Scorpio states. "Kenshin Haruta has trained another student, and he's growing in strength."

"I've heard," Stinger responds. "And you know they're becoming too much of a threat... yet you still just stand by as they interfere with our plans!"

"Kenshin Haruta was my friend," Scorpio sternly tells his second-in-command. "What you've been suggesting is out of the question!"

"No. It's what we have to do. You push the thought away... because you trusted him."

Scorpio lowers his head.

230

"You cared about him, just as I did!" Stinger continues. "But whatever friendship you had with him needs to be sacrificed for the greater good!"

Bill Williams battles his thoughts in his mind. He and Kenshin had been the best of friends, stopping crime side by side. Bill remembers how they began to argue and fight each other. He remembers the day they went their separate ways, and how the ninja master slashed his eye out. Kenshin said it was an accident, but Bill didn't believe him. Then Scorpio remembers how he came across Stinger.

"When we met," Scorpio starts to say to Stinger. "You were recovering from Haruta's brainwashing. You simply sought to learn ninjutsu, but instead, the old man pinned you against me. Then, when we met, I helped you to realize the truth about my family, the truth about the Scorpions. I tried the same approach with his new student, but-"

"But he didn't listen," Stinger finishes for him.

"Yes. However... he may if I continue to persuade him-"

"He won't if we do what we're going to do," the second-in-command sharply replies. "But you know that we have to do it. You wouldn't be able to execute your plan if we don't."

Sadness fills Bill's heart, but he goes over his plan again in his mind. As he weighs his options, he realizes that no matter what move the Scorpions make, the old ninja always seems to get in their way.

"You're right," Scorpio tells Stinger. "Gather as many of us as you believe we need, and tell them... that it's time."

****

Zach Rylar rides to his sensei's dojo past midnight on his scooter. The Gray Ninja doesn't care how dark it is; he just keeps scooting on the sidewalks and streets until he makes it to Kenshin Haruta's property on the edge of town. Zach notices the silver car parked outside of the large wooden fence and tosses the scooter next to it. Then, he rushes up the hill to the large wooden gate, opens it, and runs through the compound.

As Zach approaches the front door of his grandfather's house, a dark figure steps out of the shadows.

Zach hastily takes out his nunchucks and swings them at the figure dressed in black. The man grabs Zach's nunchucks and disarms him. Zach first thinks he is a Scorpion, but when the man steps forward, Zach realizes that it is Sensei Haruta in his black kimono.

The younger Gray Ninja takes off his helmet.

"Sensei!" he exclaims.

"Why are you here so late, Zach?" Sensei Haruta asks him.

"I couldn't sleep," Zach admits. "I have to talk to you."

All of a sudden, Zach's grandfather's head jolts the other way. The ninja master's attention diverts from Zach, and he seems to stare off into space.

"Were you followed?" he questions.

"I... I couldn't have been..." Zach says in disbelief.

Sensei Haruta promptly looks down at his grandson again.

"Put your helmet back on," he commands. "NOW!"

Zach quickly puts the silver ninja-like helmet back on his head while trying to guess the cause of his sensei's odd behavior. Sensei Haruta turns in multiple directions, seeming to search the area for something. The ninja master proceeds to rush over to his front door and yank it open. Zach hastily follows his grandfather into the dark house, and they both stop in the kitchen.

Sensei Haruta's kitchen has a big, sliding glass window, which the two ninja look out of. Zach's eyes pick up multiple figures moving through the woods behind the backyard, carrying guns and knives. Kenshin Haruta whispers something that sends a chill up Zach's spine.

"The Scorpions...are here."

Suddenly, the thundering sound of gunshots fills Zach's ears.

"FIND COVER!" his sensei yells, and Zach jumps behind the kitchen counter.

Zach's eyes search frantically for his grandfather as the teenager's heart pounds. He breathes a sigh of relief once he realizes that Sensei Haruta found cover behind the hallway wall.

CRASH!

The glass sliding window shatters into a million pieces, and a moment later, Scorpions start to step through its remains. Shurikens fly past Zach and disarm the invaders. Zach watches as Sensei Haruta lunges out from his hiding place, and rushes towards the invading Scorpions. The ninja master takes out each of them with only his hands and feet.

Zach faintly hears another crashing sound, and Sensei Haruta exclaims that it is from the bedroom window. The younger Gray Ninja moves away from underneath the kitchen counter and runs through his grandfather's hallway. Two Scorpions move through the bedroom window, and Zach hits them both in the head with his nunchucks.

This time, Zach's opponents don't fall over, so he proceeds to karate-kick both of them to the ground.

Zach's eyes then pick up another figure inching through the broken bedroom window. This Scorpion has dark-gray sleeves, a black ninja hood, and a longsword strapped to his back. He jumps to the carpet floor and stands to his feet. Zach raises his nunchucks as the figure moves towards him, but doesn't draw his weapon.

"Uhh... Sensei?" Zach calls. "This one's a ninja!"

With his nunchucks in his right arm, Zach charges at the ninja-like Scorpion. The man instantly grabs the arm and pushes Zach against the bedroom wall. Weakly, Zach watches as the Scorpion advances past him and faces his sensei in the hallway, who is wielding his staff in a defensive position.

"My old student," Sensei Haruta greets him, and Zach's heart skips a beat. "Why have you returned?"

"I go by 'Stinger' now," the ninja-like Scorpion responds and raises his fists. "And you know why I'm here!"

He lunges at Sensei Haruta and grabs the staff. They both struggle to possess the weapon, but Stinger is stronger. He rips it out of Sensei Haruta's grip and tosses the staff behind his old teacher. Stinger then hurls a fist at the older man's direction, but Kenshin dodges it.

Zach Rylar gets back on his feet and rushes towards the attacker. He shoves him at the wall, and Kenshin Haruta kicks his old student back. Stinger raises his head as if the blows had no effect on him.

"You didn't tell me you had another student!" Zach exclaims to his sensei.

"We'll talk about it later!" Sensei Haruta responds. "For now, we have to get you out of here!"

"But, Sensei, you're not in your Ninja Suit!"

"There's no time!"

The ninja master moves back to his kitchen, grabs a chair, and throws it at Stinger. As Stinger loses his balance, Kenshin Haruta grabs Zach's arm and pulls his grandson forward.

234

"Let's go!" he orders, and Zach obeys him.

Both ninja run through the house until Zach's grandfather pauses. He pulls something out of a pouch in his black kimono and raises it to Zach.

"Lock the basement," the ninja master instructs, handing Zach a set of keys, with one separated from the rest.

Both ninja look back to see Stinger getting up, and advancing towards them.

"I'll hold him off!" Sensei Haruta adds.

Zach moves over to the hatch on the floor, keeping the basement key separate from the others. He inserts it into the keyhole on and locks it. Zach looks back at Sensei Haruta, who has pushed Stinger back again. Sensei Haruta looks back at his grandson and runs over to him.

"To the car!" Zach's grandfather commands. "The dojo... is lost."

Zach Rylar and Kenshin Haruta rush out of the front door of the house and start to run through the compound.

Around them, Scorpions jump onto the ground from the top of the walls, wielding knives and daggers. Kenshin Haruta takes one of Zach's ninja swords out of the sword-holder on his back and starts to fight the Scorpions. Their blades clash with his, and Zach joins in on the fight, unsheathing the other ninja sword from his sword holder. Kenshin Haruta easily bests each of his opponents, as Zach struggles to take down his. One of the Scorpions knocks Zach's ninjatō out of his hand, but Kenshin Haruta knocks that Scorpion out with the hilt of his sword. Eventually, all of the Scorpions on the compound are on the ground, except for Scorpio.

"I see you brought your best men!" Zach's sensei taunts the gang leader.

Scorpio growls and reaches for a weapon on his back. He whips out a bladed chain weapon and swings it at the ninja master, who dodges the attack. Sensei Haruta parries another before slashing at Scorpio's weapon with the ninjatō. With great force, Sensei Haruta knocks the bladed chain weapon out of Scorpio's grip.

As this is happening, two of the fallen Scorpions get up and lunge at Zach with their knives. The first of the duo slices through Zach's arm with his blade, which causes Zach to cry out in pain. Zach tries to retreat, but the second one jumps in front of him. Kenshin Haruta's attention diverts to his grandson, and he karate-kicks the second of Zach's attackers to the ground. Zach elbows the first in the face and punches him down.

But the younger Gray Ninja's arm has started to bleed, as a stinging sensation consumes it. The teenager, already weakened from previous fights, falls on his knees while clutching the arm with his opposite hand.

While Sensei Haruta is focused on Zach, Scorpio kicks the elderly man down, and the sword slides out of the ninja master's hand. The leader of the Scorpions goes for it, and the two adversaries fight over the weapon.

Zach's vision blurs as his body gets weaker. He reaches for the bottle of Water of Purification on his Suit before realizing in horror that the bottle is empty.

Sensei Haruta grabs the hilt of his sword and smacks it across Scorpio's face. The bald, eyepatched man falls to the ground, and the ninja master aims the sword at Scorpio's throat.

"You went too far this time, Scorpio!" Kenshin Haruta exclaims angrily.

"So what will you do?!" Scorpio challenges. "Kill me?!"

Zach watches as his grandfather's expression starts to change. Sensei Haruta's eyes widen as if he fully realizes the position he is in.

236

"This fight… this fight has been going on for too long," Kenshin Haruta responds.

The ninja master looks at his sword before whispering something to himself that Zach can barely hear.

"Strive for peace with everyone."

Sensei Haruta tosses the sword aside and extends a hand to his enemy.

"Pain… is not an illusion," Kenshin accepts. "But we can still look past it… and the differences between us that have gotten in our way. Bill… I know I've hurt you, and you don't have to give me your forgiveness… but I just want to say… that I'm sorry… for everything.

Scorpio stares at his adversary's open hand but finally takes it.

Sensei Haruta lifts him up.

The eyepatched gang leader's expression turns to sadness, and a tear starts to form in his single eye. He looks up, and his gaze turns to something behind Zach.

"So am I," he replies.

All of a sudden, Scorpio moves quickly out of the way.

BANG!

Sensei Haruta flinches as a bullet rips through his chest. Zach's senses heighten as he turns around to see Stinger with a gun pointed at his grandfather.

"NO!" Zach yells weakly and moves over to his sensei.

Zach grabs his grandfather and stares down to see blood staining the older man's kimono. Tears fall out of Zach's eyes as he realizes that the bullet pierced his grandfather's heart.

And then Kenshin Haruta gives Zach a look he will never forget. As the elderly man stares into Zach's eyes, it is like he is staring into Zach's soul. In Kenshin's eyes, he says sorry. In Kenshin's eyes, Zach can tell that his grandfather has really cared about him. Sensei Haruta doesn't have to use words for Zach to know how the grandfather feels. Throughout his life, Kenshin Haruta stopped trusting people and didn't have a person that he could call his best friend. But now, as Kenshin Haruta stares into his grandson's eyes, Zach realizes that his grandfather had found one.

"Sensei... no, no, no... SENSEI!" Zach cries out, as tears slide through his ninja helmet.

Sensei Haruta's eyes slowly close, and he dies as his body rests against the ground. Tears flood through Zach's helmet, but he endures to get ahold of himself. The Gray Ninja notices that the Scorpions around him are getting up, but also realizes that he has something in one of his Suit pockets. Zach takes out the keyring that his grandfather had given him.

The Gray Ninja lifts his head to see Stinger approaching him, with his gun raised. Scorpio stands behind Zach and picks up his bladed chain weapon.

"What should we do about this place?" Stinger asks the gang leader.

"Burn it to the ground," Scorpio replies, turning his face away from Kenshin Haruta's body.

"And what about the student?"

Before Scorpio has a chance to respond, Zach leaps to his feet and kicks Scorpio's legs out from under him. Then, he tosses a shuriken at Stinger, and the gun flies out of his hands.

Zach Rylar takes off running through the compound, avoiding the Scorpions that are starting to get back on their feet. Bullets fly towards Zach as he pushes his way through the large, wooden doors of the dojo.

Zach looks back to see flames coming from Kenshin Haruta's house and then turns his gaze to his grandfather's fallen body.

238

Still in tears, Zach races over to the silver car on the street below. He advances down the hill while flipping through the keyring, and then rushes to the driver's side of the vehicle.

Scorpions move through the dojo doors as Zach unlocks the car. He notices his scooter lying beside it, which he quickly tosses into the back of the vehicle. The Gray Ninja jumps inside, slams the driver's door shut, and puts the key in the ignition. He then turns the key and puts the car in reverse. Scorpions rush up to him with guns, but Zach quickly switches to drive and slams on the gas. Zach looks behind him to see the Scorpions fade off into the distance, but also watches in horror as his grandfather's home is consumed by fire.

Zach Rylar rips off his helmet and throws it aside, sobbing, as he drives the car away towards his house.

CHAPTER 17: "PAIN"

The events that unfolded that Friday night and Saturday morning seem to play over and over again in Zach's mind. He can't stop thinking about his grandfather, and Zach's last moments with him before his death. Zach Rylar spends that weekend in solitude, not letting his mother or even his friends talk to him about it. He just wants to forget about the whole thing, but the pain doesn't seem to go away.

Later that morning, the police showed up at Zach's house and delivered the bad news to his mother. Zach listened from the hallway as a policeman described to his mother how Kenshin Haruta was killed by arsonists. Zach told his mother in passing that his grandfather had loaned him his car before the incident, so she wouldn't suspect that he was there too.

Zach stayed home from school the first couple of days, continuing to do nothing productive in his room and only coming out to grab food or use the bathroom. On Tuesday night, Zach's mother knocks on the door of his room and asks if she can come in. This isn't the first time she has asked this over the past few days. However, each time, Zach told her no. He repeats his answer, but his mother opens the door and walks in anyway.

"Hey, Zach," she greets, and her son responds with a sigh.

"What do you want?"

"Look... I know I haven't always been there for you, and I'm really sorry about that. But I just want you to know..."

"That what?!" Zach interrupts her. "That you'll actually try to be now?!"

"I hope to," she replies, staying calm. "But also that... I really do love you, Zach. Your grandfather also cared about you so, so much... and we both know that he wouldn't want you to live like this. He would want you to go on without him."

"Yeah, I know," Zach mutters in agreement, yet still annoyed.

His mother walks closer to him and stares into his eyes.

"While I don't know all of the details, I do know that your grandfather got involved with the wrong crowd. *sighs* I wish I wasn't so blasé about it before... but we can't change the past... your grandfather told me that."

Zach remembers other things that his sensei told him. About how he should press on when life gets hard, and strive to master endurance even in the toughest of times.

"Your grandpa was a firm believer in God, and I doubt he was right about everything he said... but he was right about this, Zach..."

Zach looks up at his mother.

"There is still hope, Zach," she tells her son. "I just... wanted you to know that."

She hugs her son awkwardly and then walks out of his room. Zach lies back on his bed, staring at the ceiling.

A lump forms in his throat while he thinks back to all of the good times he had with his grandfather.

Zach smiles as he fondly recalls the time when the eighty-year-old man did more pull-ups than he could. The time when Sensei Haruta decided to run alongside him around the dojo during his Endurance Training. The time when the ninja master taught him how to fight and how Kenshin Haruta was so patient with him.

Then, Zach recounts their adventures on the bike trail with Ryan, Mike, and Seth. Sensei Haruta said something to Zach that day. In this moment, his words suddenly come back to Zach.

"Enjoy these moments, Zach," Kenshin Haruta had told him. "They won't last forever."

Zach Rylar immediately bursts into tears. His heart beats faster as his emotions overwhelm him. He misses his sensei, but more importantly, his best friend. Zach regrets all of the times he argued with his grandfather. He regrets all of the times he disobeyed him, especially when he walked out of his grandfather's car.

Why did I walk away?! Zach thinks to himself, as anger builds up inside of him. *WHY DID I WALK AWAY?!*

Zach's anger shifts from himself to the Scorpions. Hate consumes Zach as he blames them for everything. *They will pay for what they've done,* he tells himself.

Zach Rylar locks his door and transforms into the Gray Ninja, putting on all of the separate armor pieces and weapons. Then, he plots in his mind what he is going to do.

While he waits for his mother to go to bed, Zach quietly does some training exercises in his room to prepare himself for the night. All of a sudden, the young ninja hears the sound of running shower water. Zach realizes that now is the time to make his move.

With his mother busy, the Gray Ninja crawls through his bedroom window and stealthily maneuvers over to the silver car in the driveway. Zach takes out his grandfather's car keys, unlocks the car, and gets in. He then removes the upper layer of his suit, setting the helmet in his passenger seat. He wants to make it appear as though a normal teenager is driving.

Zach drives his grandfather's car away from his house, and heads in the direction of downtown Old York, with vengeance on his mind.

Once he reaches his destination, he drives around to scan the area for the Scorpions. Half an hour into his search, he notices some dark figures hanging out in an alley.

Zach Rylar parks the car in a nearby parking lot. He puts the rest of the Gray Ninja Suit on, including the helmet. Before he exits the car, he opens up a secret storage compartment in the car that his grandfather had shown him one day, and pulls out a bottle of Water of Purification. Zach attaches it to his Ninja Suit and gets out of the car.

The Gray Ninja moves behind parked vehicles and stealthily advances over to the alley. He then carefully maneuvers over to it and hides against a wall.

"You fought well," he hears one of the Scorpions tell the other.

"Why, thank you," the other says, and laughs. "You didn't."

Other Scorpions join in laughing as rage overtakes Zach.

They're bragging about how they killed my grandfather! Zach assumes with anger. The Gray Ninja takes out a few shurikens and immediately lunges out from behind the corner. He launches the shurikens at the Scorpions, who flinch as the shurikens rush towards them.

One of the shurikens hits a Scorpion in the face, another hits the second one in the stomach, while the remaining two projectiles miss. Zach counts four Scorpions and watches them raise their fists. The Gray Ninja whips out his nunchucks, and swinging them, charges at the first Scorpion. He slams the nunchaku into the first Scorpion's face, and the ninja's opponent yelps out in pain. Then, the Gray Ninja forces the second Scorpion back with the weapon, but the third stops his arm. The third, a female Scorpion, tries to kick Zach with her knee, but the Gray Ninja's armor stops the attack. The female Scorpion cries out in pain as she hits the invinsium, and the Gray Ninja shoves her back into a dumpster. The second Scorpion's fist flies up to the ninja, but the Gray Ninja headbutts it away with his helmet. The Scorpion shakes his hurt hand, but Zach forces him backward with a powerful karate-kick. The fourth Scorpion rushes over to Zach and snatches one of the ninja's short-swords from the weapon-holder on his back.

"Why are you attacking us?!" the Scorpion yells at Zach. "Couldn't you see we were unarmed?!"

The Gray Ninja spins around and realizes that the gang member stole his sword. He also finds the Scorpion's voice familiar, but can't seem to identify it. Zach pushes the thought away to unsheathe his other ninjatō and lunges at the Scorpion. Zach's opponent blocks the sword with its counterpart, and their blades clash.

However, the battle does not last long. The Scorpion raises his sword for an attack, but Zach acts quicker. The Gray Ninja swings his sword at the Scorpion, and it slices through his opponent's chest.

The Scorpion grunts in pain and starts to lose his balance. He drops the sword and falls onto the cold pavement.

The other three gang members take off running. The fourth Scorpion tries to get up, but clutches his chest and immediately falls back down. Zach is about to chase the retreating Scorpions, but he notices something out of the corner of his eye. A streak of red flows out of the Scorpion's chest.

Zach freezes. His heart beats faster, his sweat moves quicker, and his eyes focus in on the wounded gangster. The Gray Ninja's sword starts to slip from his grasp, and it plummets to the ground.

The Scorpion cries out in pain, still clutching his bleeding chest. Zach remembers what his sensei had taught him about anger being deceptive, now realizing the wisdom of his grandfather's words.

The world seems to spin around Zach as all he can see is the man dying in front of him. *I never wanted to kill anyone!* Zach thinks. Suddenly, Zach turns to the Water of Purification attached to his suit and realizes what he can do. He seizes the bottle and makes his way over to the Scorpion. The Scorpion reacts quickly, picking up the ninja's sword and aiming it at him.

Zach raises his hands.

"I'm not going to hurt you!" Zach assures him.

"Oh, really?! I think you've already done that!" the Scorpion responds with a shaky, yet distinct voice.

The Gray Ninja opens the bottle of Water of Purification.

"What's that?!" the Scorpions hastily questions him.

"This will help you," Zach answers.

"And why should I trust you?!"

An idea appears in Zach's mind. *No... I can't do that!* Zach tells himself. Yet Zach knows that if he wants to save this guy, he may have no other choice.

So he does it. The Gray Ninja takes off his helmet, revealing his face.

The Scorpion's eyes instantly widen in shock. He also removes his hood, unveiling his own face. Zach's blood runs cold as he immediately recognizes the face of a long-time friend. The face of Mike Alford.

"Zach?!" Mike responds.

"Mike?!"

Tears form in both of the friends' eyes. Mike lowers the sword while Zach moves closer to him.

"I'm so sorry, Mike," Zach says, as tears roll down his face. "I'm so sorry."

"Me too, man," Mike replies emotionally before bursting out coughing.

Blood flies out of his mouth, and Zach understands that his time to act is now. He moves the Water of Purification over to his friend's wound and lets the healing water flow down onto Mike's chest.

Mike coughs up even more blood, making Zach realize that he is close to losing his friend. Sensei Haruta's words seem to slap him in the face as he watches as another one of his best friends appears to be dying.

"The water does not work if the person is past the point of recovery."

Please, God! Zach cries out in his mind. *Don't let him die! It was so stupid of me to do this! I'm so sorry!*

Suddenly, the Water of Purification kicks in. Mike's wound closes, as the coughing and bleeding stop. Mike's expression transforms from one of fear and anxiety to one of surprise.

"I feel... I feel great!" Mike proclaims in disbelief.

He looks up at Zach, who has dried up tears still on his face.

"What... what is this stuff?"

"Water of Purification," Zach words, and his expression turns into a smile.

246

"Is it some sort of healing water?!" Mike questions, with his usual enthusiasm and fascination starting to glow from him.

"Yeah," Zach replies as his smile expands.

"I can't believe it!" Mike exclaims. "You're the Gray Ninja, and you saved my life!"

Zach wants to feel good about what his friend is saying, but guilt overtakes him.

"No… no," Zach tells him. "I almost killed you."

"I shouldn't have been here," Mike states, also shifting to a serious tone. "It was my brother… I just didn't want him to get hurt, you know?"

"What happened?"

"Did I tell you why my family moved back here?"

Zach thinks for a moment, remembering that his friend mentioned it on the first day of school, and how the touchy subject made Zach feel uncomfortable.

"You lost your brother, didn't you?"

Mike nods, with sadness written all over his face.

"Yeah… my older one," Mike explains sadly. "And when my family moved here, we expected to get away from it all."

He sniffs.

"But then my younger brother started hanging with some bad friends, and I noticed that he had been sneaking out to go with them late at night. This one night... about a month ago... I followed him into an alley…"

****

Mike walks into the alley. A figure dressed in black frantically turns around and lunges at Mike.

"Marcus!" Mike exclaims, dodging the blow. "What are you doing?"

"Mike?" the figure questions, lowering his fists.

"Why are you here?" Mike asks him.

"Bro, you should not be here," Mike's younger brother tells him.

Before Mike can say anything, the side door of the building behind Marcus bursts open. Two hooded figures, wielding large guns, rush out and aim their weapons at Mike. Mike's heart skips a beat, and his hands shoot into the air.

The sound of slow footsteps fills Mike's ears as a man steps out of the doorway. His hands are folded behind his back while he casually walks by the gunmen. Mike observes that he is wearing an eyepatch over his right eye.

"You can put away your guns," he tells the gangsters. "This young man is not a threat."

They do what he says. The eyepatched man then moves past Marcus and over to Mike.

"I'm sorry, sir!" Marcus apologizes. "He must have followed me! I-"

The eyepatched man raises his hand to Marcus, and Mike's brother stops talking.

"Tell me," the man says to Mike. "What is your name?"

"He's my brother-"

"I want to hear it from him," the man interrupts Marcus again before turning back to Mike and repeating his question. "What is your name?"

"Mike," Mike answers slowly.

"Nice to meet you, Mike," the man voices with a smile and offers a handshake. "I... am Scorpio."

Mike tries to hide his fear, but when he awkwardly returns the handshake, Scorpio gives him a look of sympathy.

"No need to fear us, Mike," the gang leader tells him.

248

"No, I get it," Mike replies sarcastically. "It's not like your guys almost shot me or anything."

"Pete and Bob can get a little… tense sometimes," Scorpio responds apologetically and then turns back to the other three Scorpions. "Go back inside," he orders.

The two armed gangsters nod and start to re-enter the building. Scorpio turns to Mike's younger brother.

"Don't worry, Marcus. Your brother will be fine," Scorpio assures him, and Marcus reluctantly follows his associates inside.

"This is a gang, isn't it?" Mike asks Scorpio.

"No… we're a family. We stick up for one another, learn to grow together."

"And you're the leader?"

"In a way, yes. In a way… I am like the head of this family. We call ourselves the Scorpions, and we do this to distinguish ourselves from the others. The plural form 'Scorpions' almost shouldn't exist… since the average scorpion lives in solitude for most of its life. But we are the Scorpions. Did you know… that during the winter… some scorpions come together? Like the Arizona bark scorpions, for instance, who usually assemble in crowds of thirty."

"Fascinating," Mike responds, only pretending to be intrigued. "Why do they do this?"

"I'm glad you asked that. You see, these creatures realize that they have a common goal and resources to share. They recognize the problem of the wintertime and use what they have to work together to reach that goal."

Scorpio walks past Mike, and focuses his gaze on the street and passing cars.

"Old York is going through a winter… a winter of disorder, crime, and a corrupt government. My family does not seek to poison society, but to restore it. We may wield weapons, but they are for defense. And when they are for offense, it is for the greater good."

Scorpio turns toward Mike again.

"Mike... have you experienced injustice in your life?"

Mike remembers the death of his older brother and how his family was treated in his old neighborhood.

"I have," Mike admits.

"So have we," Scorpio responds. "Some time ago, I simply went with the flow, kept my head down, and just stood by and watched as this town fell apart. But what I've come to realize is that change starts with us! So I formed the Scorpions... a family that accepts anyone, anyone who wishes to make a difference and save this town!"

"Why are you shouting?"

Scorpio chuckles.

"Sorry about that... sometimes I get into it too much."

"I feel you."

"But do you feel what I'm feeling, Mike?" Scorpio asks him. "About how we need to rise up and be the change?"

Mike doesn't want to lose another brother. His love for his younger brother transcends anything else he is feeling. However, Mike considers what happened to his older brother when he entered a gang.

I can show Marcus how bad the Scorpions really are, Mike plans. *And then I can get him out of here.* Mike figures that if he can stay close to Marcus in the gang, he can convince his brother to leave.

****

"So I joined them," Mike tells Zach. "And I failed. I had a plan to get my brother out and take down the gang in the process. You see, I had been in contact with a police officer named Kowalski, and informed him of their location."

Zach's face turns red.

"Wait, were you the informant guy I accidentally beat up?"

"Oh... 'accidentally,' huh?"

"Okay... maybe that was on purpose," Zach admits. "But I didn't know you were one of the good guys. I'm sorry about that."

"Good guys?" Mike questions. "We're all bad, Zach. We just have the power to make good choices."

"Yeah... I guess so."

"Heh, and I almost took you down that time before!" Mike teases.

"What... no way."

"Yes, way!"

The two friends pause for a moment, staring at each other. Mike sighs, breaking the silence.

"When I came to that day, the police arrived. I bolted, but my brother Marcus wasn't so lucky," Mike tells Zach. "He's in a juvenile facility now."

"I... I don't know what to say."

"It's okay, Zach. You've said enough. It's good to know that we're fighting for the same thing."

"So... you're not with the Scorpions anymore?" Zach asks.

Mike thinks for a moment.

"I'm not, but there's something I need to figure out before I leave," he declares. "Scorpio's been planning something big... and I don't know what exactly, or even when it is... but I think it will involve Lennwood."

"What?!"

"I don't know all of the details, and I'll try to find out more... but Zach... I think there's going to be an attack."

Chapter 18: "Surrender"

"I appreciate the ride," Mike says to Zach as his house comes into view.

"No problem," Zach replies. "I'm sorry for uh-"

"Forget about it," Mike interrupts. "I'm glad it was you... it could have been worse."

Zach drives his friend to his house and parks the silver car near the Alford home. Mike Alford unbuckles his seatbelt and is about to get out of the vehicle until he stops himself.

"Oh yeah, and Zach... your sensei... was he your grandfather?" he asks.

Zach nods sadly.

"I overheard some other Scorpions talking about him," Mike continues. "They killed him, didn't they?"

Zach just nods again, forcing himself not to cry. Mike breathes a sigh.

"I wish I was there," he states. "Maybe I could've stopped it."

Once again, Zach's mind brings him back to the days he trained with his grandfather. He pushes the thoughts away, remembering how much Sensei Haruta valued endurance.

"No," Zach responds, rubbing his eyes. "We need to press on. We need to focus... on what's coming. That's what my grandfather would have wanted."

Zach turns to look at Mike.

"Find out all you can about what the Scorpions are planning to do at Lennwood," Zach tells his friend.

"I'll let you know as soon as I do."

Zach smiles.

"Thank you, Mike. I'll see you later."

Zach's friend responds with a goodbye of his own and prepares to sneak in his bedroom window. Zach watches as Mike gets in, carrying a gym bag containing his Scorpion getup.

Zach Rylar drives the silver car away from his friend's house, heading for his own. He parks the silver car in the driveway next to his mother's car, takes his ninja helmet off, and stuffs it in his backpack. Zach then stealthily exits the vehicle and maneuvers over to his window. He opens it, tosses his backpack inside, pulls himself up, and climbs through it. After closing and locking the window, the Gray Ninja collapses onto his bed.

Exhausted, both physically and emotionally, Zach just wants to go to sleep. He wants to forget about everything that has happened, but he can't stop thinking about this night's events and his grandfather's death. *I almost killed someone,* Zach thinks. His lip quivers as the incident replays in his mind. *I almost killed Mike!*

Zach Rylar tries to think about other things, or simply concentrate on sleep, but his mind just can't seem to get past it. *No! I just want to forget!* Zach fights in his mind. *I can get through this, I can beat this on my own!*

Yet as the night goes on, he realizes that he can't get beat this on his own. Zach's feelings of guilt, frustration, and restlessness all culminate as the young ninja remembers something that his grandfather had tried to talk to him about. Zach Rylar sits up in bed, and his senses heighten.

Suddenly, he freezes. His heart pounds faster as his body is seemingly entirely still. He reflects back to what his grandfather tried to tell him about, about believing. Throughout Zach's entire life, he has tried to do everything on his own, but during this moment, he realizes that he can't do this alone.

Zach Rylar moves off of the bed and lands on his knees on the carpet floor of the bedroom.

During his childhood, Zach had been taught in church about surrender. He had pushed away the concept for so long, but now it comes back to Zach, and a conviction washes over him. As Zach's eyes are opened to how he has been living, he closes them and folds up his hands.

God, he prays. *I'm not really good at this prayer thing, but if what I've heard is true… about how You love me so much… then I guess that doesn't matter. I know You're real. I've denied it over and over again because I wanted to do things my own way. I didn't want to be a nobody– no– I wanted to prove myself! But it didn't work. I thought being the Gray Ninja is what would save me from my insecurities, but that's You, isn't it? And you'll forgive me for what I've been doing… and you'll save me from all of the sins that have been holding me back?*

As Zach prays, he feels an assuring presence wash over him, and a joy starts to fill his heart as he continues his prayer.

"Then I surrender," Zach gives in. "I'm sorry for pushing you away… and I now realize that I can't do this on my own. I need you, Jesus. I believe… yes… I believe that you were a real person, and that You really did die for

254

me. I believe that God raised You back to life and that You're still real… and Lord, I… surrender…"

Zach raises his head. His shoulders feel lighter as if a burden was just lifted off of them. A spark of confidence ignites in Zach while he starts to realize what has happened.

"Whenever it seemed like no one else cared, You always did, Lord," Zach says aloud in realization. "And You still do."

Zach's hands pick up his helmet, and the Gray Ninja stares at it.

"What do you want me to do about this?" he asks God. "Should I be the Gray Ninja?"

As Zach ponders the question in his mind, he also thinks about what Mike told him. He thinks about Lennwood High, and what might happen if the Scorpion would actually invade it.

Lord… I can't just let this happen, Zach prays desperately in his mind. *Lennwood's my school… I can't stand by and watch as the people I know get hurt… please God, guide me through this…*

A minute passes, and Zach recalls the time he went with his sensei to church. He remembers the sermon and ponders over the passage.

I wonder if I could find that, Zach thinks and searches around his room. *Do I even have a Bible?*

He gets an idea and grabs his phone. Zach unlocks it and searches the internet for what was brought to his mind.

I think it was John… John something.

He finds a website with a Bible on it and clicks on the book of John. He scrolls through it for a bit, and his finger stops at certain verses.

One seems familiar to him.

"For God so loved the world..." Zach reads from John 3:16. "...that He gave his one and only Son, that whoever believes in Him shall not perish but have eternal life."

I now have this eternal life, Zach recognizes, and suddenly it hits him that Sensei Haruta had quoted this verse before.

Intrigued, Zach Rylar scrolls through the book of the Bible some more before getting to the next chapter.

A passage sticks out to him close to the end of chapter four, where Jesus's followers were urging him to eat. Jesus tells them something that impacts Zach.

"My food is to do the will of him who sent me and to accomplish his work," Jesus said to his disciples, as recorded in John 4:34.

That work was to die... Zach realizes. *God's will was Jesus's sacrifice... and for Him to come back to life and to give us new life.*

What is your will for my life, God? Zach prays. *Do you want me to be the Gray Ninja, to fight the Scorpions? Or is that just my own way?*

He thinks about how people could be in danger, about how people could get hurt if the Scorpions attacked. *I can't let that happen,* Zach repeats in his mind. *And this is the work you have for me to do, isn't it?*

A spark of energy, a desire to get through this, burns inside Zach Rylar. His eyes droop, and his body moves slower.

But Zach's determination brings him to his school backpack, from which he grabs a sheet of looseleaf paper. On the sheet, the Gray Ninja begins to draw a map of the school. Yawning, he includes the main areas of the property: the parking lot, the math building, the cafeteria, gym, library, etc. Every building at the school is connected, forming a square with an open courtyard in the middle.

256

With fatigue rolling over him, Zach forms his plan. He begins by putting arrows on all of the places he can enter and exit stealthily, and then-

Zach's head hits the paper.

****

Mike Alford sits on the bed, scrolling through his contact list on his phone. He calls a few of his friends in the gang, but they have heard nothing about an attack. He proceeds to call a fourth and gets a different answer.

"I've heard rumors that many of us are going to do something big tomorrow," the Scorpion says. "Scorpio's told us to be ready."

"What time?" Mike inquires.

"I don't know," his former associate replies. "You could ask Scorpio, you know. Remember that private number he gave all of us?"

"Yeah... yeah... I remember."

Mike thinks about when Scorpio convinced him to join, and the trust that the gang gained in Mike. As much as Mike desires to leave, he also wants this friend of his to be safe.

"Listen, man... you shouldn't go tomorrow," Mike tells him. "What Scorpio's planning isn't right, and you have to find a way out before it's too late."

"Is this a joke, Mike?! I'm at one of our bases right now! If Mr. Mustachio hears us talking about this, he'll tell you-know-who!"

"Mustachio's there?" Mike questions.

"Yes, and I'm going to pretend you didn't say what you just said," the Scorpion states firmly.

"No," Mike responds, even firmer. "Do not forget what I just told you. And do me a favor. Put Mustachio on the phone."

"What?!"

"Just do it... trust me."

A moment later, Mike hears a familiar greeting from a man with a Southern accent.

"This is, uh... Dave Smith," Mike replies with a fake voice. "I'm a part of the special team that's going to attack Lennwood tomorrow."

"Huh... I don't know if we've met before..." Bartholomew Mustachio responds with a hint of disbelief in his tone. "Dave Smith... that sounds like a fake name."

"So does 'Bartholomew Mustachio.'"

"Hey!"

"Sorry! Sorry! That was my bad, sir. I should, uh... respect your name... and mustache," Mike says while holding back a laugh.

"Exactly. Now, what do you want?"

"I forgot what time it would be. Could you remind me?"

Mike hears a loud, "UGH!" over the phone.

"12:00, you idiot! How could you forget?!"

"Do you mean noon or midnight?"

"What do you think?! The Knight's Jewel is only there in the daytime!"

The Knight's Jewel, Mike thinks. *So that's what they're after...*

Mike clears his throat away from the phone before speaking into it again.

"And why does he want that again?" he questions.

"I don't know! For power and control or something like that! If you weren't on this team, Mr. Smith... I would make sure you never get promoted. But since you're on this team, Scorpio obviously thinks very highly of you. He chose the best of us for this special mission."

"To get the jewel, right?" Mike clarifies.

258

A loud, angry growl comes from the other end of the phone.

"You may be skilled when it comes to combat, but you are the dumbest-!"

Mike Alford ends the call, busting out laughing. Yet his attitude quickly changes as he starts to comprehend what he just learned.

Oh, man, he thinks. *They really are going to attack the school... and at noon today!*

He takes a deep breath.

"I should tell Officer Kowalski about this so the police will know," he says out loud to himself. "And Zach... he needs to hear the news."

****

Zach Rylar awakes to a pounding sound on his bedroom window. He jolts himself up, realizing that he fell asleep on his floor, with his head on his 'Ninja Plan' while still wearing most of his Gray Ninja suit. Zach looks up frantically and stares at his door. He jumps to his feet to rush over to it. He runs his hands over the knob and then breathes a sigh of relief.

Good... it's locked, the Gray Ninja thinks. *I don't want my mom finding me in this.*

His eyes move up the wall until they stop and concentrate on Zach's clock.

7:47, Zach processes. *Mom's probably left for work by now.*

The person outside continues to pound on his bedroom window.

"Zach! Open the window! It's me, Mike!" Zach hears faintly and recognizes his friend's voice.

The Gray Ninja hastily moves over to the window, and pushing the curtains aside, opens it for his friend.

"I tried to call you like four times!" Mike exclaims.

"I might have uh... fallen asleep."

Mike sighs.

"That's okay... I got some rest too."

Mike Alford's expression changes as his eyes lower.

"Are you still in your suit?"

"Yeah... I was super tired," Zach tells him, feeling a little awkward. "But don't worry... my mom's not home. She leaves early in the morning."

"Gotcha," Mike responds. "Can you let me in?"

"Yeah, I'll let you in the front," Zach replies, closing the window.

He makes his way through his hallway and into his living room. Zach Rylar opens the front door to his house, but to his surprise, Mike is not the one standing there.

"Zach?!"

"Um... What are you doing here, Ryan?" Zach questions nervously.

"I just came to tell you that school was canceled," Ryan informs him, with eyes wide with shock.

He points at Zach's Ninja Suit.

"Is that... is that what I think it is?"

"Yep, it's my Halloween costume!" Zach responds and gives a nervous chuckle.

"No..." Ryan stops him. "You're that ninja!"

Zach is about to try and cover it up even more, but Mike talks over him.

"Maybe we should just tell him, Zach," Mike voices from behind Ryan.

Ryan does a 180°.

"Mike!" he exclaims in even more surprise. "Wait! Are you a ninja too?!"

"It's kind of hard to explain," Mike responds. "The bottom line is... Lennwood's in danger."

260

"I know," Ryan comments. "The school called everyone. Well, everyone from the school, I mean. The police are there today to stop some gang activity or something."

"I was the one who called the police," Mike reveals, and then looks at Zach. "I'm Roger Kowalski's informant, remember? I told them what I figured out."

"What did you figure out?" Zach inquires.

"The Scorpions are after something called the Knight's Jewel. I don't know why... I've just heard it's powerful."

Mike takes a deep breath.

"To be honest, Zach... I don't know if they'll be enough. Old York has a small police force, and the Scorpions that are going after it will be the best of the best!"

"I have to go," Zach blurts out, barely giving it a thought. "My sensei trained me for this. I wish he could be around to help me... but maybe this was God's plan all along."

"I don't know," Mike replies. "But you can't go alone... which is why I'm going with you."

"Thanks, Mike."

"Me too, Zach," Ryan declares.

"No," Mike firmly tells Ryan. "Zach and I both have fighting experience. Ryan... this gang is dangerous. You could get killed, and we don't want that to happen!"

"Yeah, well, I don't want you guys to get killed, either!" Ryan exclaims defiantly. "You guys are my best friends!"

Zach's neighbor's voice starts to get shaky.

"I care about you guys so much... If I don't go... and you guys die... how will I be able to even live with myself?!"

"Ryan... Mike's right," Zach says to his neighbor. "You don't even know why we're doing this."

"All I know... is that you guys are heroes. You both want to risk your lives for whoever's at the school that these gangsters might harm. Teachers, students who didn't listen to the call, even the police. And this powerful object Mike mentioned... what if it's dangerous? Won't people be in danger if these bad guys get it?! You're doing it for the people, right? Everyone who's in danger?!"

This really hits Zach, and his thoughts bring him back to the prayer he prayed earlier. He surrendered his life to God, and set aside Zach Rylar's will, for instead aiming to follow God's will. Zach recalls what he heard at church when he went with Sensei Haruta, how the pastor talked about how we should love one another. The pastor's words are now starting to make sense to Zach. Even though the teenager had barely opened a Bible in his entire life, and rejected this story of love until this morning, Zach is finally starting to realize God's love. He is beginning to understand how God loves him and every human being, and that Jesus died to take away the punishment that we deserve for our wrongdoings. If we choose to accept Jesus and believe what He did, God will forgive us and will start to transform us for the better. Zach Rylar accepted this, and at this moment, realizes that God made a way for him out of love. Jesus Christ died willingly, and He did it out of a selfless love for us– a broken, sinful people.

I need to do this for You, God, Zach prays in his mind and heart. *For You and other people over myself.*

"You're right, Ryan," Zach responds. "That should be our reason for doing this. Not for ourselves... but for the people. If Scorpio gets the Knight's Jewel, who knows what kind of power he may have! We can't let the Scorpions harm a single defenseless person, and we can't let them get that jewel!"

"So, what's the plan?" Ryan questions.

"The plan… is that I will train you two to become ninja, just as my grandfather taught me."

****

"Officer Kowalski!"

Roger turns around to see Police Chief Vincent Mulberry walking up to him.

They are both among the dozen police officers that are in front of Lennwood High School waiting for a Scorpion attack. Roger's friends, John Lawson and Richard Thompson, are not among the group and are recovering from being held captive. After Roger and the Gray Ninja rescued them and the other officers, Chief Mulberry graciously decided not to punish Roger.

"I don't think I've thanked you yet," the police chief tells him.

"I'm just doing my duty, sir," Roger replies.

"You see, that's just it. Thank you for doing your duty, Officer Kowalski," Chief Mulberry says to Roger. "Your dedication, even if it meant going against my poor judgment, is what helped to bring some of our brothers and sisters home. And even though I was mad at you before for disobeying me, you still gave me the message to come out here."

Chief Mulberry rubs his forehead.

"I apologize for my arrogance," he tells Roger. "And I think you'll become a fine police chief one day."

Roger chuckles.

"Maybe someday, sir," he responds. "And it's… okay."

"I appreciate your understanding," the police chief says.

"I do have one request, though, sir," Roger states.

"Yes?"

"Can I call my wife real quick?"

"Of course," Chief Mulberry answers and proceeds to walk away. "I'll cover for you."

Roger Kowalski thanks him, gets into his squad car, and then pulls his phone out of his glove compartment.

"Hi, Honey," Roger greets Amy over the phone.

"Jello?" Amy Kowalski replies, sounding as if she had just woken up.

"Oh, I'm sorry... did I wake you?"

"Yeah," she says sleepily.

"Sorry, I just wanted to give you an update."

"Update on what?"

Roger pauses, considering how to voice something he wishes would never come true.

"I'm at a high school right now. The Scorpions also will be here in a few hours."

"Oh, no."

"Yeah. Right now, we're making sure no one comes to school today," Roger adds.

The police officer exhales deeply.

"Honey... I'm tired of all of this violence. I keep praying that it will stop, but every day... it just keeps happening!" he exclaims.

"Roger..." his wife starts to say. "This world is so broken... and all of this violence... you know it's all because of sin."

"Yeah, I know. Sometimes I just wish God would stop all of it, you know?" Roger admits.

"God... is in control... but it's people's choices that are causing this. God gave us free will, the power to make choices. Oftentimes... people give in to sin and choose the wrong... choice."

She says the last part with a yawn.

"Wow," Roger responds, starting to chuckle. "That was really profound, and you just woke up!"

"Stay safe, Roger," Amy tells him as their conversation comes to an end.

"Love you, Amy," he replies.

They say their goodbyes, and Roger ends the call. He takes a deep breath, as he thinks about how his wife may have just had her last phone call with him.

Roger pushes the thought away and gets out of the police car, ready for action.

CHAPTER 19: "NINJUTSU"

"So that's why you were at your grandfather's house so much!" Ryan exclaims.

Zach nods.

"Yeah... but this gang, the Scorpions... they're the ones that killed him."

"Zach... I'm so sorry," Ryan says to him.

Zach fights the tears back.

"I can grieve later," he replies. "Right now, I need to know if you guys are in or not."

"I'm down to be a ninja," Mike states. "How about you, Ryan?"

"Of course," Ryan answers confidently.

"Are you sure?" Zach questions both Ryan and Mike. "Being a ninja will take all that you two have, as you'll both have to endure through so many physical and mental challenges. You'll have to push your bodies and minds further than ever before."

"We're not doing this for ourselves, remember?" Ryan reminds him. "I'm willing."

Zach can't help but smile.

"It's a yes for me, too," Mike adds.

"Thank you... both of you. This means a lot," Zach tells them. "I guess... I'll give you guys a crash course in ninjutsu over the next three hours, so we can go in at least somewhat prepared."

"It feels like someone's missing, though," Ryan blurts out. "I mean... are three ninja really enough?"

"Well... we do know this one guy," Mike adds.

"No," Zach replies firmly. "No way!"

"Yeah, dude! I'd love to be a ninja!" Seth Davis exclaims on the phone.

Mike and Ryan made Zach call him.

"Are you sure?" Zach challenges.

"Yes," Seth replies quickly.

"This will take everything you have."

"As long as it doesn't take my LEGOs, I'm fine with it."

"You will be tired, physically and mentally, as you are pushed beyond your limits."

"School already does that to me."

"Are you taking this seriously?"

"Zach, do I take anything seriously?"

Zach glares at Mike and Ryan, and then focuses back on the call.

"Seth... this is one thing you must take seriously. You can make jokes, but don't let them distract you. This is a matter of life and death! I know that because... this gang that we're going up against... killed my grandfather."

There is silence.

"Seth? Are you still there?" Zach asks into the phone.

"That dude was cool," Seth responds, sniffing.

"Seth... are you in?"

"Maybe… I don't know," Seth says with uncertainty in his voice.

"Mike, Ryan, and I are going to my sensei's place to get ready. Should I…"

I can't believe I'm saying this, Zach thinks.

"Should I pick you up?"

"What time?"

"In a few minutes," Zach tells Seth. "We're about to get in the car."

"Okay," Seth agrees. "And this isn't all some prank, right? You're actually the Gray Ninja?"

"Well… you're about to find out."

****

A silver car pulls to the side of a road in what seems to be the middle of nowhere. Zach Rylar opens the driver's door and steps out of the vehicle, with Ryan Hampkins, Mike Alford, and Seth Davis following his lead. The four friends trod on the ground where Kenshin Haruta's dojo once stood. Zach eyes the remains in sadness, expecting to see his grandfather's beautiful home, but instead only makes out pieces of wood and bricks scattered throughout a field of dirt.

The woods behind the property remain intact, but something else catches Zach's eye. He walks over to it, with his friends close behind him. A trapdoor is sticking out of the ground, with a lock on it. Mike, Seth, and Ryan observe as Zach grabs Sensei Haruta's keyring out of his pocket and inserts one of the keys into the keyhole. The Gray Ninja turns the key and then lifts up the door to reveal a staircase beneath it.

"Whoa!" Seth exclaims in awe. "Secret room!"

The four friends walk down the stairs and enter Sensei Haruta's basement. Unlike the rest of the dojo, the basement remains intact and looks exactly the same.

"Is that a swimming pool?" Ryan asks Zach.

Zach grabs several empty bottles near the pool and scoops the liquid into them.

"This is Water of Purification," Zach informs them. "This stuff is basically healing water."

Seth grabs a bottle and pours some of it on a zit on his head.

"But don't use it yet! This stuff is only for emergencies!" Zach adds.

"Yeah," Mike agrees. "I've experienced this stuff firsthand. Trust me, it's awesome… and we don't want to run out of it."

"Mike's right," Zach says. "And do you guys want to see something even more awesome?"

Zach brings them to the back wall of the basement.

Seth stares at him with a blank face.

"Really? A closet?"

"Not just any closet," Zach replies to Seth and proceeds to open the closet door.

Suddenly, several ninja suits fall out of the closet, making a loud crashing sound as the invinsium armor hits the floor.

"Um… these are your suits," Zach presents.

"Wow, Zach. Thank you for taking good care of them," Seth tells him sarcastically.

Zach ignores Seth's comment.

"My sensei kept these as spares. But now… If you three complete my crash course training, these suits will be yours," the Gray Ninja declares. "I also brought spray paint from my house, so you guys may choose your own colors."

"LET'S GO!!!" Mike exclaims excitedly.

****

"I will teach the three of you what my sensei taught me," Zach tells Ryan, Mike, and Seth.

Zach has led his friends above ground and into the woods behind Sensei Haruta's property.

"Listen carefully," Zach instructs. "First of all, there are six core elements of ninjutsu..."

Zach paces back and forth as a joyful feeling overtakes him.

"Strength... Speed..."

Zach imagines that his grandfather is standing beside him, proud of his grandson.

"Stealth... Endurance..."

He watches as his friends stare at him attentively; Zach returns their gaze, beaming back at them.

"Balance... and Patience," he finishes. "I will lead the three of you in a series of exercises for each of these Six Core Elements..."

For strength, Zach guides them in a push-up exercise; for speed, sprinting down the property; for stealth, fighting in the trees; and for endurance, jogging laps around the trees.

For the balance part of the training, Zach stands on one leg, as his friends attempt to follow his lead, struggling to maintain the pose.

"Alright. You guys may stop," Zach instructs, and they do so almost immediately.

Zach pulls out his phone and checks the time.

"Aw... my joints hurt..." Seth complains as Ryan breathes heavily.

"I know you guys are tired," Zach claims. "But this is why my sensei taught me the elements. The last of them is patience, and I think it's important to remember that it'll take time to accomplish our mission, but if we stay patient while enduring-"

Seth, Ryan, and Mike all stare at him. Anxiety builds up in Zach as he struggles to figure out what to say. He quickly prays for the words and reflects back on all that Sensei Haruta has taught him.

"My sensei..." Zach starts to say. "My sensei... always told me to *focus* and *press on*. And these... are words to live by. Every day... we should have our eyes *fixed* on our objective, on our goal. We shouldn't let *anything* distract us from our mission, but we should *concentrate* on completing it. It will be tough... and it will get even harder."

Zach pauses for a second, but more words come to his mind.

"So we're faced with a *choice*... we can either give up... or endure through it. And if we *choose* to persevere, we will grow... so much."

A thought comes to Zach. A reminder of the gift he received before he went to sleep. Zach feels different today. Yesterday, he felt tired, stressed, angry, and so much sorrow over his grandfather's death. But right now, Zach feels as though a peace has washed over him like never before. Zach knows in his heart that this day may take not only everything that he has trained for but everything that he has. Nevertheless, instead of continuing to feel anxious, a confidence builds up in Zach that could only be from God. He finally feels ready to fight the Scorpions, defend Lennwood, lead a team, and be the Gray Ninja Sensei Haruta trained him to be.

"Guys... we can do this," Zach assures them. "You guys did really well with training today. Even though you aren't that experienced, I'm still really impressed with you guys... especially for your willingness to do this. It's time, guys. It's-"

"Time for what? Lunch?" Seth interrupts with a grin.

"Time to put together your new ninja suits," Zach declares.

"But if the attack is at noon... when are we going to eat lunch?" Seth questions.

Zach, Ryan, and Mike just stare at him.

"Are you seriously asking that?" Mike questions.

"Yes... it is a legitimate question," Seth replies.

Zach takes a deep breath, not letting frustration consume him.

"Seth... don't let anything distract you. Don't let anything take your eyes off of the prize," Zach instructs.

"Exactly, Zach," Seth responds, smiling. "Ice cream if we win?"

Mike and Ryan can't help but laugh, and Zach lets a chuckle out.

"Okay..." Zach gives in to Seth's request. "Ice cream if we win."

****

After Zach Rylar pulls out the three identical spare Gray Ninja suits, the team begins to customize them with the spray paint Zach brought.

Ryan chooses multiple colors: olive green, brown, and tan, the colors of camouflage.

"Okay, Camo Ninja!" Seth dubs him, after looking at his suit. "I'm going with a more classic design."

At this point, Mike realizes that he and Seth are both making black ninja suits. They get into a little argument, but Zach helps them come to a compromise by suggesting a second color for the armor.

"I'm going with charcoal gray," Mike announces.

Seth turns to Zach.

"That's a good idea, Zach! And since you're silver, I'm going with gold!" Seth exclaims.

Before Zach can stop him, Seth Davis grabs the gold spray paint and uses it on the armor of his suit.

Zach facepalms.

"Well, that's not stealthily at all," Ryan comments.

Zach lowers his gaze and pulls out his phone to recheck the time.

"10:41," it reads.

Zach's heart beats faster as he realizes that time is running short.

"Guys, we have to hurry on the suits," Zach instructs. "I still have to give you guys your weapons."

"Not to worry, Zach," Mike assures him. "I gotchu."

He opens up a duffel bag he brought with him to extract two gun-like objects. He aims one at the closet and pulls the trigger.

Zach expects to hear a loud gunshot, but instead hears a faint, "Thoop!"

A familiar silver object flies through the air and bounces off of the closet door, hitting the floor.

Zach walks over to it and picks up the object.

"This... this is one of my sensei's non-lethal shurikens," Zach realizes in surprise. "How do you have this?"

"You and your sensei left a lot of these lying around when you went after the Scorpions," Mike explains. "I knew that I would eventually have to help take the gang down, so I designed some weapons of my own."

Mike Alford takes the non-pointed shuriken back from Zach and grabs a second object from his bag. He tosses this one– which resembles a small, yet thick metal shaft– to Seth.

"What is this, some kind of... *laser sword*?" Seth jokes and presses a button on it.

All of a sudden, another shaft, this one longer, comes out of one end. Seth presses the button again, and a third comes out of the other end. It is now as tall as Seth.

"Whoa! A metal staff!" he exclaims excitedly and then presses the buttons again.

Now, with each press, the shafts contract, and the staff decreases in size.

Seth extends the staff again and reaches for his gold and black spray paints.

"So... this is mine?" Seth confirms with Mike.

"It's all yours, Seth," Mike replies.

"YEET!" Seth responds, proceeding to spray paints the middle part black and the outside poles gold.

"And for you, Ryan..." Mike declares. "I have the *coolest* ninja sword."

Zach recognizes his sensei's ninjatō– or ninja short sword. Ryan takes the weapon and examines it.

"Okay, this is *definitely* an upgrade from my hunting knife," Ryan remarks.

"I've also modified it," Mike adds and points to a button on the hilt of the sword. "If you press that, you will activate a case that will slide out to cover up the blade."

Ryan presses it, and the sword does just as Mike said it would. It converts into a non-lethal sword.

"I'll just stick to my nunchucks," Zach tells Mike before his friend can offer him something. "But these are fantastic, Mike. I really appreciate this."

"No problem."

"Okay," Zach asserts, taking charge. "Mike and I will demonstrate how to use the weapons and help you to get comfortable with them," he says to Ryan and Seth. "We must do this with speed, however, because we're running out of time."

****

In a neighborhood, Sensei Haruta's silver car brakes at the side of a road, and four ninja exit the vehicle. One is silver, gray, and dark blue; the second is camouflage; the third, black and gold– the Gold Ninja; and a fourth black and charcoal gray– the Shadow Ninja.

The four ninja, grasping their weapons, run steadily through a wooded area next to them. They maneuver through the trees until they reach the edge of the woods. Peering out from the trees, the four vigilantes gaze into an open area, where the buildings of a high school stand. Zach observes red and blue flashing lights coming from the parking lot in front of the school, which is adjacent to where the four friends are.

"Let's go over the plan one last time," the Gray Ninja tells the others. "The main thing that Scorpio is after is the Knight's Jewel, which is located on a trophy. The trophy is in a glass case by the athletic director's office in the gym. Seth and Ryan: you guys are going to retrieve the jewel, and get it as far away from this school as possible. Mike and I are going to assist the police in fighting the Scorpions, and make sure they finally go to prison."

The rest of the team nods.

Suddenly, something catches Zach Rylar's eye in the distance. Behind the school, on the opposite side from the main parking lot, there is a small parking lot for teachers. Several dark vans driving together are headed straight for this parking lot, and only a few police cars are in it.

"Mike, go find Roger Kowalski and tell him we're here. Then, meet back up with me," Zach commands, and then turns to the others. "Ryan, Seth... get that jewel."

His gaze returns to the approaching vehicles.

"I'll try to hold them off," Zach concludes.

The Gold Ninja extends his arm.

"E-yah on three?" he suggests.

The rest of the team looks at Seth in confusion.

"Come on, it's like 'Hi-yah,' but better," Seth explains, with his arm still extended.

"Let's just do it," Ryan states, and extends his right arm to put a hand on Seth's fingers.

Zach and Mike give in and do the same. The four ninja are now in a circle, with their right hands together.

"Okay!" Seth declares. "Let's remember all Sensei Zach's taught us… and uh, be good ninjas or something. Um… be the best ninjas you can be!"

For once, Zach feels proud of Seth and can't help but smile.

"Yeah, guys," Zach finishes for him. "Focus, press on… and master the core elements. Alright… E-yah on three. One… two… THREE!"

"E-YAH!" the four ninja cry at the same time, and then each run off to complete their tasks.

The Gray Ninja advances towards the parking lot behind the school as Scorpions get out of their vehicles. The gangsters approach the school with their hoods on, masks up, and weapons raised.

Three policemen step out from in front of the building to face them. With their guns aimed at them, the officers order the Scorpions to freeze.

"Put your guns down," a familiar voice among the gangsters commands.

Scorpio, Zach recognizes.

The eyepatched leader steps forward, with his hands folded behind his back. Over a dozen Scorpions stand around him. Each of the gangsters has their own firearms pointed at the officers, while more of them emerge from the vehicles.

"What do you three fight for?" Scorpio challenges the policemen. "Because *we* fight for justice, and *we* all know that there doesn't need to be any unnecessary bloodshed. So please... put your guns *down.*"

Zach sneaks behind a wall, watching as the three officers slowly put down their guns. A couple of Scorpions pick up the weapons and attach them to their Scorpion outfits. Then, a large group of Scorpions starts to enter the school.

The Gray Ninja enters the school through a different door but stealthily maneuvers over to where the Scorpions are walking. The inside of the school is dim, with no lights on and only the sunlight keeping it somewhat lit. Fortunately for Zach, he has been familiar with the school for over two years.

He sneaks quietly through a hallway as the back doors of the building open. The Gray Ninja finds cover behind the end of a row of lockers, detecting the sound of multiple footsteps moving into the building. Zach peers out of his hiding place to see Scorpion after Scorpion step into the dark school. The ninja waits patiently for a moment to attack, but the sound of footsteps is coming closer.

Suddenly, the Gray Ninja makes his move. He slides out from where he is hiding and tosses multiple shurikens at a group of four Scorpions. Before they have a chance to fire their guns, a barrage of non-lethal shurikens rushes towards them. Two of the Scorpions are disarmed, while the others are hit lightly by the throwing stars. Then, the Gray Ninja whips out his nunchucks and beats down three of the gangsters before they have the chance to make a move. The fourth Scorpion fires his gun at Zach, but Zach's quick movements don't give his opponent an easy target. The Gray Ninja lunges at the fourth Scorpion and whacks him down with his nunchucks.

Unfortunately for Zach, more Scorpions are advancing into the hallway, and Zach realizes that he is outnumbered. He bolts back to his hiding place while more Scorpions pursue him. The Gray Ninja quickly puts his nunchucks away and whips out two of his sais. As a couple Scorpions begin to move around the corner of the row of lockers, Zach gets the jump on them. He slams the hilt of one of the sais into the forehead of one of the Scorpions, knocking him to the ground. The second one fires his gun, and a bullet scrapes Zach's side. The Gray Ninja kicks the Scorpion back, and then hurls the sai at his opponent, disarming him.

A familiar stinging pain torments Zach. He limps away, as the sound of running footsteps gets louder. The Gray Ninja runs into the darkness of the hallway as he hears Scorpio shout from behind.

"STOP HIM!"

****

Ryan Hampkins holds onto his new ninja sword tightly as he and Seth rush through the hallways of Lennwood High towards the gymnasium. They approach the gym, only to find two figures dressed in black moving toward them.

Seth gasps.

"Scorpions!"

Ryan squints at the figures.

"No, those are police officers," Ryan corrects him.

The Gold Ninja breathes a sigh of relief.

"Okay, good," he says.

Seth then walks up to the policemen, not stealthy at all.

"Hey, guys!" he calls. "We're here for the Knight's Jewel!"

278

The two officers raise their guns.

"These must be Scorpions!" one of the officers exclaims.

"So this is what they look like!" the other comments.

Ryan and Seth take off running, with the policemen chasing after them. The ninja maneuver through the dark hallways, passing lockers and climbing up and down stairs until they finally feel as though their pursuers have lost them.

The two friends just breathe heavily with their backs against a couple of lockers.

"Wait... a second," Seth blurts out and scans the area around them in realization. "This is the math building!"

Ryan's stomach sinks. He imagines a layout of the school in his mind and realizes that they are at the front of it. The gymnasium is located close to the back of the school.

"Come on!" he tells Seth, and the two friends take off running again.

****

Mike Alford is running stealthily through the empty, dark hallways of Lennwood High, in his new Shadow Ninja Suit. He met up with Roger Kowalski, and now the police officer is accompanying him, with five other officers behind them. The heroes have their weapons raised as they approach the back area of the high school.

They change their pace to move forward slowly and carefully, while gunshots and fighting sound in a stairwell several yards in front of them.

A figure in black is on the ground, dazed. Roger Kowalski hurries over to him and handcuffs him almost immediately. The policeman looks up the stairs before turning to the other officers and Mike.

"There are more up above!" Roger informs them.

The Shadow Ninja raises his two' shuriken-shooters.'

"I got this!" he proclaims and proceeds to run up the stairs.

Once he makes it to the second floor, Mike watches as two Scorpions send a barrage of bullets at a silver blur. The silver blur dashes into a doorway, out of the attacker's reach.

Mike activates his own weapons, letting multiple shurikens launch towards the two Scorpion invaders. They are disarmed, so Mike quickly attaches his shuriken-shooters to his suit and lunges at them with his fists.

The Gray Ninja sneaks out from the doorway and aids Mike in the fistfight.

"It's good to see you again," Zach tells Mike, after the two ninja defeat their opponents.

"Are you alright?" Mike responds, noticing red on Zach's suit.

Zach Rylar takes out a bottle of Water of Purification and pours some on the wound.

"I am now," the Gray Ninja responds.

Mike snickers.

"Dude, that's so awesome," he comments, and the two ninja run down the staircase.

****

"Gray Ninja!" Roger Kowalski exclaims when he sees his familiar ally.

For Roger Kowalski, this mission has taken an unexpected turn. He did not anticipate that he would encounter multiple ninja, and that his informant is one of them. Then, he was even more surprised to be told that the Scorpions were after some red jewel. However, Roger

knows that this mission could be it. This could be the day
that the OYPD finally takes down the Scorpions, or this
could be the last mission that he lives through.

"Get this guy in a squad car," Roger orders one of
the other officers and passes the handcuffed Scorpion to
him.

"There are more down that hallway," the Gray Ninja
informs him, pointing left.

Roger turns to the remaining officers.

"You four: find and handcuff as many Scorpions as
you can," he instructs them.

"Yes, sir," they say, almost in unison, and exit the
scene.

Roger turns to the ninja.

"I'll be with you guys," he tells his allies.

"Okay," the Gray Ninja replies. "I heard the
Scorpion leaders heading past here earlier. I don't know
where they are right now... but I know where they will be..."

"The gym," Roger's informant, the Shadow Ninja,
finishes for him.

"Exactly," the Gray Ninja confirms.

"I have an idea," Roger announces. "But you guys
will have to follow my lead."

The vigilantes agree to Roger's idea, which
involves the three of them to take an indirect route to the
gymnasium, which they do with speed. The three heroes
start to see figures moving through a hallway in front of
them, so Roger and the two ninja put their backs against a
wall.

Roger Kowalski recognizes Scorpio's shape as the
gang leader walks through the darkness with his men.

"This is our chance," Roger whispers to his allies.

The Gray Ninja appears very focused as he stares into the darkness in front of them.

"The gym is almost directly in front of them," the Shadow Ninja observes. "We have to go now!"

"No," the Gray Ninja almost cuts him off. "There's not enough cover, and too many of them."

Roger's heart beats faster, realizing that this is the moment that he has anticipated.

"Right now... we have a choice to make," he tells both of the ninja. "If we don't go, we may lose our chance to stop Scorpio. And if we do, we'll be risking our lives trying to stop him."

Something his wife told him this morning comes to Roger, as he continues to speak in a quiet voice.

"God gave us free will for a reason. And with this, comes the power to choose. What choice will you make?" he challenges.

Then, the blonde police officer turns back to the Scorpions moving in the darkness.

As the dark figures continue to advance through the hallway, Roger realizes that Scorpio is escaping his view.

"Well..." the policeman declares. "I'm choosing... *to go*."

Roger Kowalski quietly speedwalks toward the Scorpion leaders with his gun raised.

Chapter 20: "Showdown"

Seth Davis's lungs feel like they are about to explode.

Man, he thinks. *I haven't run this much since…*

He can't think of a time– but tells himself that it doesn't matter– since he and Ryan are about to make it back to the school gymnasium.

This time, the policemen from before are not there.

"Where's that trophy case?" Seth asks Ryan.

"It's down this way," the Camo Ninja replies and leads Seth down a short hallway next to the basketball court.

They pass by the boys' locker room to enter a dark area that Seth recognizes.

This is where the gym teacher's offices are, he thinks, recounting all of the instances he had to meet with his gym teacher for misbehaving. *Fun times.*

"There it is!" Ryan exclaims.

Seth notices that his friend is pointing at a massive glass case along the wall.

The two ninja approach it and examine the case.

"It's locked," the Camo Ninja points out.

Seth swings his staff against the glass, and it shatters.

Ryan looks up at him in disapproval.

"What? It's for the greater good!" the Gold Ninja defends.

He reaches through the broken glass, and pulls out a gold and silver trophy, with a red rock-like object on the top of it.

Suddenly, a bright light shines upon the two friends and the broken trophy case. They turn, blocking the glare with their eyes.

"What do you two think you're doing?!" a familiar voice sternly questions them.

"Mr. Earnheart?" Ryan whispers out loud.

As the figure walks into view, Seth remembers seeing this teacher around the school. Seth is initially concerned that they will be recognized before remembering that they are disguised behind their ninja helmets.

"I heard that some thieving little scumbags were trying to steal my jewel!" the orange bearded man exclaims. "Do you guys have any idea how much I've been studying it?!"

"Um..." Seth starts to say.

"I take it with me every night to research and try to find out as much as I can!" Mr. Earnheart continues. "And you know what?! This thing is dangerous! It was tampered with already... before it came here!"

"You mean before it hit the school in a meteor?" Seth questions while removing the jewel from the trophy.

"Yes, and you'd better not mess with it!" the teacher orders.

****

Roger Kowalski advances valiantly towards the figures in the dark. He expects to be doing it alone, but to his surprise, the ninja choose to accompany him. The Gray Ninja unsheathes two ninja short-swords and hands one to the Shadow Ninja. Roger smiles as the three of them face the Scorpions.

Seven Scorpions are in front of them, including Scorpio, Stinger, and Bartholomew Mustachio. Roger Kowalski gets behind the armored ninja and fires his gun at the hands of their opponents. Weapons fly out of the Scorpions' hands as the two ninja lunge at the Scorpions. The Gray and Shadow Ninja use their swords to knock out the remaining guns, and then the hilts of their swords to knock three of them down. After Roger tases a fourth, only Bartholomew Mustachio, Stinger, and Scorpio remain.

Scorpio turns to Stinger and Mustachio.

"Deal with them," the gang leader commands, and then starts to run towards the gymnasium.

Roger Kowalski disarms Bartholomew Mustachio, but the mustached Scorpion puts up a fight. He kicks Roger in the chest with his knee and then punches him down. Roger gets back on his feet to block a second punch. The brave policeman struggles to drive Mustachio to the ground, as the Gray Ninja and Stinger lunge at one another beside them.

Wielding his longsword, Stinger clashes his blade against the Gray Ninja's ninjatō.

****

Mike watches through both of the fights as Scorpio gets closer and closer to the gym.

"I'm going after Scorpio!" Mike declares.

He pushes away fear and rushes after the Scorpion leader.

Scorpio turns around and fires a pistol at him. A bullet ricochets off of Mike's invinsium helmet, and then he takes out one of his shuriken-shooters. Shurikens sail towards the gang leader, and the pistol flies out of his hand. Scorpio unsheathes a dagger and lunges towards the Shadow Ninja. Mike puts his firearm away to embrace the short-sword Zach gave him with both of his hands. Scorpio lunges at him, but Mike blocks Scorpio's attack with the sword. However, the Scorpio retaliates by forcing his dagger against the ninjatō. The Shadow Ninja struggles to maintain his grip, as the gang leader's might shoves the sword out of Mike's hands.

Scorpio swings the dagger at him two more times, but Mike blocks both attacks with his invinsium wrist armor. The Shadow Ninja moves even closer to Scorpio, and with both hands, grasps on to the hilt of Scorpio's dagger. He twists the gang leader's wrist and disarms him.

"ARGH!" Scorpio cries out in pain before kicking Mike back.

The force of the kick is so great that it sends Mike flying against a wall. He falls to the ground, and his ninja helmet slides off of his head.

Sweat rolls down Mike's forehead as he understands what has just happened. Towering high above him is the bald, eyepatched man that let him in his family. Scorpio eyes Mike with shock and disbelief, as the gang leader recognizes the ninja's face.

Mike's heart beats faster as he detects another emotion coming from Scorpio.

Anger.

****

Zach Rylar's silver blade clashes against Stinger's longsword. Emotions build up in Zach as he acknowledges that this is the man who killed his grandfather. Zach tries to force the feelings away and focus on the fight, but sorrow and anger consume him. With every movement of his weapon, he slams his might against Stinger's longsword with a fierceness that Sensei Haruta warned him about. Nevertheless, the Scorpion second-in-command easily counters and copies each of the Gray Ninja's moves. While Zach uses tactics Sensei Haruta taught him, the Scorpion ninja is familiar with all of them and knows how to counter each one.

The Gray Ninja misses a block, and the Scorpion slices through part of Zach's suit. Zach cries out in pain yet continues to keep his sword raised. Stinger also holds his blade in the air, and Zach can tell that his opponent is trying to anticipate his next move.

Zach takes a deep breath, quieting his mind. He grips his sword, realizing that he can't beat Stinger like this. So the Gray Ninja lets go of the blade with one hand and takes out a handful of shurikens with the other.

"Hey!" Zach calls to the Scorpion ninja. "If you've really been trained by Sensei Haruta, did he teach you this lesson?!"

Suddenly, Zach flings all of the non-pointed shurikens at Stinger, who shields his face with his longsword. Zach proceeds to throw his sais at the other ninja, and then his nunchucks. Stinger wobbles from the projectiles, as Zach charges at him with his sword.

"E-YAH!" he yells, slamming the ninjatō down hard against Stinger's longsword.

The longsword falls out Stinger's hands, but the Scorpion second-in-command fights back with his fists and feet, showing off some martial arts that Zach has not seen before.

"Heh," Stinger snickers. "What kind of lesson was that?"

"To be ready for anything," Zach responds and then headbutts Stinger with his invinsium helmet.

The impact of the blow sends the Scorpion second-in-command to the ground.

Zach Rylar, weak from the battle, slowly picks up his weapons and attaches them back to his suit. He raises his head to see Roger Kowalski struggling to handcuff Bartholomew Mustachio.

But then, Zach observes a brutal fight in front of the gymnasium.

The Gray Ninja rushes over to Mike, who is getting beaten badly by Scorpio. Mike tries to block the gang leader's mighty blows but ends up on the ground, defeated.

Zach watches as Scorpio stands over his weakened friend. Zach's heart cries out as he longs to go over and help him.

But just as Zach is about to, a hand yanks Zach's left foot and pulls him to the ground. The Gray Ninja spins around to see Stinger slowly getting up. Zach whips out his nunchucks, but Stinger kicks him back.

****

"I let you into my family, and this is how you repay me?!" Scorpio shouts at Mike.

Mike coughs in reply, while lying on the ground, beaten.

Two figures run behind Scorpio, and the gang leader quickly turns around. He pauses, and then Mike watches as Scorpio's head slowly turns back to him.

"Soon... you won't have a choice," he tells Mike. "Soon... the only choice anyone will have will be to fight for my cause! When I make it to the roof with that jewel... I will have control, and everyone will fight for good!"

288

Scorpio turns again and pursues after the two figures, whom Mike recognizes as Ryan and Seth.

****

The Camo and Gold Ninja run through the gymnasium with the Knight's Jewel. They hear two gunshots, and both of them fall to the ground. The Knight's Jewel slips out of Seth's hand and rolls across the floor.

"Ow..." Seth moans.

Grunting in pain, Ryan reaches for his Water of Purification and unscrews the lid. He pours some on his wound, then some on Seth's.

A bald, eyepatched man towers over them, and the two young ninja fearfully observe as a hand reaches down and picks up the red, sparkling jewel.

Scorpio grins before walking away with the Knight's Jewel.

****

Back in the hallway, Stinger and Zach both rise to their feet. The Scorpion second-in-command karate-kicks the Gray Ninja again; this time in the face.

Zach's back hits a wall. The Gray Ninja raises his nunchucks and swings them at his opponent, but Stinger grabs hold of the nunchucks and tosses them aside.

The Scorpion ninja whips out a knife, and then-

BANG!

Stinger clutches his side, and the knife falls out of his hands. Zach quickly turns his head to see Roger Kowalski, with his gun in his hand and Bartholomew Mustachio in handcuffs beside him.

Wounded, Stinger limps away and escapes into the darkness. The Gray Ninja then picks up his nunchucks and goes over to Roger Kowalski.

"Thanks for the save," Zach tells him.

"No problem," Roger replies with a smile.

Zach's eyes turn to Mike.

The Gray Ninja rushes over to his friend, with Roger Kowalski following him.

"Mike? Mike?!" Zach questions, as a lump starts to form in his throat. "Are you okay?"

Mike coughs, but slowly shakes his head.

"Yeah, I'm fine. Just… need…" Mike struggles to speak.

Zach realizes that he is reaching for his Water of Purification attached to his suit, and helps him to drink some.

The Gray Ninja turns to Roger Kowalski.

"He'll be okay, but can you make sure the Scorpions don't get to him?"

Roger nods.

"I'll do my best."

"Wait…" Mike says weakly, and Zach leans in. "Don't let Scorpio reach the roof… and activate… the jewel. If he gets there-"

"What?!" Zach questions. "What's going to happen?!"

"No… time," Mike stammers. "He went after… our… friends…"

Ryan and Seth! Zach realizes in alarm.

He sheaths his second ninjatō and immediately takes off running through the gymnasium. The Gray Ninja's eyes pick up his friends on the other side, who are starting to get up.

"Are you guys okay?!" Zach demands with a shaky voice.

290

"Yep, since we have this awesome water!" Seth exclaims, tossing the bottle to Zach.

Zach thanks his friend and attaches the extra bottle to his Ninja Suit.

"We're fine, Zach, but that eyepatched guy took the jewel," Ryan tells Zach. "He went out to the compound."

"Sorry about that," Seth apologizes.

"No," Zach firmly responds. "I'm the one that should be apologizing, and I should've said this a long time ago. Seth... I underestimated you, and I'm really sorry about that. And Ryan... I shouldn't have pushed you away. I-"

"It's okay, Zach," Ryan interrupts him.

"No, it's not!" Zach disagrees, his voice still shaking. "I should have treated you guys better. Recently God showed me that I was just doing whatever I wanted, living only for myself... when instead... He wanted me to be loving you guys like brothers."

A tear falls out of Zach's eye and slides down the interior of his helmet.

"Ryan... Seth... I just want you guys to know that... whatever happens today... you guys and Mike are... my brothers."

Before his friends have a chance to respond, Zach turns and starts to walk away. The Gray Ninja heads straight towards the front doors of the gymnasium that lead to the outside compound. He stops in front of the doors, noticing four Scorpions standing guard in the middle of the large, open area. However, Scorpio is walking past them, headed straight for the tallest building in the high school: the math building.

Zach also realizes that his only cover is behind the Scorpion guards, and there is little of it.

I have to do this fast, Zach thinks. *I could try to run through the buildings that surround it... but that would take longer, especially if there are more Scorpions in them.*

291

Zach starts to understand that if he wants to get the jewel from Scorpio, he only has one option. An overwhelming anxiety builds up inside of Zach as he concentrates on what is ahead of him: Four Scorpions with large guns. A flagpole in the middle of the compound. A statue of a knight on the other side. But there is no cover in front of the guards.

Zach pushes the fear away, as a voice in his mind tells him that he can't do it, that he's not good enough.

No, Zach tells the voice, and then begins a prayer. *God… be with me through this. I need you! I can't do this without you…*

All of a sudden, Zach seems to be taken back to when he and his sensei were debating about pain. Sensei Haruta's words come back to him:

"Do not let the idea of pain stop you. Pain is an obstacle that tries to prevent you from carrying out your mission."

Zach takes a deep breath and gets in a running position. He concentrates on what is in front of him: four Scorpions, little cover, and Scorpio getting away with the Knight's Jewel. Zach remembers what Mike said about the jewel, about how he should not let Scorpio get to the roof with it.

"Pain can be defeated if you persevere through it," he hears Sensei Haruta's words in his mind. "Discipline your mind, Zach."

Zach's heart seems like it is going to explode, as it beats faster and faster. Zach repeats the six core elements to himself, as he focuses through the glass door. His eyes are locked on Scorpio, who is getting closer and closer to the building on the other side.

The Gray Ninja takes out his nunchucks and pushes the door in front of him as he recalls his sensei's words:

"Reduce pain to an illusion."

Wind rushes past Zach as his feet fly through the compound. With great speed, the Gray Ninja sprints up to the Scorpion guards. These Scorpions almost immediately spot him, and bullets rush towards the ninja. One impacts him, but Zach repeats the phrase in his mind that Sensei Haruta had taught him.

Pain is an illusion.

Zach's flight response kicks in, and the Gray Ninja forgets his weakness to fly even faster.

Another bullet pierces through his suit.

Pain is an illusion.

A few bullets ricochet off his armor, while others scrape against him. Zach jumps at the first Scorpion and beats him down with his nunchucks. He quickly swings them at two other Scorpions and takes them as well. The last of the Scorpion guards fires at the ninja again, and Zach loses his balance.

Pain is an illusion.

Zach gets back on his feet, maintaining his balance as blood pours out of him.

Pain is an illusion.

With all his strength, the Gray Ninja shoves the Scorpion back. His opponent falls to the ground, and the Gray Ninja continues to run through the compound. An intense, stinging sensation overtakes Zach's entire body.

Pain is... an...

The Gray Ninja attempts to endure through the overwhelming sensation weighing down his entire body, yet he feels like he is going to collapse. Zach's vision blurs as the world seems to be fading around him.

No... this can't be it, God... Zach prays as he feels weaker and weaker. *Please, Lord! I don't want to do this my way anymore! Just Yours... please give me the strength to keep going!*

Zach's legs continue to fly forward as he starts to close his eyes, without realizing that Scorpio is entering the math building. All of a sudden, Zach Rylar collapses on the ground behind him.

Weaker than ever, Zach slowly reaches for the Water of Purification on his Suit and unscrews the lid.

Zach's hand lowers as the Water of Purification begins to flow from the water bottle and onto his bloodied body. The teenager's head lowers as his heartbeat slows down.

Suddenly, the Gray Ninja opens his eyes. He looks down to realize in disbelief that his wounds have been healed.

Thank you, Lord, Zach prays.

The Gray Ninja rises to his feet and rushes over to the math building in front of him, quietly opening one of its glass doors.

Scorpio has already made it over to a staircase and is beginning to climb up the stairs. Zach maneuvers over to it without making a sound, and stealthily pursues the gang leader.

Scorpio glances behind him to spot his pursuer. An all too familiar sound to Zach fills his ears, as the gang leader fires upon his adversary.

The bullets ricochet off of Zach's helmet, and the Gray Ninja reacts with a barrage of shurikens. The gang leader's pistol flies out of his hands and falls down to the floor below.

Scorpio growls in frustration, but instead of going for it, he continues to advance up the stairs.

Zach races after him, unsheathing both of his ninja swords as Scorpio puts the Knight's Jewel in his pocket and takes out his daggers. Zach charges up to him, but

Scorpio slams down hard with his daggers, causing Zach to lose his balance.

The Gray Ninja falls down, but lifts himself up to send his ninja swords clashing against Scorpio's blades. Both fighters try to swing their weapons high and low, but end up dodging or blocking each others' attacks.

Scorpio proceeds to attack much quicker, causing Zach to be unable to keep up with the more experienced fighter's movements. Both of Zach's swords are forced out of his hands and the eyepatched gang leader kicks him down the stairs.

The Gray Ninja tumbles down the stairs but gets up once more to see Scorpio dashing up the staircase. Zach whips out his sais to pursues him, but the gang leader turns around again, causing Zach's sais to meet his daggers. Zach knocks one of Scorpio's daggers out of his hands, but in the process, Scorpio grabs Zach's arm and flips him over.

More pain shoots into Zach as his back lands on the edge of a stair. He disregards it, setting the concept aside to crawl up the stairs. The Gray Ninja then lifts himself up and continues to pursue the gang leader.

Scorpio reaches the top of the staircase and steps onto the roof. Zach lunges at him to yank Scorpio's second dagger out of his hand. The gang leader reacts by raising his fists and proceeds to rapidly punch his opponent. Almost instantly, Zach's sais fly out of his hands, landing on the other side of the roof and out of the ninja's reach. Zach tries to grab his nunchucks from his belt, but Scorpio yanks them off of the Gray Ninja Suit and tosses them away.

The gang leader shoves Zach down and pins him to the ground.

"Stay down, Gray Ninja!" Scorpio tells Zach. "You know I fight for justice, and yet you still fight back!"

Scorpio lets go of Zach only for the Gray Ninja to push himself to his feet again. With a powerful kick, Scorpio forces Zach down again. The gang leader proceeds to take the shiny, red Knight's Jewel out of his pocket as he walks to the other side of the roof. However, Zach reaches to grab his nunchucks and gets up one more time.

Scorpio turns back around to him and throws up his arms.

"There aren't any students here. No one had to be harmed today!" the gang leader continues. "Even if the school was in session, I would make sure that no one would be harmed!"

He raises the Knight's Jewel.

"I just wanted this."

"What does it do?!" Zach demands.

Scorpio focuses his gaze on him as the ninja approaches slowly and cautiously.

"When your sensei and I fought crime, I suggested a solution for peace," Scorpio starts to explain. "To create a *family*, where former gang members could go to get out of crime... and fight for a cause that is *actually* worth something."

Scorpio lowers his gaze to examine the jewel.

"Recently... there was talk of a powerful object... that can provide another solution. This jewel– if used correctly– has the power to make anyone... believe what I believe. After Old York is impacted by the power of this jewel... anyone that has a desire to do evil... will instead desire to do good!"

"Hypnosis," Zach analyzes. "You're using it to control other people!"

"BECAUSE PEOPLE NEED TO BE CONTROLLED!" Scorpio shouts. "If I don't do this, Old York will continue to be destroyed by violence, by

296

corruption! But if I activate this jewel, I will
make *everyone* strive for peace, and *everyone* will only
want *to... do... good!*"

Scorpio shakes his head.

"Don't you see, Gray Ninja? This is what I've been
fighting for! This is how Old York can find peace!" he tells
Zach, who stops moving. "When I unleash the power of
this space rock, its energy will connect my will to all of
those I target. And from this height, I will be able to
concentrate my will to target most of Old York! Soon, every
person in this town will only want to DO GOOD!"

"If what you're saying is true," Zach replies. "Then
you're forcing other people to believe what you believe,
forcing other people to do what you want them to do."

"What's so wrong about wanting people to do the
right thing?" Scorpio argues. "If you had the ability to make
everyone do this, wouldn't you do it?!"

Words come to Zach's mind, something that Roger
Kowalski had told him earlier.

"God... gave us free will for a reason," Zach
repeats. "My sensei believed in the Bible, in God, while I
always rejected that kind of stuff. But last night I realized
that I was wrong... and that I kept following my own way,
which brought me nowhere. I thought of myself as inferior
to everyone else, but God thinks of us differently. I now
realize... that God loves all of us, and *that's* why he gave
us the power to choose! He doesn't want to force us to do
good... or force us to follow him! No... He longs for us to
come to Him willingly!"

Scorpio looks at him curiously.

"So... we have a choice," Zach continues. "Which is
already awesome, because we don't deserve a choice, we
don't deserve to be able to be with Him, because of how
messed up we are! But He chooses to forgive us, if we

believe in Him… He loves us so much that he died… to *save us*."

"I know of what you're talking about," Scorpio responds. "But it doesn't solve the problem. Even if you're saved by your God, you will continue to do evil. You will continue to fight against peace, fight against justice!"

"Yes, but now that I'm following God, I don't have that same desire to sin anymore," Zach defends. "I may give in to it sometimes, but now I... I want to commit to what God wants me to do."

"Which is what?" Scorpio questions. "Does God want you to fight me, to stop me?!"

He throws up his arms again.

"Is that your so-called God's plan?!" he demands. "To go against my plan?!"

"No," Zach replies. "Right now, that's my plan… I want to fight you… but God doesn't want me to do that."

Zach now realizes what God is calling him to do. Something inside of him fights the will, but Zach pushes away his selfish desire to submit to his Savior.

Zach drops his nunchucks and walks closer to Scorpio. He takes out his remaining bottle of Water of Purification and hands it to Scorpio.

"He wants me… to forgive you."

The eyepatched gang-leader gives him a look of confusion as he cautiously takes the water bottle with his empty hand.

"Use it on your right eye," Zach tells him, and his former enemy looks at him with surprise.

Zach Rylar takes off his Gray Ninja helmet.

"Trust me."

Scorpio puts the Knight's Jewel back in his pocket and lifts up his eyepatch. He unscrews the bottle of Water of Purification and pours the healing water on his scarred

298

eyelid. Almost instantly, the eye is healed, and Scorpio's eyesight is restored.

"My right eye…!" Scorpio exclaims in disbelief. "I can see through it again!"

Scorpio's face beams with joy as he throws the eyepatch off of the roof.

Then, he pauses and turns back to Zach. Scorpio takes the Knight's Jewel out of his pocket again, looks at it, and then looks up at the Gray Ninja.

"Why would you do this? After what I did to your sensei, to your teammates, and to *you*?" he wonders.

"Why did Jesus die for us?"

"Well… *if* He really did, He did it out of grace, I suppose," Scorpio replies.

"So what should we do?" Zach asks, pointing at the Knight's Jewel. "Should we try to control what other people do, and force them to believe what we believe, or should we try to convince them to do so in other ways, more loving ways?"

Scorpio raises the Knight's Jewel, still examining it. He sighs and then lowers it.

"You may be right, Gray Ninja," he says. "I don't know about everything you're saying, but you are right about that."

The gang leader walks to the edge of the roof, and Zach watches as his grip gets looser and looser. The shiny, red space rock slides out of his hand and then plummets towards the ground below.

"Please…" Zach pleads to him. "Call off the attack on my school."

The gang leader turns around again and looks into the pain in Zach's eyes.

"I'll do as you ask," Scorpio gives in. "Perhaps I can establish peace another way."

Zach smiles.

"Thank you. I trust… that you can."

****

Roger Kowalski charges up the stairs of Lennwood High's math building, with five policemen behind him. Once they reach the top, Roger expects to see a fight. Instead, he only sees the back of the Gray Ninja, as the ninja slips his helmet back on.

"Lower your weapons," Roger tells the other policemen and then walks over to the ninja.

The Gray Ninja turns to face him.

"We captured Bartholomew Mustachio and many of the other Scorpions," Roger informs his ally. "But Stinger got away."

"I wasn't able to defeat Scorpio," the Gray Ninja admits, before redirecting his gaze to stare off into the distance. "But actually… I don't think I was supposed to."

"I'm not sure I understand."

The young ninja turns back to Roger. As Roger looks beneath the ninja's eyes, he can tell that the young ninja is smiling behind his helmet.

"I'm grateful for your words… God can give words a lot of power, you know?"

"Why, yes… I suppose… you're right," Roger responds, surprised by the vigilante's response.

"Scorpio may still be out there… but I'm not sure that he'll be a threat to Old York anymore," the Gray Ninja says to Roger.

"What about that jewel thing? Was it destroyed?"

The ninja nods in reply.

"Well… there's a chemistry teacher down below who won't be happy," Roger chuckles, and then offers the vigilante a handshake. "Thank you for your help, Gray Ninja."